PRAISE FOR F
MY NAME ON A GRAIN OF RICE

"Voigt thrives in crafting this honest and composed coming-of-age novel. It's a reminder that 'putting your name on a grain of rice' instead of up in flashing lights isn't always a bad thing; sometimes it's enough to know you exist, and simply be content with existing for another day...A brisk and well-written novel dealing in reality and relationships."

Audrey Davis, *Independent Book Review*

"Richard Voigt builds a story of transformation, change, redemption, and growth...Voigt creates a powerful tale that revolves around death, a renewal, and choices that had unforeseen consequences for future...happiness...an engrossing novel especially recommended for readers interested in stories of family influences and change."

D. Donovan, Senior Reviewer,
Midwest Book Review

"Richard Voigt tells an absorbing tale of a young man trying to find purpose in his life but struggling to adjust to his circumstances. *My Name on a Grain of Rice* is a story about self-discovery, about making your own mistakes and carving out the right path for yourself. The narrative is well-paced and feels like a breeze to go through. This is a character-driven drama with nuanced and in-depth characters who have complex layers in their personalities. Harry (the narrator) feels like a real person with conflicting morals. Yet, despite his many flaws, you can't help but root for him. The bittersweet ending only adds charm to the story. If you enjoy well-written slice-of-life stories, this is the book for you. FIVE STARS ***** "

Pikasho Deka, *Readers' Favorite*

"Voigt is an exceptional writer. His intellect, under-standing of human nature, and empathy emerge in chapter after chapter. His protagonist...is humanized by Voigt's wit, wisdom, and innate ability to imply restraint where lesser scribes would embellish. This is a novel worth reading for the writer's voice as well as his story. both are quite memorable."

Joe Kilgore, *The U.S. Review of Books*

MY NAME ON A GRAIN OF RICE

A NOVEL

Richard Voigt

atmosphere press

FOR ANNEMARIE

"The pure admire the pure,
and live alone."

Theodore Roethke

MY NAME ON A GRAIN OF RICE

When exposed to air, blood darkens and thickens. I knew this simple fact from childhood when I watched scabs form. But those scabs came from only a few drops of blood, which coagulated quickly. A pint of blood that runs from a man's mouth and then stiffens into a maroon jelly is something different.

Nothing in my childhood prepared me for the fact that human beings are made of flesh. I thought that the human body was not simply that of another animal. Because people could talk and think, because we had been made in God's image, the shape of our bodies was ordained. I now know that we can be easily ruined.

I remember staring at the two dead men with numb, unintended concentration as I looked down into an excavation as rescuers picketed their way through pieces of steel to get to them. It is still difficult for me to believe: in an instant, the two men had been replaced by mangled corpses. In a blink of my eyes, their eyes had become fixed. How could something so terrible, so tragically significant have happened so fast?

But I knew that it was going to happen. Not the specific moment. Not the specific men. But I knew enough to know better than to be there and see it all. Yet, I stayed. I keep trying to explain to myself why I ended up in these horrible circumstances and why, in some ways, I should be blamed for them. I keep trying to explain to myself how my current life should account for this history and whether it should matter to anyone.

The events rush through my mind just as they rushed through my life at the time. So maybe what I am about to tell you leaves out something important. Maybe I use the speed with which things happened as an excuse for some of what I did. But I know enough to know better than to think that it can excuse everything.

CHAPTER ONE

If you have to, blame me for wanting to feel the rush that comes from making something out of nothing, and that something would be me. Not do what was expected of me so that my life could become a true adventure. I feared that if I did what was expected of me, what would pass for experience in my life would be nothing more than a pathetic sequence of purchased, contrived events akin to bungee jumping or of scheduled tee times at the club for manicured recreation with my parents. Maybe, this fear was an overreaction. So, if you have to, blame me for losing control over myself until resistance became fate.

The cliché is that a journey of a thousand miles begins with a single step. Those words would have been lost on me because, at the time, I didn't think that I was embarking on some type of long trip with a simple first step. For me to have had that thought, I would have first needed a destination. In fact, I had no specific objective, just a general objection to my probable future.

Along with my co-worker Sterling Nesko, I quit my job at the Speed of Light, or SOL as we called it – a software startup. Paul Matel, the swanky guy behind the company, kept insisting that SOL was a "strategic software play, Einstein in cyberspace" and that "right now, right here I am putting you to your highest and best use".

Sterling didn't buy it. "Our highest and best use? That's a joke. All that he wants from us is zero drag-coefficient. And then there is all of his talk about us annihilating the competition, taking no prisoners, burning their crops. Total bullshit. If we end up like him, we won't have any relationships deeper than a spread-sheet. I say fuck this cubicle crap."

"Say what?" I answered.

"Fuck this. Let's quit. I know that you agree with me."

"Well...I...."

"OK, then it's decided."

"But...I...."

"And, by the way, I'm looking for somebody to move in with me. I'll give you the first month for free."

For better and worse, something was mesmerizing about Sterling. It was not his eyes which held my attention, although they had a certain sharpness. In fact, his face, which was framed by a casually tended beard, divided by a modest nose, and topped by curly brown hair, could be easily overlooked in a group photo. It was his swagger that got to me.

According to Sterling, if you are going to do anything important in life, you must have illusions, not dreams. He had not used those exact words, but that was what he was driving at. He boasted about how he could handle anything that life threw at him, about how he was going to live life at "ramming speed". To hear him tell it, he had overcome situations, avoided situations, created situations simply through a burst of outrageous energy. The trick was to convince yourself that you could do it. Believe your own bullshit.

So, as boneheaded as it may sound to you, Sterling and I quit SOL with nothing else on the agenda. In my self-inflated way, I came to regard my stumbling willingness to follow Sterling out the door as a bold maneuver.

Even before Sterling arrived at SOL, I was unhappy. Sure, I wanted the money, but the long, sunless hours on the job seemed like an increasingly large price to pay. And then came the gnawing feeling that I needed to get out of there so I could determine whether or not I had any character. But, in reality, my bolting from SOL was a form of play-acting, pretending not to be intimidated by uncertainty, of pretending not to need time to sort through important factors. It did not take long before I came to recognize that I could no longer pretend about such matters and that my rushed, flagrant change of direction had also been inept.

CHAPTER TWO

I hated to admit to myself that I tended to be a spectator. Smart enough to recognize true ability in others, whatever it might be, but not smart enough to display any exceptional talent myself. And no doubt, there was an element of spectator sport in going off with Sterling. His defiant, mocking exuberance was a draw. But there was more to it than that. To be in the game, I would have to do something myself.

I wanted to try. No doubt, up to that point I hadn't been truly competent or engaged. I didn't even expect to be. Initially, at my father's urging, I had attempted some substantive courses in finance and economics in college. I dropped the one on the structure and valuation of stock options after I found the course material to be uselessly complex. From what I had heard from my father, no one in business used any of the terms or formulas in the textbook to make decisions about stock options, so to me, the only point of the class had been to create contrived difficulty which would allow some students to do better than others and eventually make claim to academic awards. As for the rest of us, our role was to fill out the grading curve with mediocre, inconspicuous performance or worse.

My father grudgingly paid the tuition, room, and board as I drifted into marginal courses of useless simplicity. For a giddy year, I felt liberated from the expectations of success which had weighed upon me since I had been enrolled in a selective pre-kindergarten program with other hothouse flowers who were being watered, pruned, and fertilized so that we would show well. For that irresponsible year, I was also liberated from the company of the self-congratulatory ribbon winners who had no apparent concerns beyond reminding themselves and everyone else of their high rankings. I made my little point and graduated as a knucklehead.

* * *

Ray's Oasis was the neighborhood bar where Sterling liked to do his drinking. The sign above Ray's simply said "BAR," although the "oasis" theme was displayed by plastic palm trees in the corners and cut-out plywood camels on two walls.

"I hereby call this meeting to order," Sterling declared as we sat, post SOL, in a booth at Ray's. He always did his drinking according to Robert's Rules of Order. "We are now in session. We will dispense with the reading of the minutes. No committee reports. No old business. The Chair has new business, so I will recognize myself." He paused; then continued. "So recognized."

"Excuse me, but I was wondering how you can dispense with the reading of the minutes if there aren't any minutes?"

"How can I not dispense with the reading of the minutes if there aren't any?" Sterling signaled to Ray for two drafts. "Are you volunteering to become the recording secretary so that we can have minutes in the future?"

"No."

"Then you're out of order." Sterling leaned forward as if to emphasize his point. "As I was saying, the Chair has new business."

"So what is it? You've already recognized yourself to speak for Christ's sake."

"I've signed us up to be piledriver apprentices."

Now I leaned forward. "Say that again. I don't think I got it.

"Yeah, you got it."

"Did you say piledriving? What do you know about piledriving?"

"I had an uncle who was a piledriver. A man's man. I'm ready for that type of work. I went on the internet and got what I needed to know about how to get started in an apprenticeship program. It's mostly on-the-job training, but you can get paid doing it and at the end you can do some heavy shit."

"Do you really have any idea of what you are talking about? You're a computer jock. Piledriving? Don't be ridiculous."

"That's exactly what I'm going to be."

"OK, OK, so you wanted to get out of SOL. So find another computer job. Why go into construction? It doesn't make sense."

"Because I want to learn how to build something solid. Understanding the engineering. Be clever with my hands. Get some stories of my own to tell. If I have to spend any more time hanging around guys like Paul Matel, I'll end up in the Institute and you'll only be able to see me during visiting hours."

"And did I hear you say that you had signed us up to be piledriver apprentices? You and me? The both of us?"

"Correct. I thought that I would do you a favor."

"You're whacked out. If it's ridiculous for you to go into piledriving, which it is, it's even more ridiculous for me."

"What else do you have going? Finding an entry-level data-entry position somewhere? Working for a temp agency? Hitting up your dad for his contacts so you can run errands for a hedge fund trader? Fuck that shit. Time for you to broaden your horizons."

"But getting to the end of every day, exhausted and covered with mud is not exactly the kind of life I am looking for....and that assumes that I get to the end of the day. We're talking a whole different thing here."

"Well, if you can't hack it, quit. If you can quit SOL, you can quit piledriving."

"I would probably wash out before I quit. It's not much of a plan to go into something knowing from the get-go that you've got no business being there."

"Look, do what you want to do. I don't care. I'm making you a good offer. You turn it down, fine. I don't owe you anything; you don't owe me anything." Sterling bristled with determination. "I'm going into the apprenticeship program. You can join me or not."

Sterling downed his beer theatrically and sat back to wait for the carbonation to work its way up to a belch. Some of his weight had been deposited in his face, pushing his cheeks up and his eyebrows down, narrowing his energetic blue eyes. He signaled to Ray for refills. By getting drunk at Ray's, he was going to tell me and everybody else to get the hell out of his way.

* * *

I got out of Sterling's way and I got out of my own way as well. He was right. I had nothing else going for me. Of course, that was no reason, in and of itself, to try something new that I had no business getting into. But there was no way that I was going to join in my father's manic pursuit of admission to the Glenn Knoll Country Club, which was one step above the one he already belonged to. So, in a decision that I cannot fully explain other than as some sort of discount protest against life as envisioned by my father, I told Sterling that I would join him in his piledriving caper. For sure, Sterling made it easy for me to follow him. In fact, he had had an uncle, Art Nesko, who had worked as a piledriver and whose reputation with the union Business Agent greased the skids for us to get into the apprenticeship program.

I dreaded telling my parents about my new plans. I held off until I joined them for dinner at the fake chateaux they had built for investment purposes after I moved out of their old place. When my father greeted me at the double-door entryway, he seemed diminished by his slight stoop, bifocals, and disorganized eyebrows with long hairs going in all directions. My mother also seemed smaller than I usually thought of her. Her dyed orange-brown hair glistened like a marmoset's coat. The skin around her wrists looked to be made of canvas, unflatteringly accented by a tennis bracelet. She had a look of frantic wealth.

Their appearances made me uncomfortable. But then my father shook my hand and embraced me with genuine emotion and my mother greeted me with her cheek which I dutifully kissed. When she drew back from me, there was a tender look in her eyes.

Our conversation over dinner was restrained, polite, and without significance. At times it stopped altogether. Then it was so quiet that I could hear the air coming out of the ductwork in the house. Finally, I screwed up the fortitude to tell them about the piledriving apprenticeship program. My father clenched his jaw as he listened to me. When I finished, a new silence fell on us. My father appeared as if he were trying to calm himself down to the point where he could deliver his emphatic opposition in complete sentences.

"If you stay with this crazy decision of yours...," he finally began but then stopped and then started again. "If you stay with this crazy decision of yours, you're going to end up as a bottom feeder. That's not what I raised you to be."

"I'm just trying to find a life for myself which you have not already lived for me. I wished you wouldn't use the term 'bottom feeder."

"What I'm telling you is that you should make as much money as you can as fast as you can and then, if you want to do manual labor, you can buy yourself a chain saw and some land somewhere and cut up deadwood. And if you also want to use money for some charitable purpose, you'll have it."

"Look, I've quit SOL and I'm not going back. Maybe that will turn out to be a mistake; maybe it won't. Either way, it was my decision."

"But following the lead of this guy Nesko is no plan; it's just messing around."

"You think that I'm the only guy my age trying to figure things out? Give me some credit: I'm not moving back in with you. I'm not asking you for money."

"Are you looking for some sort of prize for that?"

"No. I have just gotten to the point where if I'm going to be living with mistakes, they might as well be my own."

"Say whatever you want to, you're still throwing away the opportunities I have given you."

It was only later that I learned that my father was sleeping apart from my mother in a downstairs bedroom because she correctly accused him of having an affair with the real estate agent who had sold them the property on which the new house had been built. This sad information surfaced when my parents, each in his or her own way, told me that they were getting a divorce. Put in that miserable context, my father's instructions to me about what I should do with my life were not persuasive. Nevertheless, to this day, his words stick with me – an accusation, a plea, a prediction all mixed together

CHAPTER THREE

When Sterling and I met with Don Crispin, the union Business Agent, at the local's office, Sterling played up how much he admired his Uncle Art and the work he had done even though Sterling had told me that he had barely known the man before he died after suffering a stroke and leaving his widow with a mortgage on a house, a Ford F150 with 112,000 miles on it, and an overdue Master Card balance.

"Art Nesko was a no bull shit piledriver," Don Crispin said as he moved a toothpick from one side of his mouth to the other, which, along with his stuffed torso, made him appear as if he had just finished a large meal. "You guys can only hope to be half the piledriver he was. You'll be startin' at the bottom of the ladder and I don't mean the bottom rung of the ladder. Just standin' in front of the ladder, lookin' at it. Might get on it. Might not. And even if you do, it'll be years before you can become a journeyman. But you're lucky bastards to even have the chance."

As Crispin talked, my eyes briefly drifted away from him and to the walls of the union office which were covered with photographs of groups of men attending district conventions, regional conventions, national conventions, and training workshops. Then my gaze returned to Crispin. I noticed that two of his fingers were amputated at the second joint.

"You got your eyes on these?" Crispin asked as he held up his hand with the two blunted digits. "I've done my time in this business. If you don't keep your noses clean, you won't have any fingers at all."

I smiled slightly at his screwed up reference to multiple body parts.

"Understand something, junior," Crispin shot back at me. "People don't laugh when I talk. You fuck with me and you'll be standin' at the end of the line at the unemployment office."

* * *

So Sterling and I went into the apprenticeship training program and were instructed in the basics of the trade. I will spare you the details other than to admit that I found a peculiar satisfaction from operating an acetylene torch and from being told not to wear pants with cuffs on them so that hot metal would not get caught in them and set me on fire. About four weeks into the program, we were told that we would be assigned to work for Thornton Construction as "punks".

Some people might look at what I was doing and want to compliment me for showing some backbone by venturing into something that would force me to become a different, perhaps even a better person. Ridiculous. I got hired to do construction work. Nothing special in that. Happens all the time. And there is nothing special about me. Growing up, I had two parents. There was always food on the table and a bedroom for me to sleep in. I tested at grade level. My emotions were contained and appropriate for the situation. Most days, I could get out of bed in the morning and face the day. Other than the fact that ultimately I caused men to die, I'm as ordinary as they come.

But, as someone once said, "Every life is a problem to be solved." Ordinary people have to decide how they are going to earn a living; if they are going to get married and to whom; if they are going have children and then how to raise them; how they are going to bury their parents; how they are going to manage their own deaths if they ever get the opportunity to do so. Every day, ordinary people make other decisions, including how we deal with our inevitable failures, which, in sum, determine whether or not we are assholes. That has got to count for something.

"Not really," you say, because to you many of the stories are run-of-the-mill, because to you they are not big enough. No doubt, most of us simply try our best not to be a burden to others, and, with some luck, not to be forced to do things we don't want to do. Motivational speakers exhort us to "reach for the stars", but that is a lot to ask when we are struggling with the facts of our lives on earth. Certainly, I cannot claim that becoming a piledriver apprentice was aiming for a celestial goal. And certainly, I cannot claim that the fact that I caused the death of others converts me into an extraordinary person. Therefore, you still might not be convinced that anything in my life is worth the notice.

You are entitled to your opinion. Maybe, there is no deeper meaning in what happened to me other than what happened to me. Maybe, I cannot offer anything other than my account of just one person trying to solve the problem of his own life. But maybe, if you think about it, there is something bigger embodied in this singular accounting because I am so ordinary. I could be wrong about that, but I'm in no position to resolve the matter here.

* * *

On that first Monday morning, Sterling and I were to report to Thornton Construction, I found myself lying on my side in bed, folded in uneasiness at the prospect of getting up and going to a construction site. Reluctantly, with a stiff moan, I rolled to the edge of the bed, straightened myself, and then stood up. Twisted around my body were boxer shorts and a corduroy shirt. I tried to get things into focus as I looked into a small mirror on the wall. Gazing back at me in the gray glass were dark eyes set near the surface of my brow and cheekbones. There was the face of a man in his twenties, both youthful and mature, who you could tell had slept in his clothes from the corduroy pattern of his shirt sleeve embossed on his face.

I blended in with the disorder in the room. In an "in for a dime, in for a dollar" way, I had moved some of my things into Sterling's apartment even before my lease had expired so that we could get up early together to go to work. He had an extra room and had offered me a rent-sharing arrangement that was more than reasonable if you overlooked the fact that the place was a sty with only minimal furnishings and the litter of Sterling's life piled into most of the corners. I had tried to avoid mixing any of my things with his, which explained the clutter in my quarters. Shoes in a pile; clothes in a pile; magazines in a pile.

I regarded the room with disdain and then shuffled off to the bathroom. In the sink, a delta of rich, alluvial soil had formed around the drain. I ran some cold water over my face and then fumbled for the towel. When I eventually found it on the floor, I started to wipe my face but stopped when the mildew smell became too strong.

The next thing was to see what shape Sterling was in. The night before, he had gone on a bender. Dead-end drinking, elbows-on-the-bar, talk-to-yourself drinking. I had told him to stop, that we had to go to work in the morning. Sterling said to leave him alone, that he had "momentum." Then he declared that he was "outta control" — his public service announcement about the amount of alcohol in his system.

I walked out of the bathroom, down a short corridor, and into the living room. Actually, there was no way that you could tell that it was a living room since it did not have any furniture. There was an air mattress on the floor, on top of which was Sterling, still asleep, having barely moved since passing out the night before.

"Get up," I said.

He flinched and then turned on his side.

"I know you're awake."

Sterling opened one eye and then the other. He worked his tongue around his mouth and made a face as if he had just eaten a sock. "Go away."

"You're not bailing out on me now. Get up!"

"Don't lecture me." Sterling rolled off the mattress and onto the floor. He stayed there and seemed to be getting comfortable again.

"No way." I grabbed him by the leg and pulled him out straight. He got to his hands and knees and started to crawl dog-style in the direction of the bathroom.

I returned to my bedroom and sat on the edge of the

bed to put on my new work boots. They were heavier and stiffer than any shoes I had ever worn and I worried that I looked club-footed when I walked in them.

With weighty steps, I stumbled into the galley kitchen and foraged for a donut. I ate the last one and then trudged out of the apartment, down the stairs, and out to the street curb where I waited for Sterling next to his car, a dented Charger with empty soda cans piled in the back seat.

Although, as I said, Sterling had made it easy for me to follow him, that didn't mean that I still didn't have doubts and anxieties about what we were doing. I was going into what, for me, was a wilderness where I had no special survival skills. Was I nervous about what lay ahead for me? Damn straight.

Sterling finally came down displaying a bad case of bedhead and started the car. I flopped onto the passenger's seat and leaned limply against the door. Through dim eyes, I looked at the street as Sterling drove us to work. Although I had been on the street before, none of it seemed familiar to me; I noticed everything as if I were seeing it for the first time.

* * *

A large sign at the corner of 16th and Calhoun promised that a twenty-story office building was being built on the property. As I walked with Sterling through the gate to the site, I felt adrenalin rush into my veins.

In the middle of the area was a huge excavation. Holding back soil walls and foundations of adjacent buildings were massive steel beam piles anchored by other steel beams set against the piles at an angle. The size of the excavation was unsettling. It seemed to challenge nature in a way that invited retribution. I backed away from the edge as we walked towards some trailers.

We approached one of the trailers and then hesitated at the base of the steps leading up to the door. "Let's get it over with," Sterling finally said. With slow feet we went inside.

"We're looking for the piledriving foreman," Sterling said to the first man who paid attention to us.

"Wrong trailer. He's next door."

We backed out and then went to the adjacent trailer where Sterling repeated his announcement.

"I'm the piledriver foreman," a man leaning against a door jamb said. That man was Lloyd Sollis.

Sollis appeared to be in his thirties, and even though he had thick arms and tarnished skin, he did not fit the image of the hardened construction worker. His glasses and high forehead gave him a bookish air. "You guys the apprentices Crispin told me about?" Without waiting for an answer he continued, "Go over to the piledrivers trailer. It's right behind this one. I'll be there in a few minutes."

So once again we backed out of a trailer and entered another one.

The interior of the piledrivers' trailer was beaten-up and spartan. Dented lockers along the walls bracketed several benches in the middle of the floor. The air carried the smell of yesterday's cigarettes.

A thin man in his early forties sitting on a bench looked up. As he did so, tendons and veins stuck out in his neck. He looked at us with clear, sharp eyes. He raised the Bible in his hands and said in a confident, matter-of-fact voice, "He staggered not at the promise of God through unbelief; but was strong in faith, giving glory to God. Romans 4:20."

I did not know how to respond. "Ah....ah."

Then Sterling stepped forward and extended his hand. "Sterling Nesko."

I followed. "Harry Travers."

"We're apprentices," Sterling added.

The man put his Bible into a locker, then turned to face us and shook our hands. "The name's Malcolm Snipes."

Another man who was standing next to Snipes nodded at us but didn't say anything. There was something inaccessible about him. His features were crowded into the middle of his face leaving much wasted space on his forehead and chin. Malcolm seemed to sense the awkwardness of the moment. "That's Early Ford," he said. "Don't pay him no mind. The man's goin' through a bad time. His girlfriend moved out on him and took all his furniture. He figures he can't do much about it because she's got brothers."

"Who are these clowns?" a guy standing in the back of the trailer asked. The man's eyes were widely spaced in bony sockets and had a leaden dullness which said that they could watch pain without blinking. His nose was bent in two directions.

"They say they're new," Malcolm said coolly.

"Who hired them?"

"Don't know. Ask 'em yourself."

"So who hired you guys?"

I noticed that the man had "TNT" tattooed across the knuckles of both hands.

"Lighten up on these guys, Drager" an older man sitting at the end of one of the benches said while looking at the man with tattoos. "They're obviously punks."

Drager sneered and turned away. The older man stood up and offered his hand. "Carl Baltimore. The smartest damn piledriver on this crew." Carl's bulky arms stretched his T-shirt at the seams and his bulging stomach forced his belt buckle to face the floor. His legs were short, making him look as if he was about to tip over.

The last man in the trailer, who was putting a jacket into a locker, turned and laughed. "The smartest piledriver, my ass." His eyes, his feet, his hands, his mouth, his ear lobes, everything about him was large. The only thing small about him was his voice. When he talked, no air came out. "Ellis Harding."

Lloyd Sollis appeared in the doorway. "Gentlemen." He stepped into the trailer and stood next to Sterling and me. "I assume you met everybody." He swung his leg over a bench and sat down. "Harry and Sterling here are apprentices. I expect you to do what you can to help 'em out."

"Crispin know about this?" Drager asked with an edge in his voice.

"Everything's been worked out with the union," Lloyd answered. "One of these guys is Art Nesko's nephew."

"That don't mean squat."

"Maybe to you. But to Crispin and maybe some of the rest of us it does. I told you that everything has been worked out with Don."

Drager looked at me with a mean directness. I had not said a word to him. I had never met the man before. Yet he appeared to despise me. The irrationality, the inaccessibility of his hostility made it seem truly threatening, even though there was also something rote about it.

His focus made me feel uncomfortable in a way that was new to me. For sure, I had never liked to be conspicuous in any setting. When I went into a room of strangers or even people I knew, I usually ended up leaning against the wall near the door. Drager's singling me out made me feel exposed and vulnerable. In a self-protective impulse, I was tempted to walk out of the trailer and abandon this strained attempt to define myself apart from my parents and their two-story foyer.

But, at the time, self-protection was not my top priority. Instead, I was all about defying expectations for me. Everyone's expectations, even including those that someone like Drager might have. If he wanted me off the crew, I would stay on it. If he wanted to intimidate me, I would resist him. I wanted to show him, Sterling, my family, myself something that we would all remember.

I looked away from Drager and at the other men around me. I noticed that several of them had a missing tooth. Ellis Harding was in the worst shape with his remaining, damaged incisors and bicuspids reminding me of stalactites in a small cave.

This also made me uncomfortable but not as uncomfortable as Drager's invented meanness.

Lloyd gave the crew their work assignments, spending some time discussing special precautions and procedures that would be necessary to get the job done safely. When he got around to Sterling and me, he said that because we were punks, he would only give us some simple shit to do as our initial assignment to see how we handled ourselves.

In fact, our work was simple shit. Our job was to hold onto tag lines attached to pieces of steel that were being lifted by a crane. The point was to not let the steel swing out of control. As I walked the pieces to where they were going to be landed, I watched the piledrivers whenever I could as they made their muscular calculations as to how to move and secure the heavy steel shoring which would hold back the sides of the excavation.

As the name of the trade indicates, a significant element of this work involved driving piles into the ground. In this case, driving steel beams down to bedrock. The beams had to be positioned into huge guides at the top of which was a power-driven weight that pounded the beam into place. Cross girders would be installed when necessary and then wooden shoring inserted between the vertical beams. The sound of the piledriver doing its work was steel on steel, intense and sharp. All of the crew, including Sterling and me, were given earplugs to wear.

While Carl Baltimore was rigging the tag line to a new piece of steel, I watched Drager climb up the guide attached to the piledriving machine. I jumped when I heard Sollis yell at Drager to "get your ass down to the ground." I continued to watch as Drager picked his way down the ladder on the guide and then as Sollis confronted him when he reached the bottom.

"Goddamn it!" Sollis barked at Drager. "Pay attention to what you're doing up there! You were leaning over the top of the pile. If the hammer had come down, you would've been nothing but a grease spot. I'm keeping you on the ground for the rest of the day and writing you up for a safety violation."

Drager turned his head away from Sollis and caught me watching him. He gave me another nasty look before I could point my eyes in another direction.

CHAPTER FOUR

At the end of the day, Lloyd set up a tab at a bar near the job site and invited the crew to drop in for a little welcoming party for the punks. While I appreciated Lloyd's gesture, I worried to myself that I was spending too much time in bars. My mood lifted when I saw that Drager was not there. I ended up sitting at a table with Carl and Ellis.

"It's been a month of Sundays since I worked with apprentices," Carl said. "And I ain't complainin' about that fact neither. Nothin' against punks, but I always feel like I gotta keep an eye on you because you don't know jack shit about piledriving. I ain't lookin' out for you. I'm lookin' out for me."

"Relax. We all started out as punks," Ellis said.

"What were you doing before that?" I asked.

"I was working in a factory putting together electric meters. Pretty easy, not very dangerous, no bad weather. But I wasn't learnin' shit. And a measly dollar an hour raise after a year. So I said the hell with it and signed up as a punk piledriver. It turned out OK. Ain't been a bad life."

"Agreed," Carl added and then turned to me. "And I got somethin' to show for it." Carl slapped his stomach as if it were a big melon. "How old do you think I am?"

"Forty-five. Somewhere around there," I answered.

"I'm forty-eight. See, Ellis, everybody thinks I'm younger than I am. If you had a full head of hair and better teeth, you'd look a hell of a lot younger too."

"At least I ain't so fat that I can't tie my own shoes."

"Good livin'. Big belly. I ain't ashamed of it."

Carl started to rub his stomach with both of his hands as if he were polishing it. He really was proud of his gut.

It turned out that he was from West Virginia, but for years he had moved up and down the East Coast following construction work and accumulating more addresses than either the post office or his creditors could keep track of. Carl said that all that moving around has been hard on his family, wife always having to pack things up in boxes, and his kids always having to drop out of schools. "But it kinda made us close," he said. "Everywhere we went we was strangers 'cept to ourselves. I told my wife that there was just one thing I won't put up with. There weren't no way I was ever gonna use anything but two-ply toilet paper. May cost more but it's worth it."

Lloyd was making the rounds and eventually got to our table. He sat down in the fourth chair as a new round of beers was delivered by a woman chewing gum on the tip of her tongue. "Not bad for a first day," he said addressing me. "Just keep an eye on Drager. He ain't right in the head and you seem to bother him."

"What have I done? I haven't said a word to him."

"It ain't nothin' you've done; it's just the fact that you're here. He's always worried about the company hiring guys to catch him stealing stuff."

"Why focus just on me? What about Sterling? We came in at the same time."

"I guess he doesn't like your looks. No offense, but I have to say that you are little bit of a pretty boy. What do

I know? I'm just bull shitting now...probably making too much of it."

"Drager is something you'd find crawling under a sink," Ellis blurted out. "I can't believe he' still being sent out to jobs. Lloyd, have you heard that Drager lifted some bricks off a job so that Crispin could build a patio behind his house, and now Crispin won't let anyone touch him?"

"That one has been goin' around for months. Might be true, but I think that Crispin's price is higher than a few patio bricks." Lloyd tilted his head back for a swallow of beer and then looked me in the eye. "What did you do before you signed up for piledriving?"

"Worked for a computer software company," I answered uneasily.

"Desk job. Must have been decent money, Why quit? Or were you fired?"

"I quit. I needed something completely different."

"Well, you got it now. I'm not sayin' anything against computers, but it just seems like too much sittin' around. At least with piledriving I'm on my feet and moving. And I got to use my head too. But no denying that it's a lot of bull work. You really understand what you're getting' into?"

"I'm not sure"

"Maybe you'd be better off working somewhere else."

"I didn't mean it like it sounded," I said, backpedaling.

"Pay real close attention to what I'm gonna say. I'm good at piledriving. Real good, but not much else. So this has got to work out for me and I'm not gonna let anybody, particularly guys I hardly know and probably I'm not gonna see again five years from now, fuck it up for me." Lloyd tilted his head back again to finish off his beer and then slammed the empty glass on the table. "Got to run. My sister's here. You guys stay as long as you like." He stood up from the table, pivoted on his right foot almost as if he were performing a military maneuver, and walked toward the front of the bar.

"That was cold," Ellis said.

"I get what he was saying," I responded as I watched Lloyd pick his way through the tables, and then join a young woman who appeared to be waiting for him in the front of the bar. She was standing in one of the few well-lighted spots in the establishment so I could see her face. It was exquisitely feminine with curves from her cheek-bones to her chin bent along a gentle oval. She held her head with a slightly upward tilt which accented the line of her neck.

"Is that Lloyd's sister?" I asked.

"Yea, I think that's her," Carl answered. "Lloyd said that she works at some clothing store around here...sells uniforms for security guards or something like that. Lloyd says that he likes this Thornton job we're on because he can meet up with his sister every now and then after work."

Sterling walked over to my table and took the chair which had been vacated by Lloyd. "I assume that you guys are interested in staying here and building up some momentum on this free tab."

Although I nodded weakly "yes", my mind was really on Lloyd's sister. Even from a distance, I was attracted to her. She was wearing some kind of smock from work. Her hair was cut close to her head suggesting that she was less interested in glamour than in being able to dry it quickly so that she could get to work on time. From my distance, it was hard to get a good look at her eyes. But from my limited vantage point enhanced by my imagination, she appeared to be someone who was playing the hand she was dealt in life so that at the end of the game she would have a stack of chips in front of her. I had this odd sensation that she was being beautiful just for me, as if I alone could recognize this beauty, and that I needed to do something about it or otherwise she would not receive the admiration she deserved.

When Sterling and I returned to our apartment, I went online and searched for a uniform shop in the general vicinity of the Thornton project. I came up with Arlene's World of Uniforms on Market Street about six blocks from the job site. Arlene's website did not have either photos or names of employees so I was not sure that this was the business where Lloyd's sister worked. I wrote down the address with the thought that I might drop by the place to see if she was there. Don't ask me how I let my mind run away like this based on seeing this woman across a bar room for less than two minutes because I don't understand it myself. All I know is that I was determined to give her the attention that was her due.

* * *

"Drager isn't comin' in," Lloyd announced to my relief the next day when he entered the trailer.

"He arrested again?" Ellis asked.

"No, but he came damn close. I'm told that he was messed up on something and was going after people. They were just about ready to call the cops."

Carl Baltimore turned to me. "You know that Drager

thinks that you and Nesko ain't really punks. He thinks that you're Pinkertons or something like that. That you're going to turn him into the company, get him arrested."

"Lloyd already told me something like that."

"Well, if you aren't spying on him, you probably should be. Can't prove it but I'm sure that on a couple of jobs, he was fencin' the compressors. Got so bad the company started hangin' them from crane lines at night so that no one could get to 'em. Next day tools is missin'. I'm tellin' you if it ain't nailed down, he'll lift it. The company even set up security cameras but they still couldn't catch him in the act."

Carl finished off his coffee and pitched the empty paper cup into a plastic bucket at the end of the bench. "Even if he ain't a thief, he's twisted in the head. Ernie Corso told me that Drager's old man beat the crap out of him. It was so bad that after the guy died, Drager went to the gravesite and fired off a few rounds into the dirt about where he thought he would hit the bastard in the heart."

"I figure that he was just born nasty," Ellis said. "Getting knocked around as a kid probably didn't help things."

Malcolm reached into his locker, pulled out his Bible, and held it up in front of us. "For all have sinned, and come short of the glory of God. Romans 3:23."

* * *

For our next assignment, Lloyd took Sterling and me over to a pile of steel and told us to "burn it" into pieces. The job was to use torches to cut through the beams at places that Lloyd had marked with a piece of chalk. "This is simple shit too. Torch work won't get any easier than this. But don't forget that you're gonna be blowin' hot metal out of the backside of the cut."

This was not welding work so I felt that the training we had been given about handling a torch was sufficient to allow me to do the job. That is, right up to the point where I was supposed to actually start working. I just stood there, jammed up by the fact that a digital guy like me was on a construction site with a torch in my hand and a face shield attached to my head.

"Travers!" Lloyd yelled from a distance. "Any day now!"

With tentative motions, I lit my torch. It felt like a weapon in my hand. I flipped down my shield, put the torch to the steel, and held it there until molten metal blew from the side of the beam.

To avoid the obvious danger of the burning operation I tried to focus on the details. The blue flame at the end of my torch. Adjusting the gases in the feeder lines so that the flame came to a perfect point. Steadying my hand so that the cut through the steel was as straight as possible. After a while, I developed a rhythm that made the job move more quickly. To my surprise, I was able to work with the simple discipline that comes from thinking no more than ten minutes into the future and with the simple satisfaction that comes from doing the job correctly.

* * *

The day was hot. Nervous heat rose within me and the July heat rose around me so that by 10:00 a.m., I had saturated my shirt and by the lunch break, had sweated through my pants.

Everyone else on the crew was suffering from the heat. At the lunch break, Early drank everything in his thermos without stopping for air. When Ellis took off his hard hat to wipe his brow, his thin hair was wet and flattened against his head. He looked like a bird that had just climbed out of an egg.

I was breathing with my mouth open like a panting dog. The fumes from the burning work had done nothing to help the situation. Sterling and I had picked up a sandwich and a Coke from a street vendor even though neither one of us had much of an appetite. Looking pale and unfocused, Sterling said that he was going back to the vendor to get another Coke. I remained sitting on a steel beam feeling a little forlorn.

"As it is written, there is none righteous, no, not one. Romans 3:10". I looked up and saw Malcolm Snipes standing in front of me. He had a benevolent smile on his face which suggested that he was going to attempt a conversion. He sat down on the beam next to me. "You look lonely over here all by yourself. There is never a need to walk alone if you accept...."

"Thanks for coming over to keep me company," I cut him off before he could finish his sentence. "So how long have you been a piledriver?" I asked hoping to steer the conversation away from matters of faith.

Malcolm did not take offense at the interruption, now displaying benevolent patience as if this might be a necessary step to establish a connection with me. "Ten years or so."

"You ever been hurt?"

"A few cuts and bruises. Nothing serious. But off the job I was shot in the leg," Malcolm stated as if making a proclamation. "Right in front of my mother's place. A drive-by. Still don't know who did it or why. It felt like somebody hit me in the leg with a baseball bat. A few inches higher and I'd be singin' soprano. I started to sleep with a gun under my pillow. I was livin' with my mother then and she comes into my room with some laundry. I wake up and see this person standin' next to me and before I know what I'm doin', I kick her in the head. Knock her backward into a closet and I already got my gun in my hand and takin' aim before I realize that it's my mother lyin' in that pile of shirts. I knew then I had to get out of there. Praise Jesus, I found a wife who had her own place in a better neighborhood. I say 'thank you, Jesus,' by being a lay preacher on Sundays. I tell my story to anybody who'll listen."

Once again, Malcolm had brought me up short and I did not know how to respond. But he wanted to keep me engaged and kept on talking. "Yea, it's been about ten years. I've worked with some of the guys on this crew on and off. Different jobs. Don't know much about 'em 'cept for Early. I know him from way back. Piledrivin' money is the best he's ever had but he's never been able to hang on to it. Gone before he evens counts it. Girlfriends drained him. Now he's got himself a new woman called Velveeta. He talks serious about her."

I appreciated the shift in Malcolm's focus, as if he sensed that a religious message might be lost on me. Maybe he was abandoning the effort or simply biding his time. Regardless, he now appeared to be deserving of respect and possibly, at some future moment, deserving of being considered a valuable source of insight on some appropriate topic.

Sterling returned sucking on a can of Coke. Malcolm excused himself and walked away.

"I didn't mean to break up the party," Sterling said with disappointment in his voice. "So how are you feeling?"

"Not great."

"Me either."

* * *

Malcolm's story stayed with me when I returned to work. Although it was well beyond my experience and full comprehension, I was grateful that he had shared it with me, as I was grateful that Carl and Ellis had shared something of their life histories with me. All three of the men had spoken in an open, easy tone, which served as an invitation for me to try to understand them. But what could I share with them which would help them understand me? I was only just starting to collect stories.

One story that I wanted to be able to tell, hopefully not one of hardship, would involve Lloyd's sister. Her face had become more real to me in contemplation than it had been in seeing it from a distance at the bar. It was almost as if I had created a hologram of her that was beginning to interfere with my ability to see what was actually in front of me – not a good thing on a construction site.

I was saved by the weather. At about 1:00 in the afternoon, it began to rain which caused the job to be shut down early. I decided immediately what I wanted to do with the time off. I would walk to Arlene's World of Uniforms. I knew that this might not be a good idea. I was wearing my work clothes and a hard hat. I did not have anything in mind to start a conversation with Lloyd's sister if she were actually working at Arlene's. But in my obsessed state of mind, I could not postpone trying to get closer to her. So I told Sterling that I wanted to run some errands and that I would get back to the apartment on my own. "Whatever" was his full response with the sound of small surprise in his voice.

I spent a few bucks on a cheap drugstore umbrella so that I would not get drenched on the walk to Arlene's. As I made my way down the street, I became increasingly uneasy with what I was doing. I admitted to myself that I was probably on the prowl because as a business slave at SOL, I had been denied the pleasures of female company and now might be hyperventilating. An encounter which should have been carefully planned was happening on the fly with the potential for it to turn into a disaster. And what would Lloyd do if he found out, which he would, that I had stalked his sister to her job? What if she were already involved in a serious relationship and had no use for me? What if she chewed gum with her mouth open? What if she thinks that my coming to her like this was strange, which I had already concluded that it was?

As the questions kept coming, my feet kept moving and I soon found myself standing in front of my destination. Arlene's World of Uniforms, which was wedged in between A&M Liquors and the Perfect Cut Hair Salon, was identified by a small neon sign showing Arlene's florid signature. If there were a world in there, the window display warned that it might be somewhat bizarre. Neither of the window mannequins, respectively dressed in uniforms of crisp meter-man khaki, and crisp security guard blue, had all of his rigid anatomy. One was missing hands and one an ear. The one with both hands but only one ear demonstrated his double-jointed virtuosity by twisting his right palm 180 degrees in the wrong direction. The fact that their hats were two sizes too big in no way discouraged the dummies, who, with their chipped complexions and fixed smiles, stared resolutely ahead toward a distant and bright horizon.

I decided that I would walk past the shop just for a closer look but that I would not actually go in. I tried to peer through Arlene's window, but the reflection from the sky kept me from seeing in. Approaching the door to the shop from the other direction was a woman in a smock. I stopped in my tracks. It was Lloyd's sister.

"Can I help you?" she asked.

"Ah...ah."

"It's okay. I work here. I'm just coming back from a break. Can I help you?"

"Well...ah...I...ah."

She smiled, almost laughed at me. "Don't be afraid to ask. Come on in." She waved her arm towards the interior of the shop and waited for me to go first, which I did.

Inside, she went behind a counter and told an older woman, who I assumed was Arlene, that she would take care of me. She motioned for me to step up to the counter. "So let me try again. What are you looking for?"

I heard her words but was lost in her face. Her full mouth was centered under lively, dark brown eyes. A few small blue veins could be faintly seen through the delicate translucent skin on her temples. Her teeth were slightly buck which promoted her smile. She wore a name tag which had "Minnie" stamped in gold lettering on a green background.

"If I brought in a suit, could you tailor it?"

"Sure. You don't have it with you?" Again, she smiled, almost laughed at me.

"Actually, no. I thought that I would stop by first to see whether you could do it. I was in the neighborhood, so it was no big deal."

"So bring the suit in when you're ready." Even though our transaction was basically completed, she did not move away from the counter but instead looked directly into my eyes. A wordless moment passed between us. My breathing became shallow. I wanted to touch her but did not move. Finally, I was able to muster out a few more words. "Thanks for your help. I'll come back with the suit."

"You do that. I'll be here."

I walked out of Arlene's because I felt that I had to, not because I wanted to. I had nothing else to say to her that would have made any sense. Attempting to go any farther with this first encounter would have made me seem to be the even bigger fool than I feared I already appeared to be in her eyes. Minnie Sollis. Minnie Sollis. Her name kept rolling around in my head.

CHAPTER FIVE

Upon entering the apartment, I found Sterling asleep on the "living-room" floor. He was snoring lightly with his hands folded behind his head. I stepped over him, walked into my bedroom, and stripped off my dirty clothes so I could shower.

I took a soaker during which Minnie's face appeared before me again. The energy in her eyes, the movement of her eyebrows, the way she ran her tongue over her lips gave sensual animation to her profile and held my attention to the point where I concluded that, in fact, I was losing it. I started to invent little facts about her to make her seem more approachable. That she was unattached, that she was longing for something really different in her life, that she was interested in me. I reminded myself of the look she had given me, that it seemed to be beckoning me in some way. Almost without me knowing it, she had become a beacon of rescue.

As I stepped out of the tub, Sterling yelled through the door to the bathroom. "Time for Ray's."

"I'm making a laundry run tonight," I yelled back.

"So just put your stuff in the machines and then we'll convene a meeting at the Oasis."

"Try not to get totally hammered tonight," I answered, doubting that it would make a difference.

* * *

Sterling said that the apartment manager had referred to the laundry room as a special advantage to renting in the building. Well, maybe. I had to brush aside strips of lint from dryer screens in order to find a place on top of the machines to put my bundle. The gray tile floor was covered with black streaks left by people who had put out cigarettes with their shoes. Empty detergent boxes were piled into a corner along with lost socks. About half the machines had "OUT OF ORDER" signs on them and a middle-aged woman on a plastic chair seemed to be in a similar condition. I filled up two top-loaders with dirty clothes, jammed in some quarters, and then left to meet up with Sterling at Ray's.

At the Oasis, several men were standing near the front door, taking long drags on short cigarettes. Since I had been there before, my entrance merited only casual inspection by the men at the door and the people inside. I did not know any of the regular patrons by name but nevertheless had imagined specific lives for many of them. I put them all on the edge of some kind of trouble - a car about to be repossessed, a wife about to walk out on the family, an unemployed brother about to move in for a long and difficult stay. It was the preoccupied looks in the faces that convinced me I was near the truth.

But tonight, Ray's was jumping with an end-of-the-month, new-money-in-the-pocket crowd. I dodged a waitress and two couples who, judging by the way the men rubbed the women's shoulders, were on their way to some serious sex.

"Lucky bastards," Sterling said as he slid into a booth. I sat down across from him. Sterling shook his head at his sorry circumstances, and got the attention of a waitress. "A pitcher of beer for me and my buddy here. Bring some pretzels too."

The beer was delivered and Sterling poured two glasses from the pitcher, and then he banged the pitcher on the tabletop. "This meeting is hereby called to order."

"Yes, I know: we'll waive the reading of the minutes..."

"The Chair has new business." There was a bounce in Sterling's voice.

"Get to the point."

"See that blonde number standing at the door? She's been eyeing us. I think she and her friend are coming over here."

I turned and saw two women approaching the booth. That's right. Women, not girls. They appeared to be past their middle twenties but just how far wasn't clear. What they lacked in attractiveness they made up for with ripeness. Their spiky hairdos made them look as if they had just stuck their fingers into a 120v socket.

"Excuse us, but all the booths are full and we were hoping that you might be willing to share yours."

"Make yourself at home," Sterling said.

"Mighty decent of you." The women parted and slid into the booth, each on one side of the table, with the woman who had done the talking sitting next to Sterling. "My name's Crystal and this is Dawn. What's your names?"

"I'm Sterling."

"Harry."

The waitress delivered two bags of pretzels and turned to Crystal and Dawn. "You ladies drinking to-night?"

"We'd like two bourbons and ginger ale," Crystal answered.

"They're on their way." The waitress returned to the

bar counter, leaving an awkward silence as Crystal fiddled with something in her purse. Finally, without looking up, she asked, "Sterling? I like that name. Sounds expensive."

"My mom used to say that I had it because I was the only thing that was 100% in her life."

"Good reason," Crystal replied.

"I haven't seen you two in here before," Sterling said in an obvious attempt to keep the conversation going. "Where you from?"

Crystal answered still looking down at her purse. "Trenton. We've been here for just a couple of weeks. Still getting used to this town."

"Dawn ever talk?" Sterling asked.

"Of course, she does, but she lets me do most of the talkin' when we meet strangers." Crystal snapped her purse closed. "How about yourselves? You been livin' here long?"

"Probably too long."

"What you do for a living?"

"Construction. Heavy stuff. Just started."

"Hey, I hear there's good money in construction. A guy I used to date worked construction and he drove a real nice Camaro. Too bad his wife decided to come back."

The bourbons and ginger ale were delivered.

Crystal centered her glass on a coaster. "Like I was sayin', I hear there's good money in construction."

"Yeah, pretty good ... if you can stand the work. What brought the two of you to town?"

"Wanted a change of scenery. Better job if we can find one," Crystal answered.

"What are you looking for?" Sterling asked.

"Just about anything that'll pay above minimum wage."

"Yeah, that's right," Dawn said after emptying half her glass, Her sudden willingness to use language destroyed what little energy there was in the conversation. The ensuing deadness was finally broken when Crystal ordered another round of bourbon and ginger ale.

It was slow going. But beneath the surface, there was some suggestive sexual play. Dawn, who was sitting next to me, rubbed her leg up against mine. Crystal told Sterling that she thought that he was "cute as a bear" and had "bedroom eyes."

The second round of drinks moved things along a little farther. Crystal declared that if she didn't get squared away soon, she was might take a job at the Pajama Game Massage Parlor. No, she had never done anything like that before and no, she wouldn't go all the way with the customers but she wasn't about to starve or go back to Trenton. Dawn agreed that they shouldn't starve or go back to Trenton. Crystal said that she liked men who wore tight jeans.

Crystal tipped back her second drink and put down the glass. "You'll excuse us, I'm sure, while we go to the ladies' room." Crystal tapped Dawn on the shoulder and helped her get oriented so that she could make it to the john. Dawn downed her drink and both of them set off toward the back of the bar.

Sterling waited a few seconds until they were out of hearing range. "I like Crystal. She's kind of frisky. This could go somewhere, so you gotta help me out here."

"I'm sorry but I can't come to the phone right now.

Leave a message and I will get back to you."

"Come on. Help out a friend in need."

I fiddled with a pretzel and considered the idea. How would I ever explain to Minnie Sollis or to myself the fact that I had spent the night with a woman like Dawn? "Those women are sure taking their time in the bathroom. Dawn probably can't figure out how to get herself out of the stall. Don't be dependin' on me to occupy her attention, such as it is, when they get back."

The waitress walked up to the booth. "Here's the check, gentlemen."

"That's OK, we're not finished yet," Sterling answered. "Matter of fact, we'd like to order another pitcher."

"Well, I thought you were done since your lady friends left and said you would pay for everything."

"They did...said...what?"

"Yeah, those two women that were sitting in your booth left a few minutes ago."

"They said they were going to the ladies' room."

"Well, they went out the back door and they said that you were picking up the tab for their drinks. It was your treat. So here's the bill."

"No way," I insisted. "They invited themselves to sit down with us. We didn't ask them over here. Never seen them before in our lives."

"Look, that's what they told me. If you want to work something out with Ray, that's fine by me, but I gotta account for these drinks."

I smacked the table. "Damn it! I can't believe we got suckered like that. It's pathetic." I pushed myself out of the booth and started to make my way for the door.

"What about some money for the drinks?" Sterling

yelled after me.

I turned around, went back to the booth, threw some cash on the table, and headed back for the door.

* * *

A steady rain was falling outside. Still furious, I stood in front of Ray's and looked at the apartment building across the street. Damp masonry gave the structure a dim, lifeless appearance. On the third floor, I saw the face of a boy staring out to the street through the glass. The face was framed on one side by a crooked line of masking tape covering a crack in the window and on the other side by a potted flower sitting on the sill. He waved to me as if we were friends.

I opened up my cheap umbrella with too much force and ripped some of the fabric off the end of one of the spokes. The rain was doing nothing to help the appearance of the neighborhood. Instead of looking washed, the streets looked greasy and the exposed roots of the thin trees by the curbs were covered with wet litter. On my way back to the apartment, I passed several people who appeared to be oblivious to the rain. Walking along in saturated shirts, stepping in all of the puddles, hair stuck to their foreheads, going nowhere in particular. The idea behind leaving SOL had been simple: everything real. The boldness of it all! But maybe this was too much reality.

At the laundry room, I found my wet clothes piled on top of several washing machines. I began to untwist the piles so I could throw the stuff into a dryer. As I tried to work out the knots, my mind went back to Minnie Sollis. I kept thinking that I had come close to cheating on her even though we had no relationship. It was a ludicrous sensation, but one that told me where things were headed.

As I threw the last of my shirts into the dryer, I looked at a young mother, who was folding baby's clothing with a surprising, almost poignant neatness. I felt that both of us should get out of the neighborhood.

* * *

Truth be told, the neighborhood was not all that bad. The buildings were in generally good repair and free of graffiti. Yes, there were some burger wrappers and empty soda cans on the ground, but no worse than in other parts of town. Small businesses seemed to have a steady stream of customers. And with the exception of the people I saw sloshing through the rain, most of the people walking along the streets seemed purposeful.

Yet, as I had done with the patrons at Ray's Oasis, I imagined difficult lives for all of them. Perhaps, not with the specificity I used at Ray's, where I had more time to focus on individual faces, but with enough conviction to give me an attitude. That attitude seemed to become more defensive as I stumbled forward with my own life. I had to imagine that other people were struggling more than I was so that I would not seem like such a fuck-up myself. Misery loves company, but loves to see people worse off even more.

As usual, I was slightly disoriented when the alarm sounded the next morning. Lying in the rumpled sheets, I had the backward sensation of having awakened into a dream because my actual surroundings seemed unreal to me. I closed my eyes again and hoped that the next time I opened them I would see something different.

When that did not happen, I struggled not to sur-
render to my urge to pull the top sheet over my head.
Finally, embarrassed by my own dithering, I threw back
the sheet and pulled myself up and out. I stood next to
the bed for a few seconds almost as if I were trying to get
my balance and then moved my feet forward without
lifting them. Slowly, I made my way to Sterling's
bedroom. He was completely zoned out. He stirred after I
yelled "Wake up!", so I continued my shuffling into the
bathroom.

I used the toilet but did not have the willpower to
shave. I figured that there was also no point in going into
the kitchen because I had no appetite and there was
nothing to eat anyway. I went back into my room, put on
my work clothes, and waited for Sterling to present
himself.

Eventually, he surfaced like a gray carp coming up
through murky water. He looked at me through my door.

"We got anything to eat?" he asked.

"Not unless you bought it last night on the way back
from Ray's."

"Why can't you buy something for once?"

"I did and you ate it."

"I don't remember that," Sterling appeared genuinely
perplexed.

"There are a lot of things you don't remember. The
fact is that the refrigerator is empty. So just get ready
and we'll get something to eat on the way in."

Once again, I left the apartment before Sterling to
wait for him beside his car. As I leaned against the
fender, I contemplated the early morning. I knew little

about this time of day because I had not seen very much of it. I was familiar with the gaudy orange drama of sunsets. But sunrises, at least the few that I had seen, had stiller colors, quieter light, and seemed to occur almost without being noticed. Or was it because people are more affected by departures than arrivals?

* * *

At the job, the crew seemed a little on edge when we walked into the trailer. Drager had returned. He sat at the end of one of the benches in the trailer and stared into a middle distance beyond the few feet which separated all of us in the trailer. He did not look at me; he did not say anything to me. For a minute I thought that I might have misjudged him, thought that I had seen hostility in him towards me when, in fact, there had been none. But Lloyd had seen it too and had warned me about it even though he had said that perhaps he was making too much of it. What to think? I chose to hope that Drager's refusal to acknowledge my presence was a sign that I was no longer of any importance to him.

Lloyd assigned Sterling and me more burning work. I was OK with the assignment because the job was familiar and manageable. I started it with the best of intentions. But then it became uncomfortable as my crouching position strained my back, the fumes from the burning metal strained my lungs, and the monotony of the work strained my brain. I knew that I had to pay attention to what I was doing and for a long time I was able to. But it was inevitable that my concentration would wane and then I would try to force myself back into the right zone.

I was scared that if I didn't, I would melt part of my leg away with the torch.

At the end of the day I was exhausted. As Sterling and I were walking off the job I told him that I needed to go to the portajohn. Sterling said that he would wait for me in the car.

After stepping out of the toilet, I walked in the direction of the gate to the project. As I came around the corner of a trailer, I saw Drager coming in the other direction. He immediately straightened up and looked at me. "Why are you following me?" he asked with anger in his voice.

"I'm not."

"So then why are you still here?"

"I just got done using the portajohn."

"You little fuck, why are you and your asswipe buddy on this job?" Drager stepped forward to block my way.

I tried to step to his side but was able to move only a few feet before Drager blocked me again. "I asked you a question."

I stiffened. "Ah, because I needed to work."

"I heard that you already had a job, so you didn't need this one. Don't bull shit me. Ain't a mark on your shoes."

"My shoes are new because I'm a punk."

"So you've got no time invested here. No better time to quit."

"I don't get what this is all about. Why should I quit? I just started."

"Because I'm tellin' you to."

"Well, I'm not a company plant if that's what you're worried about." I regretted this remark as soon as it was out of my mouth.

"Why would you be sayin' something like that to me?" Pieces of spittle flew from Drager's tongue.

"I didn't mean anything by it. All I'm trying to say is that I'm here just to do the work. I don't want any trouble." I tried again to slide by him.

Drager blocked me again and poked his finger into my chest. "I don't like people following me."

"I wasn't. I wasn't. I just want to be left alone."

"I don't give a shit about what you want." He grabbed my shirt.

I rammed my head into his face. My forehead cracked his nose straight on. Drager reeled and cried out in pain. I looked at him in disbelief at what I had just done. Drager stuck out his lower lip to collect the blood running from his nostrils. Before I could move away, he spit the blood into my face. I lurched backward. Drager moved in and slapped me on the side of the head. I put up my hands to cover my face. "You little fuck!" Drager slapped me again. I tried to get beyond his reach, but he kept coming after me. Another slap snapped my head to the side.

"Break it up!" Lloyd yelled from a distance.

Drager hit me again.

"Enough!" Lloyd yelled as he ran up to us.

"This little fuck head-butted me!" Drager yelled back. He stuck out his lip again to catch the blood which was still running from his nose and then spewed the red mess into my hair.

"Damn it! Back away from him!" Lloyd shouted as he stepped in between us.

Drager wiped blood from his chin. "No punk is going

to try to fuck me up and just walk away!" He winced with pain as he let loose the threat.

Lloyd did not move. "I'm handling this now."

Drager spit more blood, this time onto the ground.

"We're done here," Lloyd said with authority. "You need to go to an emergency room and get your nose looked at."

Drager made a move as if he was going to try to push by Lloyd to get at me.

Lloyd stood his ground.

Drager continued forward but then stopped. "The punk head-butted me," Drager repeated.

"I got it. I got it. Now go on out of here and get yourself cleaned up."

"I ain't finished with him!"

"You are for today!"

Drager glared at Lloyd. For a second, I thought that Drager was going to take a swing at him too. Then Drager spat again into the dirt, this time close to Lloyd's shoes, turned and stomped off towards the gate.

Lloyd looked at my face. "You're a mess too."

"It's not my blood," I said as I tried to catch my breath. "It's his. He spit on me. I was trying to protect myself."

"I saw him go after you Otherwise, we wouldn't be having this conversation. You'd be out on your ass." Lloyd took off his hard hat and ran his finger along the oil-stained liner. "What did you say to him?"

"He thought that I was following him. I tried to explain that I wasn't, that I just gone to the john."

"Drager isn't gonna let this sit. You want to deal with the shit that is coming your way?"

I did not respond.

"What I'm askin' you is whether you still want to keep this job."

I still did not respond.

"OK, then, I'll decide what to do as things stand now. I've got your cell phone number. I'll call you in the morning and tell you whether or not to come in. Where's Nesko?"

"Waiting for me at the car."

"Might be a good idea if the two of you stayed together if I let you come back to work."

*　*　*

As I walked to the car, still breathing heavily, I felt off balance, as if I were tipping beyond my center of gravity. Physically, emotionally going so far that I would just keep going until I fell over. I had never been in a fight in my entire life. Never hit anybody. Never drew blood. Never gave anyone a reason for taking revenge against me. Only a few minutes earlier, Drager's hatred of me had been totally invented, pointless, inexplicable, random in a way that had given me hope that it was temporary, maybe not even real. No more. Now, if only because I had defended myself and had hurt him, he had a reason to hurt me, to pursue me until he drew my blood. My brain began to reel with grotesque images of big skulls on small bodies. I was worried that if I moved my head to the side, it might fall off. My legs wobbled as I walked out the gate.

Sterling was pacing in front of the car when I finally approached him. "What in the hell happened to you?" he asked when he saw my face.

I had trouble finding enough words to answer his question but was able to describe how the blood got onto my face.

"So this was Drager's doing," Sterling said with specific concern in his voice. "I suppose he thinks the same thing about me and it's only a matter of time before it's my turn."

"I hurt him pretty bad, so he'll want to get back at me before he ever gets to you. You're welcome." I faked a light tone in order to bring this exchange to a close.

I got into the car, but I could still feel the wet spray of Drager's bloody spit and the hot sting of his hand on my face. It could have been worse; he could have closed his fist. I figured that by using his open hand Drager had intended to humiliate me because slapping was something he would do to a woman. Next time he would use his fist; next time he would not stop until he had injured me permanently, branded me with a scar.

* * *

The following morning I got a call from Lloyd. "Don't come into today," he began. "You're suspended without pay for the day. We can't tolerate fighting on the job. You get into a situation like that, you're supposed to walk away from it and find me."

"I tried to get away from Drager but he blocked me."

"I already told you that I saw what happened. And I already told you that if I hadn't, I would have fired you on the spot. Don't push your luck here. Take the suspension and consider yourself lucky because I convinced Crispin to move Drager to a different job. I also told Don that when that new job is done in a few weeks, he should get Drager into a dry-out tank. You broke his nose, by the way."

Did I think about quitting right then and there? Of course, I did. How could I not? But Lloyd had made a special effort on my behalf; Drager was not going to be on the job when I returned, and there was even a chance that he would never come back. These reasons occurred to me so that I can itemize them now, but, at the time, they were not carefully assembled or assessed. Instead, I experimented with bravado and said nothing to Lloyd, leaving him to conclude that I wanted to keep my job and leaving me to hope that the whole episode would fade away as if it were a bad dream. I also said nothing to Sterling other than to tell him that I had been suspended for a day. He did not suggest that either one of us quit, but he did say that he had not bargained for anything like this happening when we signed up as punks and that he was sorry that I was tangled up in it. Maybe, in the end, I didn't quit because it would have been too embarrassing to do that, particularly if Minnie Sollis found out about it.

CHAPTER SIX

I served my suspension. After Sterling left for work, I remained in the apartment until its desolation forced me to flee onto the streets. I walked to a nearby McDonald's and ordered an Egg McMuffin and a small orange juice., which was the best breakfast I had had in weeks. I nibbled and sipped as slowly as possible in order to make the time pass because I had nowhere else to go. I tried to shift my mind into neutral so that I would not obsess about Drager. I could not do it and kept slipping back into gear with futile attempts to make sense of what had happened.

Finally, Minnie Sollis appeared in my thoughts, once again offering to rescue me. I was grateful for her appearance even though I knew that most of what was going through my mind about her was in the realm of fantasy. In order to move into the realm of reality, I tried to focus on what I should do next to pursue her. I had told her that I had stopped into Arlene's to inquire about the tailoring of a suit. But I didn't have a suit with me at the apartment and the one I thought might be in a hall closet in my parents' house had already been tailored, so I needed to get an untailored suit. I welcomed the mission as one which would consume some of the day.

I found a men's store on the internet which was not too far away and which advertised a suit sale which included an extra pair of pants for free. At the store, I slowly selected a wool-blend, charcoal, traditional style which I thought communicated substance. Then I made my way to the neighborhood near Arlene's where I found another McDonald's where I could get a Filet-O-Fish and burn another hour so that I would not appear at Arlene's too early in the day, thereby raising the question: why wasn't I at work?

When I swung the door into Arlene's, Minnie looked up from where she was standing at the counter and, much to my relief, recognized me. She welcomed me back to the shop as if she had expected that I would return and then, in a business-like way, took charge of the fitting. "The changing room is in the back. Why don't we start with the pants."

After I came out of the changing room wearing the suit pants at the awkward length I had created by folding the excess fabric, Minnie positioned me in front of a big mirror and asked me whether I wanted cuffs with a medium break. I said that I did and she kneeled to pin and mark the legs. "How does the rest of it feel? Do you want to take in the waist?"

"I think it's OK," I answered even though I would have liked her to feel my hips.

"OK, let's try the suit jacket."

When I put it on, she asked me to button the front, and then she stood close to me in front of the mirror. Our eyes connected through the reflection on the silver glass. She ran her hands over my shoulders and down my torso. Her head almost touched mine. I could smell her perfume.

"I don't think that we will have to take in too much. Pretty good fit as is." She made a few markings and pinned a few folds on the sides. "So do you work around here?"

"Yes. I do construction."

"My brother's in construction. What kind do you do?"

I knew that if I went any distance with her eventually she would find out that I worked with Lloyd, but I was worried that it was too early to tell her because nothing was established between us. "Heavy construction."

"You live around here?"

"It's not far. I'm renting a place with another guy. How about you?"

"I've got my own place. I'm probably paying more than I should, but it's worth it being able to have the apartment all to myself."

"You don't have to convince me."

"I would think that construction pays well enough for you to be able to afford something like what I have."

"I'm just starting out. Actually, I'm in an apprenticeship program."

"You have to start somewhere."

"How long have you worked here?"

"A year and a half. I'm saving up to get an associate's degree, and, if I can swing it, a four-year degree after that."

I was relieved that she did not appear to think that my question was too personal and had responded with an easy directness. I wanted to follow up on her answer by asking her what she wanted to study but I was concerned that that would prompt her, in turn, to ask me questions which would force me to admit that even though I had four years of college under my belt, I still didn't know what I wanted to do with my life. "How did you decide to work here?" I was finally able to ask.

"Arlene is a family friend. I'm pretty good with a

thread and needle. The pay is decent. And I don't know how she does it but Arlene gives me health insurance." She ran her hands over my shoulders. "I think that we're all set here." She stayed close to me even though the fitting was over. I sensed that she knew that she was having an effect on me.

I figured that I might as well go for broke. "I know that this is kind of sudden but I was wondering whether I could take you to dinner on Friday night. I'm sorry....I know that this is.... I'm sorry if I'm making you feel uncomfortable..." I was starting to get tangled up in my words.

"I don't feel uncomfortable. If I don't want to join you for dinner, all I have to do is to say 'no,' which is what I'm going to do. I'm busy Friday night."

"I'm sorry...I generally don't do things like this...it just came out. You shouldn't have to put up with something like this from a customer. I won't bother you like this again."

"Stop apologizing. You were polite. And don't give up so quickly. You never asked me about Saturday night."

"What about Saturday night?"

"I could make it, but I won't be able to make a long night of it. Just for coffee and maybe a dessert. I will pick the place and will meet you there and I will go home by myself. No offense, but I don't really know you. Give me your phone number so that I can text you."

I was dumbfounded by this response. A complete and final "no" from her, maybe even a warning to leave her alone, would not have surprised me. But she had said "yes".

For hours after I left Arlene's, I still could not believe

that Minnie was going to go out with me or even that I had asked her to. Her acceptance of my invitation suggested that she was going to make the most of every opportunity that came her way; that she was going to take herself beyond the predictable. And me too.

* * *

When I stepped into the trailer the day after the suspension, Carl immediately had asked me "How did you do it?"

"Do what?"

"Break Drager's nose." Obviously, the word had gotten out.

"I don't want to talk about it."

"Why are you puttin' a 'Closed for Business' sign in your window? We all know that Drager is a whack job. No one here is gonna give you any shit about standin' your ground with him."

"I've lived through it once and I don't want to live through it again by talking about it."

"So just give us a few details. We heard that you head-butted him. True?"

"True."

"And that he was tryin' to take your head off."

"True."

"And that you bloodied him pretty good."

"I told you that I don't want to talk about it." I meant what I said. The topic was giving me nausea.

"Lay off him," Malcolm interjected.

Lloyd walked through the door. He said nothing about Drager but simply proceeded to go over the day's assignments. I was sent back to burning work, the same type of thing that I had been doing before. Sterling was given a new assignment of working with Carl rigging steel for crane lifts. He would be learning a new skill while I would be stuck with simple shit. I worried not only that this was part of my punishment but also that Lloyd was rewarding Sterling for being a better worker, which started to irritate me. But I understood that Lloyd expected me to keep my head down and to do the job without incident, which is what I did.

At the lunch break, Carl returned to my run-in with Drager. "I believe that you may be the only piledriver who has ever done any damage to Drager."

"Carl, I told you to lay off him," Malcolm interjected again. "Everybody knows the story about Drager. No use to keep bringin' it up."

Carl straightened up. "I was about to say before you interrupted me that we had Travers' back...that we'll keep an eye on Drager. I was going to make him feel better about this whole thing."

"Both you and I know that we can't watch Drager all the time. We've got to pay attention to what's in front of us and can't be lookin' around the job to find where Drager is. I'm sure that Trimmer has got that figured out. So just drop the topic."

Actually, I had figured that out and that someday I might be a sitting duck. But Drager was not on the job at that moment, so I tried to drop the topic myself.

In the afternoon, Sterling was reassigned to burning work along with me. As I watched him spark his torch, I felt a little better about my own assignment and was able to get through the rest of the day.

To get through the rest of the week was more of a challenge, but I kept reminding myself that I was going to see Minnie Sollis on Saturday. The good luck of her availability, of her willingness to meet me, did a lot to cancel out the bad luck of what had happened with Drager. Or, at least, this was the calculation that I allowed myself.

* * *

On Saturday evening, I showered with rare thoroughness. I even soaped my feet. After drying off, I combed my hair back in hopes of getting the perfect look, put on my only pair of pants with a crease in them, and put on my only shirt with a clean collar, rearranging the shirt so that its buttons were in a line with the pants' zipper. I relished every minute of this preparation.

I left the apartment without telling Sterling where I was going and drove to Donato's Café, the place Minnie had picked for us to meet. She was waiting for me just inside the door and greeted me with a sly smile. I smiled back and then checked the alignment of my buttons again. Then my eyes returned to Minnie. I was having trouble believing that there she was, right in front of me.

As we walked to a corner table, I tripped over my own feet when I was watching Minnie instead of looking where I was going. I continued to watch her, even after we had been seated.

"It's not polite to stare," she said, snapping me back into the moment.

"Minnie...I haven't met many people with that name," I finally said.

"I was named after my great grandmother Minnie Copeland. Lots of stories about her, probably exaggerated, but my family believes them just like they'd been certified by an accountant." Minnie rearranged her silverware to make all of the pieces parallel to each other. "She married a guy with big plans but not much else. He walked out on her and left her with the two kids. So she made money by doing piece work in her apartment and tried to get a high school degree. She was in and out school when things went right or wrong for her but she finally graduated. And because of some teacher, she had a thing about books. The story is that when she died, her place was full of them, just like my place. 'You and your books,' my mother always says. 'Minnie is the perfect name for you.'"

I was surprised, excited by the detail in Minnie's answer. I couldn't remember hearing anything quite like it from other women with whom I had had casual conversations. There did not appear to be any calculated ambiguity or evasion in her words. There did not appear to be any apologetic or defensive tone in the sharing of her family history. I sensed that in her directness was a message to me that if the two of us were going to have any kind of relationship I had to talk to her in the same way.

Minnie eyed me carefully. "I like the way your hair is pulled back straight off your forehead. It looks kind of foreign and domestic at the same time if you know what I mean."

I did not respond because I did not how to and because I was still thinking about what she had said about her great grandmother. I was amazed that Minnie

Sollis knew something about Minnie Copeland because I couldn't tell you a thing about my great grandmother or even very much about my aunts and uncles. It was as if my parents had wanted to have nothing to do with relatives because they had lived in two-bedroom starter homes all their lives.

"Harry...kind of an old-fashioned name," Minnie offered.

"Some people call me 'Henry', which irritates me."

"Don't worry. I'll stick with 'Harry'. So how did you get into construction?"

"Nothing particularly impressive to tell." Despite what I had sensed about the need to be open, I was hesitating.

"You've got to tell me something or otherwise I'll never get to know you."

"I guess I was just restless," I began without choosing my words carefully. "I could see my life all ahead of me. Take a desk job and make a lot of money like I was supposed to, get married to somebody with a lot of money like I was supposed to, spend lots of money like I was supposed to, have kids and get them into some country day school and a college worth bragging about like I was supposed to, and play some golf and tennis along the way. It was like I had already lived it. So I say to myself: what's the point if I already know how it's going to turn out."

Even as I was talking I knew that I had gone too far too fast, but the words had just kept coming out of my mouth as if I didn't have any control over them. I watched Minnie's eyes widen with surprise and confusion. I became upset with myself and could feel perspiration starting to seep out of my forehead.

"Country day school? College? Golf? Tennis? So you come from money and you're working construction? I don't get it."

"It's my parents' money, not mine."

"I still don't get it."

"It's hard for me to explain." I wiped my forehead with my napkin and prayed that Minnie would give up the topic.

"So your family has money and you're trying to show them that you can make it on your own. Is that it?"

"That's part of it, I suppose."

"Do you really think that working construction is the answer? I mean don't get me wrong here. My dad's a piledriver and so is one of my brothers and I respect what they do. But it's a hard way to make a living. Why do that to yourself? If your life ends up like my father's, you'll never see anything west of Detroit."

"I apologize. I'm not very good at describing what's going through my head. I can tell you that it's important to me that I decided...decided on my own...to sign up for the apprenticeship program. I'm sorry. I shouldn't have gotten into some deep subject like this right off the bat."

"No need to apologize. All you did was to answer my questions."

"Ah...ah..so, you said that you like books."

Minnie smoothed the napkin on her lap. "Yes, I like books. Started collecting them when I was in seventh grade. Library sales, throw-aways. I love to read and that's another reason why I want to go back to school. As I told you, I'm trying to save now so that I can cover the tuition. I know that my folks aren't going to help me because they can't and even if they could, I doubt that they would. My dad says that I should let employers train me on their own dime for what they want. We argue about it but it doesn't make any difference because there's no money there anyway. So I'll pay for it myself. You know how people say that God helps those who help themselves. That's what I believe..."

I knew that was not my father's view. "Some people get a lot of help from family contacts."

"Of course, who you know can make a difference, but I don't know anybody important, so what am I supposed to do? Throw in the towel? Besides, at this point, I am used to taking care of myself. Done it for years. I keep telling my parents that they should be happy that I'm on my own and stop expecting me to explain myself all the time." She suddenly sat up straight. "I'm curious: you asking me out...is this some sort of rich boy/poor girl adventure for you? See how the lesser lights live?"

"No...no. I swear it. I asked you out because I thought that you are beautiful."

"That's a nice thing to say. At least for now, I'm going to choose to believe you."

Sitting across the table from her, I suddenly imagined Minnie moving to be by my side; but then, wary of me, retreating for cover. On my way back to my apartment after she had declined my offer to escort her back to hers, she kept appearing and disappearing in my imagination like a doe feeding in a forest.

* * *

When I opened my apartment door, the place was dark. "Sterling?" No answer. I walked into my bedroom and sprawled onto the bed, thinking of Minnie, Minnie, Minnie; it was almost laughable. Finally, I fell asleep in my "good" clothes.

"Hey, man, I'm fuckin' outta control!"

I opened my eyes.

"Fuckin' out of control!"

Sterling was back.

I got up to assess the damage. To my surprise, he was not alone. Propped up against him was a short, red-haired woman, who was about as wrecked as he was. There was no focus in her eyes and she looked like she might pass out on the spot.

Sterling attempted an introduction. "This here's my friend ... Harry Tr ... Tr ... Travers." He did not bother with the woman's name.

She smiled weakly, showing short teeth and pale gums. "Pleased, I'm sure."

I put on a pleasant face. "Didn't catch the name."

Sterling pulled her in the direction of his bedroom. "Harry, we'd like to talk, but you'd better ex ... excuse us. Right?"

"Right. You two being outta control and all. Don't mind me."

"OK." Sterling did his best to steady himself as he felt his way into his bedroom and then closed the door. The whole thing was sleazy. The woman had to be a pickup from Ray's Oasis.

I went back into my bedroom and tried to listen through the wall for what was happening in Sterling's bed. There were a few moans but not much more. I listened until my little remaining self-respect forced me to turn away from the wall, crawl into bed, and turn out the light.

The woman was gone in the morning and Sterling was ready to go to work on time. He acted as if the previous night had been totally routine, which, in some ways, it had been. He made no mention of his guest. Finally, as we were riding in the car to work, I brought her up almost out of a compulsion to add a little respectability to the whole thing. "So where did you meet her?"

"Who?" He appeared to have real difficulty remembering.

"Who do you think? The redhead from last night. I would have used her name, but you didn't introduce her. So where did you meet her? Ray's?"

"Yeah. I went down there to see if I could find Crystal."

"Crystal! The one who stiffed us for the drinks?"

"Yeah. I told you I kind of liked her. The drinks don't matter that much to me."

"You've got your head wedged. I can't believe you would go looking for her. She's trouble for sure."

"You're just bitter because she put one over on you."

Sterling suddenly turned into the entrance for a Wendy's, causing the car behind us to honk and swerve. "I want a cup of coffee."

"Next time try signaling first."

Other than talking to the Wendy's employee as we drove by the service window, Sterling said nothing. He sipped his coffee through a small hole in the cup lid and then placed the cup between his legs. "I'll tell you why I'm interested in Crystal," he finally said as he drove back onto the street. "Because I think she's interested in me."

"Then why did she walk out on you?"

"I intend to ask her that when I see her again." Sterling paused to reach down to get his coffee. He drove on silently, sipping his coffee until he finally finished it, crushed his cup, and flipped it over his shoulder into the back seat of the car.

"So what about the number last night?" I asked. "She left kind of early."

"Said she had to go to work." Sterling shrugged his shoulders. "Who knows? She might be telling the truth."

CHAPTER SEVEN

I saw Minnie again the following Wednesday. This time she suggested that I pick her up at her apartment. I read everything I could into her suggestion. As I approached her door, I felt a little light-headed. I stood in front of her door for more than a moment before I could bring myself to push the buzzer.

She opened her door wearing a loose-fitting green blouse which exposed her neck in a way that made me think of her whole body. I did not move.

"Why don't you step in for a second," she said. "Would you like a beer or a soda?"

"Whatever you're having." I walked across the threshold to her apartment and tried to take in as much as I could as quickly as I could. The place, a one-bedroom on the third floor, was consistently furnished in used blond furniture, which, she said, her aunt had given her. Everything was relentlessly in order. Throw rugs perfectly parallel to the walls, curtains parted just so, doilies centered, bric-a-brac arranged on wall shelves according to size and general subject matter (a collection of ceramic cats on the first shelf and a spoon collection from the states and territories on the second – this second collection bequeathed to her by the same aunt who had given her the furniture), pillows on the sofa free of dents and carefully placed next to each arm rest, artificial fruit in a bowl on the dining table stacked in a neat pyramid, towels on a kitchen rack folded in a line just above a shining, crumb-free toaster, clean plates in a sink drainer all inserted in their proper slots, new soap with the letters sharply outlined sitting in a dry dish.

And then there were the books. Several shelves of them, reflecting a range of serious topics. Art, history, music. There were novels squeezed in next to one of the bookends shaped like a dolphin. If she had actually read all of these books, she was much better educated than I was.

Standing inside her apartment, I watched everything she did with an aching appreciation for being there. When she pulled her hair off her ears or when she adjusted the blouse on her shoulders, her hands moved with smooth, elongated gestures that enhanced the shape of everything they touched.

I wanted to know the source of this simple elegance. Minnie bore little resemblance to her mother, who watched everything from her ornately framed studio portrait sitting on a bookcase in the living room. The photo showed a flat-faced woman with a short neck and dark eyebrows located some distance from each other. There was nothing in the picture that suggested any of Minnie's gracefulness. Her father could be seen in a smaller photograph stuck inside the frame of her mother's picture. He had the same stretched look that I had first noticed in Lloyd and the same animal alertness that I had first noticed in Minnie. She favored her father.

The photographs were displayed on a middle shelf. In order to look at them, I had to take them off the shelf because late sunlight angling through the window on the opposite wall reflected off the picture glass. I felt uncomfortable doing this. Minnie had gone into her bedroom for a minute and I thought that I could return the photographs to their original position before she came back into the living room. But as I was still studying them, she returned.

"Those aren't very good photos. They're old and don't really capture what my parents look like. After my mother saw hers, I could never get her in front of a camera again."

"I'm sorry. I didn't mean to disturb them."

"Don't worry about it. I just wished that I had better ones for both of us to look at."

We were going out to dinner and once again Minnie chose where we would go. This time she selected a bistro within walking distance from her apartment. On the way there she stayed close to me, several times allowing her shoulder to brush against mine. At the restaurant, she sat to my side rather than across from me and frequently touched my wrist while making a point. After I paid the bill, she invited me to return with her back to her apartment for Irish Cream, which was all that she could offer.

Once again, when I walked through the door to her apartment, I felt a rush. This was her private world and I was being admitted to it. I watched intently as Minnie poured some liqueur into two small glasses. When she handed me my glass she also motioned for me to sit down on her couch. I did and she joined me but in a somewhat awkward arrangement since both of us were facing forward. The air in the room was fresh, flowing through an open window, lifting the lace curtains with delicate, invisible fingers. I tried to relax but could not.

"There is something I should tell you," I finally said.

"Sounds serious."

"Maybe it's not that big a deal, but it's something that you need to know."

"Whatever it is, get on with it."

"You know how I told you I was working construction...well, the construction work I was talking about was piledriving and my foreman is your brother."

"You're working for Lloyd! Why didn't you tell me right from the beginning?"

"I didn't want him to know that I had met you. In fact, I don't want him to know now."

"Why not?"

"Because I'm basically a stranger and it's because of him that I found out about you. I saw you when he met you at the bar near the Thornton job. Me tracking you down.... coming to see you at Arlene's might look like I was kind of...might look like I'm stalking you."

"So did you really have a suit that needed to be tailored?"

"Well, yes." In a certain narrow sense that was true, since after I brought the new suit it needed to be tailored.

"But you came to Arlene's to meet me?"

"Basically that's it."

"Why?"

"I saw you in the bar. I wanted to meet you in person."

"I suppose that somewhere in all of this there is some type of compliment. Thank you."

"Are you going to tell Lloyd?"

"Not now if you don't want me to. But eventually, he is going to find out from somebody and the best person is probably you."

"You still want to see me?"

"You've come clean. Now we can move on. I want to find out whether you were really telling the truth about why you asked me out. And besides, I decide who I spend time with, not my brother." As she talked, her eyebrows lifted as if to emphasize her points. "So do you have any brothers or sisters?"

"No. It's just me."

"You close to your parents?" Minnie turned and leaned against her end of the sofa. I leaned back against my end of the sofa so that now we were looking directly at each other. I knew that I had to say something of apparent substance. But I was also not very good at talking about my family. "As for my parents, let's just say that they're something of a mystery to me. They seem to like buying things and making shrewd investments, but beyond that, who knows?"

"You can tell me more than that. What's your father like?"

"He's made a lot of money in real estate and investments. He wants to show me the ropes. I know that it frustrates him, maybe even breaks his heart that we never seem to connect. And I don't have a clue as to why I see everything backward from the way he does."

I paused even though I was tempted to say more about him. I could have said that I thought that he wanted, in the worst way, to see me develop a lifestyle to which *he* was accustomed. Blend in with his routines, golf and dinner at the club, winter vacations in St. Barts and Telluride, acquaintances with capped teeth and more than one house. A superficial, one-dimensional caricature of him to be sure, but it reflected what I had to work with. For years, I had nurtured the hope that he and my mother were more principled than they seemed. That at some point, they would share with me the deeper values that had shaped them, explain why they had made the compromises they had, how they had gotten to where they were, what it was worth to them. Did I ever ask them questions which would have allowed them to discuss such matters? No. Instead, I expected them to deliver, without any prior expression of interest on my part, a carefully rehearsed, coherent, persuasive justification not only for their lives but also for mine. As if they owed it to me.

"Anything else?" Minnie asked trying to get me to rejoin the conversation.

"There are a lot of things that I don't understand about my father, so it's probably not a good idea for me to pretend that I do."

"What about your mother?"

Once again, I hesitated, since there were some things to sort out there too. Beautiful nails, tweezer-perfect eyebrows, "Didn't Justin give me a nice cut?" hair. Comforting herself with scotch, she could talk on and on. Rambling commentaries about matters of style and appearances, delivered in a tone of weary necessity that was supposed to make her seem to be an arbiter of such issues. Her home was a showcase in which a husband could be manipulated to function as her provider. Once again, a one-dimensional, superficial caricature.

"Harry, what about your mother?" Minnie repeated.

"Ah ... my mother. Well, she drinks a lot."

"And?"

"Well ... I suppose that I'm partly to blame. When I was small I probably was too much trouble for her and when I got bigger, I was even more trouble. I wasn't a bad kid, just not the easiest. She says that it was my father who decided that they would not have another child but I think that it was both of them. I know it may sound that I'm being pretty down on her, but every time I think about her I feel lonely. I think about how lonely all three of us are. I keep telling myself not to take it personally ... that some people are just not cut out to be parents."

I confess that there were times when my parents spoke in a way which suggested an invitation for me to listen, maybe even to provide help. These moments came and went even though they begged to be clarified. I did not connect with them because I was drenched in my own concerns and was impatient with them not because they were guilty of everything I accused them of, but because they weren't. I was not ready to deal with the possibility of their poignant vulnerability; I did not want them to be complex. Why couldn't they allow themselves to be summarized simply and just leave it at that? It was almost as if I were trying to turn myself into an orphan.

"I'm sorry about your mother," Minnie said sympathetically. "I still haven't made my mind up about my own. I know that she cares about what happens to me ... but she wants me to think a certain way ... so we'll always be able to talk the same language ... so we can gossip and gossip about how other people are screwing up their lives. I can only take so much of it."

"I know that my mother is having a rough time of it now," I said. "She and my father are getting a divorce. He is basically acting as if their marriage just ran out of gas. It's like he's left a car on the side of the road and he doesn't even want to call a tow truck. Just lock it up, take the plates off, and walk away."

Minnie dropped her legs off the couch and moved in my direction. She slipped her hand into mine. I felt my pulse quicken. The skin on her palms was warm and smooth.

"People get divorced all the time," I continued. "So, I suppose I should not try to analyze it too much. Still, I always thought of them as being together."

"You felt that way because you're their son," Minnie said, squeezing my hand. "You know how they say that parents can't live their kids' lives for them. Well, kids can't live their parents' lives for them either." She moved closer to me, bringing with her a scent of lilacs. "Right now, you're going to have to think about yourself ... what's best for you."

"Right now, I think that you're what's best for me."

"Ooooo. That's slick." She smiled and then ran her tongue over her lips. "Do you think that you ever looked at somebody like both of you were in a dream?"

With her so close to me, with our hands touching, every circuit in my body was switched on.

"Well, you did," she answered before I did. "When you first came into Arlene's, I could tell that you were watching me with special ... I don't know what to call it ... concentration. Again tonight, you did it. It was like you saw something in me that I didn't even know was there. It's hard to ignore."

"I have to apologize again."

"Actually, I like it. I feel noticed."

With her free hand, she pushed her hair away from her face. "I don't use much makeup," she said. "Maybe some blusher but no eye shadow."

I smiled slightly. "Why are you telling me this?"

"Well, I want you to know what kind of person I am."

She seemed to be suggesting that she was plain, when, in fact, she knew that at that moment she was dazzling me. I thought that I could actually see her pupils expand as if to gather both light and my attention. My heart began to race. Our bodies were almost touching. She put her arms around my neck, and then ever so gently, touched her lips to mine. My hands moved up her spine until I ran them through her hair and over her shoulders. Her lips moved along my face until they found my ear. I kissed her neck and then the smooth hollow formed by her collarbone. I could feel her stretching with a sigh. She gave off radiant warmth which was as sensual as skin itself. And into this warmth, I vanished.

CHAPTER EIGHT

When I returned to my apartment, Minnie's perfume was still in my clothing, in my hair, on my skin. It was an intimate scent that requested that I return to her as soon as possible.

On the floor in front of me was a trail of dropped shoes and socks to Sterling's bedroom. I followed it, poked my head through the door, and saw that he had passed out on the floor. I pulled a blanket off the bed and covered him.

I could not get to sleep myself. Rolling from side to side, I thought about what I was thinking. Thoughts bumping into thoughts, coming and going, keeping me awake and restless. Once, I had guessed that I might be in love with a girl named Jeanine Brockton, but the feeling had turned out to be something more like excitement. In her own pert way, she had eventually made it clear to me that seeing me was simply some sort of amusing, preliminary event in her life. I suppose that she deserves some credit for communicating this conclusion to me in an effective sequence of unanswered e-mails, declined invitations, 'I'm sorry but I can't talk right now; can I call you back" phone conversations followed by no call back, and then finally a brief "I hope that we can still be friends" wrap-up text. In my own quick sequence, I was hurt but then, as I focused on the specifics of how she interacted with me, relieved because she had done what was necessary to prevent us from wandering into an emotional desert with a half-empty canteen.

But there was nothing preliminary about that look in Minnie's eyes. One way or another, she was going to demand serious things of me. And I wanted serious things to be demanded of me, but maybe not too quickly. Strangely, as we drew closer to each other, I could see more clearly the distance that separated us. She was prepared for what was happening; I was not. She perceived a direction in her life; I did not. She had instincts and trusted them; I did not. While I would be kept awake by my colliding doubts, she would be sleeping soundly.

I admired her faith in herself, but at the same time, felt some apprehension that perhaps her view of things was too straightforward. At times, I had been concerned that my parents were more complex than I wanted them to be; now, I was worried that Minnie was less complex than I wanted her to be. Where were the doubts of a kind that plagued me? How would she react to me as she learned more about the drift in my life? How would I react to her as I learned more about the certainties in hers?

* * *

In the morning, Sterling first moved on his hands and knees and then slowly evolved into an upright, bipedal homo sapiens. It took him a long time to find something to wear and an even longer time to put it on. "Maybe a cup of coffee would help me out," he speculated.

"What you need is a blood transfusion and a liver transplant. The sight of you on the floor last night was pathetic."

"I miscalculated. So you've never made a mistake?"

Sterling drove us to work in fits and starts. I offered to take over the wheel, but he refused. I shut up and looked over to him as I always did on these rides. He was biting his lip. I could not tell if he was about to cry or about to scream.

The early morning traffic was still light. On the sidewalks, I could see store owners rolling up security screens and getting ready for business. Doors were being unlocked, boxes being moved by people who seemed to be confident that they were doing something useful. As I watched these various preparatory rituals, I felt a strange connection with them, as if I were moving in time with this necessary rhythm. I was going to work.

I could actually remember a time when my parents discussed work. I could not have been more than eight years old at the time. My father and mother had been standing in our kitchen, talking with animation in their voices about making ends meet. My father was wearing a gray T-shirt, khaki pants with frayed cuffs, and a pair of scuffed deck shoes. My mother was wearing a plain, cotton print dress and clogs. I cannot remember them ever looking better.

Our house at the time was a two-bedroom Cape Cod in a neighborhood that has since suffered from the widening of a commuter thoroughfare. I loved that house. It had everything I thought that I needed at the time. My own bedroom, a television in the living room, a table in the kitchen, and a backyard big enough to pitch a tent in. And it was right next to other houses with kids in them. On a summer evening when the windows were open, I might hear a family argument coming out of the

Sartinski's house, but there never seemed to be a problem the next day when I walked through their unlocked back door to play with Gerald, who was my age.

I remember my father saying that our Chevrolet was good for a few more years. I remember him saying with equal pride that he had gotten a pay raise and that he was going to save the extra money. While he talked, my mother organized grocery store coupons she kept in a folder. Then she talked about taking a part-time job as a bookkeeper in a dentist's office. The job would allow her to be at home when I returned from school.

I don't remember much more than that except that they seemed to be happy and therefore I was happy. Money had been something real to them then. Their sensible use of it, their sensible pursuit of it seemed to bind them together. They were worried but not desperate about their finances. They drew confidence from each other that they would do better and better until they had done well enough. I admired them.

And then they did better and we moved and then moved again. The number of bedrooms multiplied. We acquired a game room, a big TV with surround sound, and an acre lot with neighbors only dimly visible through the trees. My mother stopped working and my father worked even more.

I can't say that initially I was unhappy with these developments. My parents were certainly excited by their success when it first appeared. But eventually, everyone's attitude changed. I felt marooned on our property and my parents began to act as if they had lost their bearings. With so much money coming in, it was no longer something real to them. It could now be spent without careful calculation; it could be wasted without regret.

Without talking about it, I recognized that something was increasingly wrong. I remember we had just returned from a trip to Florida when my parents decided to go right back a month later for some more pampering. I had been bored on the first trip and wanted nothing to do with the second one. Trying to be polite, I had simply said, "I don't deserve this."

* * *

As if through some telepathy, Sterling mentioned Florida while I was still thinking about it as we drove to the job site. "This car is paid for, so I'm going to use my money to go down to Florida."

"Florida? For what?"

"Sun, surf, and the track. You know what really kills me? I've never done any serious gambling. Pulling in five bucks a month from you on some loony bet is personally satisfying because it's taking your money. But that's chicken shit. Now I'm getting ready for some big-time wagering. It just hit me. Why should a guy like me save money?"

"To be able to take care of yourself, for one thing. You end up broke, what are you going to do then? Go on welfare?"

"All I said was that I wanted to go down to Florida to bet on a few horses. I'm not talking about becoming some wino living in a fleabag hotel. Give me credit for some sense."

"Well, you didn't have enough sense to keep from getting shit-faced last night. Yeah, I could see you as a wino."

Sterling looked exasperated. "I said that it was a little miscalculation on my part. No reason to insult me. Besides, even if I end up as a wino, I'll still be able to think about that great time I had in Miami before things went into the dumper."

Now I was exasperated. "Not too long ago, you were telling me how much you wanted to do real work you could get your hands on. Now you're talkin' horse racing in Miami."

"You think that I'm berserk, don't you? Well, I deserve to be. My father abandoned the family. My mother died with a tube in her mouth in a cancer ward. I don't have a clue what she wanted out of life other than to win the lottery. Give her a glass of warm, flat beer and she would drink it. That's what her life was like: piss in a glass."

"That's pretty harsh."

"I'm not saying that she and my father are an excuse for me to be a fuck-up. I know that I'm responsible for what I do. Well, maybe 'responsible' is not a word that should be applied to me. Enough of this soap opera shit. It's not as if I'm heading south on I-95 tomorrow morning. No reason to get into a big discussion. What I really want to know is where in the hell were you last night anyway? You never told me where you were going. You never asked me to go along. You just left again."

"I didn't think you'd be interested. You always want to go down to Ray's."

"I wasn't getting any other offers. Besides, we could have started at the Oasis and then have done something else."

"I don't want to go drinking every night," I replied defensively.

"What's her name?"

"I never said that I was seeing anybody."

"Cut the shit," he demanded impatiently. "What's her name?"

"Minnie."

"Minnie who?"

"Minnie Sollis." I figured that he was also bound to find out sometime anyway.

"Lloyd Sollis' sister? For real? Your boss' sister?" Sterling took one hand off the wheel and slapped his leg. "How did you meet her?"

"Long story. It just kind of happened."

"You saw her in that bar Lloyd took us to, right?"

"Correct. But don't be acting like it's some big deal."

"Well, it is a big deal. And a complicated one. Going out with your boss' sister! I'm not sure how this will play out with Lloyd."

"That makes two of us."

CHAPTER NINE

I had gone to college and now was a piledriver apprentice -- a fact that I accepted as a placeholder in my life. It never occurred to me in those early weeks that I was or would become a real piledriver. If, as I had unfairly concluded, a person's job is the most important fact about him or her, I did not want to be thought of as a heavy construction worker, at least at that point in my early-life crisis. Since I recognized that this reluctance was based on stereotypes and limited encounters, I worried that it might reflect some type of residual effect of my parents' expectations for me. Of course, the effect was of little consequence because, despite those expectations, I was now showing up every day to work on a construction site.

I am not embarrassed to say that I was interested in what was going on around me and developed an admiration for the expertise involved. In his tight-lipped way, Lloyd Sollis had charisma. It was a charisma that came from being able to make decisions with a calm confidence and without needless display. He said little to the older piledrivers - Carl, Ellis, and Malcolm - because they knew what they were doing. He said more to Early because he was trying to move him along to the journeyman level. And he was patient with Sterling and me because he chose to be.

"Patient" may be a little off target. "Tolerant" would be closer to the mark. By necessity, he was reluctant to give us challenging work because of our inexperience.

For nearly a week on the 16th Street job, we did nothing but burning work - cutting steel into pieces. Basically, it was the metal equivalent of chopping wood. Even though it was dumb-ass work which was virtually impossible to fuck-up, I tried to perform it to an exacting standard which I had created for myself. Make the cut as straight as possible so that it made a 90-degree angle with the flange. Lloyd appeared to take no particular notice of my efforts, but that was almost beside the point.

After the burning assignment, we were told to move some lumber so that steel could be stacked on it. Then we were assigned to shadow Carl when he was rigging steel to be lifted. Carl would ask me to hand him a larger wrench than he had in his tool belt or to perform some other simple task. Then Lloyd assigned me to walk steel with the tag line as it was being unloaded from a truck. For each one of these small assignments, Lloyd's instructions were clear and impersonal as if he wanted to have the work done the right way but did not care that I or anyone else in particular did it.

Whenever I could, I tried to pick up on the little maneuvers the men used to position steel, the hand language they used to communicate with each other when they could not be heard, the way they steadied themselves on a beam to avoid falling, even the method they used to unwrap a sandwich so that it would be kept clean during a lunch break. Each man had his own posture and angles of movement which allowed me to recognize him from a distance. I liked the fact that at the end of that day, I could see what had been accomplished.

While I was watching the crew to pick up some of the tricks of the trade, they were watching me to see whether or not I was legit. I suspected that each man had his own definition of what he was looking for, but ultimately it came down to something like whether I could be trusted. Slowly, most of the crew seemed to become less wary of me if for no other reason than I had not made any big mistakes and kept showing up for work every day.

The novelty of the situation sustained me minimally through the early weeks. I did not think of the piledrivers as representing my future. To me, they simply represented themselves and that was fine. It bothered me that I was a peon in their trade, even though Don Crispin had laid it all out so that I could not have expected anything different. But given that other guys my age were in law school, were working in a bank, were leading a platoon, I felt an urge to assert myself so that I could move forward more quickly. Forward to what? My ambition was now sharing space with a new desire to acquire specific skills and that, at least for the moment, seemed to be a good thing.

Although I cannot say that I liked what I doing on the 16th Street job, I did want to stay on it longer so that I could see the project completed. The piledrivers did no finish work, no work that required close tolerances, elegant design or fine polish. Ours was the brute -- and eventually invisible -- work of construction. When the structure on 16th Street was finally finished, no one would be able to see the piles and support steel; it would be buried. A mason must take considerable satisfaction in driving by a building, pointing to an ornamental arch framing the entryway, and saying "I built that." Although none of the men on my crew would be able to enjoy similar reminders of his skill, they showed pride in their work, pride that they were daring, practical engineers of a sort.

As I walked along the 16th Street excavation, I felt the same sense of awe that I had experienced on my first day on the job. Silently, I appreciated the rugged beauty of the piledrivers' accomplishments. The rust-red of the rakers and whalers was strikingly handsome when the sunlight hit the beams, and the overlapping shadows that fell below laid out an intricate, angular puzzle. The wooden lagging boards in between the piles were arranged in tight, regular rows, which from a distance, took on the appearance of giant paneling. Here was a geometry of competence and power. I took satisfaction from the fact that I knew how this work had been done.

* * *

"Jeeesuss Keeeyrist!" Ellis was not happy. Although I was trying to take him seriously, I wondered if a Saudi Arabian construction worker who stubbed his toe would yell "Mooohaamed!" But Ellis was unhappy for other reasons as well. Lloyd had just told him that the crew's next job, if we wanted to take it, would be working for Elbell Construction on an underground job in the middle of downtown.

The crew was collecting itself in its trailer for the workday. The air inside the trailer felt as if it had already been exhaled. Breathing it a second time made me wish that I could go outside. I inched my way towards the door with the intention of pretending that I needed to go to the john. Before I opened the door, Lloyd did it himself and motioned for all of us to step outside. "Getting a little dense in here," he said.

Outside, we formed an irregular circle around him. Carl and Ellis sat on a pile of lagging boards. Early sat on a piece of scrap steel. The rest of us leaned against the side of the trailer. Even though diesel fumes were mixed in with the outside air, it seemed clean compared to the used atmosphere in the trailer.

"Elbell! They're for shit," Ellis declared. "It's no wonder they need a whole new crew. They've been going through piledrivers like my wife goes through pantyhose. I know at least ten piledrivers who were either fired or quit over there. And last year, they killed a guy. Not a piledriver, but it still counts."

"Yeah, I've heard they've had some problems, but they're workin' on them," Lloyd responded in a low tone.

"The place is a dump. Ever drive by it? Junk all over the yard. No organization whatsoever. A week doesn't pass that they don't send somebody to the emergency room. Jimmy Meder, he worked over there for two weeks and he told me that most of the superintendents and foremen don't know their asses from their elbows."

"But the job's got some real pluses, Ellis. They tell me they've got at least ten months of work for piledrivers. Where else you gonna find anything that steady? Nothing close to it."

"Tunnel work is a lot trickier than this stuff we've been doing lately," Ellis said emphatically. "I don't like the idea of doin' that kind of work for somebody that don't have their act together."

"I'm not trying to force you into anything. If you don't go over there, somebody else will show up. You all can do what you want to. I was only trying to help you out."

"I appreciate that, but I'm just sorry that Elbell is what you're offering." Ellis yanked up his pants to support his point.

"So what do I tell them?" Lloyd asked.

Ellis took off his hard hat and scratched the back of his neck. Carl rubbed his belly. Early folded his arms across his chest. Malcolm rearranged some dirt with his shoe. They were thinking.

Ellis hitched up his pants again. "You're probably right, Lloyd. Work that steady don't come around very often."

Carl shook his head. "My wife would probably kill me if she knew that I turned down a chance for a big job like that."

"Count me in, too," Malcolm said.

"Aw right," said Early.

"We included?" I asked.

"If you want to be, I suppose that it can be arranged," Lloyd said. Then he looked in the direction of Carl and Ellis and said, "OK, that's done. I'm puttin' in everyone's name. Don't worry so much; things will work out fine."

* * *

More time in another bar. This one was decorated with various items which appeared to have come from the garage of an old house. Rusted signs for Robin Hood flour, Bromoseltzer, and Nehi soda. A bicycle horn, a wooden pitchfork, a fishing pole, a saw, a madras fabric golf bag, a baseball bat and glove, and license plates from New Mexico and California. The wall hangings strained unsuccessfully and needlessly to create some type of nostalgic authenticity in the place. Regardless, they were a damn sight better than the worn-out wilderness scenes that covered the cracks in the walls of the bar Lloyd had taken to me after the first day on the job.

A tab had been set up for the crew by the general contractor on the 16th Street job who appreciated that the crew had finished our work ahead of schedule. We were also provided with a tray of chips and dips and a tray with red pepper slices, carrot sticks, and ranch dressing in a cup. It was a nice spread. There was no table big enough to take all of us, so some of us ended up in a booth, and some of us standing at the bar. I found myself at the bar next to Ellis. He ordered a beer from the tap. I started to do the same but then decided I'd try something different and ordered a gin and tonic.

"A gin and tonic? You're ordering like a businessman on an expense account," Ellis cracked to me when our glasses were delivered.

"Basically, we are on an expense account, aren't we?"

"You've got a point there." Ellis tilted his head back as he drained a quarter of his glass and then wiped the corner of his mouth. "Makes up for some of the shit we have to deal with. I guess that I shouldn't be surprised that none of my kids has any interest in construction. You're a young guy. Why you interested in doing this?"

I didn't have the heart to tell him that it almost came down to nothing more than a random impulse and was never intended to be long-term. "The money's decent."

"You're gonna earn it on the Elbell job. Totally different animal."

"What do you mean?" I asked with some apprehension in my voice.

"It's an underground job. Like workin' in a mine. Hardly any daylight, no direct overhead crane lifts, no room to maneuver. Everything's more complicated. The air's dirtier. The sightlines ain't for shit because it's so damn dark and there's so much crap in the way." Ellis went back to his beer, but this time only took a small swallow. "The Elbell job," he resumed, "will be a bitch. I'm thinkin' that I'm getting a little old for that kind of situation."

Ellis finished his beer and gestured to the bartender for another one. "There are times when my back acts up that I've thought about giving up piledriving. I get so I can't stand straight after a couple days on the job. I have trouble sleeping and am worthless around the house. But then I load up on aspirin and I go back. It's not just for the money. I think of myself as a piledriver. If I quit, then what am I gonna do?"

"I don't know. I'm just a punk. But I can tell you that the lagging walls on the 16th Street job are really impressive. You can be proud that you helped to build them. I mean it. No bullshit."

"I appreciate you saying that. But like you said, you're just a punk, so I don't think that you really understand what I am trying to say here."

Malcolm came up behind us and slapped both of us on the shoulder. "You guys look like you got the weight of the world on your shoulders. Why so serious?"

"Just talkin' about Elbell," Ellis answered. "You should be serious too."

"I am. I am. But not every minute of the day. I'll let you guys wrestle with that for now," Malcolm slapped me on the shoulder again and walked away.

The bartender delivered to Ellis his second beer.

I let Ellis focus on the wet glass for a few seconds and then asked him the question that had pushed itself to the front of my mind. "Have you heard anything about whether Drager will be working on the Elbell job?"

"No, but I heard that he's back at the union hall. If Crispin can't find something else for him, he will probably send him to Elbell. Lloyd probably knows more than I do."

"He hasn't said anything to me."

"Wouldn't expect him to."

"Well, I was thinking that because of my run-in with Drager, Lloyd might give me a heads-up that he is coming back to the crew."

"Maybe the fact that you haven't heard anything is a good sign. God knows, I don't want Drager to come back. Like I said, the Elbell job will be a bitch and when I said that I wasn't even thinking of how Drager could make things a lot worse than they're already going to be."

* * *

Ellis' comments about the Elbell job stayed with me through every other conversation I had in that bar. There was something about his tone of voice that communicated more than concern, more than dread. Even though, at the time, I had not envisioned something horribly specific, I had fallen into a low mood, which Sterling sensed as we left the bar and walked back to the car. "You worried about Drager coming back?"

"Yes."

"I am too. I still think that he will eventually get to me."

"But you didn't break his nose."

"He's been gone a while, so maybe he's moved on to target somebody else."

"That's a big 'maybe'. But even if you're right, I'm still not thrilled about this Elbell job. Lloyd keeps telling us that we're only doing simple shit; eventually, we're going to have to do something more difficult and I'm not sure that the place to start is working for a company like Elbell on a tunnel job."

"That thought crossed my mind too," Sterling said.

"And ...?"

"And it got to the other side and kept right on going. I admit that so far piledriving has not exactly been a dream job and that I keep thinking about going down to Florida. But Florida is too hot this time of year."

CHAPTER TEN

Minnie and I started seeing each other every day after work. I would shower and change clothes at my apartment and then go to hers. At the end of the evening, I would return to my apartment. We were taking things a step at a time, almost as if by moving slowly we would be moving surely. But each time we got together, it was more and more difficult to be careful, even though I still left around 10:30 every night.

After Sterling and I finished our discussion about the prospect of working for Elbell, I called Minnie and told her that I was running late. Then, as was the routine, I showered and pulled on some clean clothes at my place before heading off to Minnie's. Even though this was now the regular sequence of my day, I was still amazed, thankful that Minnie would be waiting to see me.

When I stepped into Minnie's apartment, she greeted me at the door with a kiss. Then she guided me to the living room couch and motioned for me to sit down. After she joined me, she began talking about her day. "My mother called me again at work today to complain about something my father did which irritated her. It's harder and harder for me to listen to her going on like that. Half the time, I don't agree with her that my father did anything wrong, and even when I think that she might be right, what can I do about it? Nothing. I told her that her complaining has grown old and that she should stop it, but she ignored me, so I hung up on her. Then she calls me when I get home to tell me that I hurt her feelings by hanging up on her and then tells me the same story about my father. Sometimes I think that my mother got married and had a family just so she could always have people nearby who disappoint her."

Minnie adjusted the neckline on her blue T-shirt, leaned back on the couch, and draped her legs over mine. Her hair was still wet from the shower and it gave her a playful sleekness. She looked like an otter getting ready to slide into a lake.

She touched my arm and spoke softly as if to invite me to move closer. "I want to tell you about the dreams I had last night. I've been thinking about them all day. It's like they've taken possession of me."

"I'm listening."

"Well, the first dream was in the water. I was swimming in clear, warm ocean water like in the Bahamas. Sometimes, it looked like a coral reef, and sometimes it looked just like my own neighborhood. I could breathe in water just like air. I swam through thousands of fish. Small, silvery fish with fan tails. They were very calm; they didn't dart away when I came near them. They let me swim through them and as I did that, they stroked me with the soft part of their tails and top fins. All over me. I was swimming naked."

She ran her finger along my arm. "If you're thinking that I'm looking for a man, you're right, I am. And if you have any sense, you're looking for a woman. Nothing wrong with any of that."

"You tell me these things out of the blue. I don't know how to ..."

She put her finger on my lips to quiet me. "I also had a dream about you last night."

"What kind of dream?"

"Ah … well … kind of erotic."

I was afraid to respond. If Minnie was going to tell me about the dream, she should do it on her own.

Minnie drew her legs closer to her own body. "When we first met, I could see right away that I had gotten to you. I'm not sure what it was, but I could tell. The way you just appeared like that…I figured there had to be some reason behind it all."

"What kind of reason?"

"I don't know…I don't know what to call it."

"For sure, you got to me when I came to Arlene's. I tried not to make a fool of myself, but I guess you saw through me."

"I didn't think that you were a fool. You were there to see me. That was really smart." Minnie smiled but then straightened her lips. "As I said, I feel that there had to be a reason behind it. It was like this has to happen."

Minnie reached back and snapped off the floor lamp. The evening light that penetrated the drawn shades cast a low yellow glow over the room. She moved closer to me. Minnie's heartbeat was visible through the skin on her neck. She brought her head next to mine, blew softly below my chin, and then with the tip of her tongue drew a small circle under my ear. She opened her mouth so that her teeth rested in the wet circle. And then slowly, gently, she bit me.

I flinched and then took her into my arms. I kissed her neck, her shoulder, her arm, her fingers, her lips. She stretched and turned to make her body more available to me and then she held my head close to her so that I would not stop. In a moment, we were astonished by our

nakedness. Sensations came from everywhere and reso-
nated through my skin.

* * *

Afterward, we lay together, not saying a word. In a few
minutes, we had abandoned the restraint of prior days.
We had been seized by something animal, risky, essential.

"I should leave," I said, breaking the silence.

"Why?" Minnie asked with shock in her voice.

"I just think that it would be better if we slept alone
tonight." I could not rid myself of the feeling that the fact
that we had not spent the night together was one last
necessary protective boundary between us. "It's ... it's
just that we need a little time to get used to what's
happening."

"It's happened."

"But right now, I feel...feel a little overwhelmed."

"So do I. We should feel that way. We should want to
feel that way."

"Just let me have this one night to collect myself."

"I still don't understand. I just don't understand,"
Minnie looked truly sad.

I got dressed and then looked back at Minnie, who
was still lying on the couch. She was a sight. Every line of
her body flowed smoothly into the next. Every curve
beckoned with a promise of pleasure. Of course, this was
not a night for us to be apart. But I kept walking towards
the door, silently denouncing myself with every step.

* * *

I was still denouncing myself when I walked into my building. I stuttered with disappointment at how I had mangled the night as I trudged up the stairs. The couple on the third floor was having another one of their loud, lacerating arguments. "I hope you roast in hell!" "Shut up, you bitch." I thought that I should buy one of them a handgun; a domestic murder would probably be a good solution for everyone in the building, including the victim.

I unlocked the door to the apartment and swung it open, revealing in sequence: bare feet, slightly pulpy legs, lace panties, a bra stretched by full breasts, a creased neck, and Crystal's glossy face.

"Hi, Honey," she said casually.

Sterling came out of the bathroom in his shorts. "Close the door. You remember Crystal, don't you? We met her at the Oasis."

"I'm real sorry, Henry," Crystal offered.

"Harry."

"I'm really sorry, Harry, about our little misunderstanding. I guess we kind of forgot to say goodbye to you fellas." She located her purse under some clothes and opened it up. "Here's a dollar to help pay you what we owe."

"I'll take it. Where's your friend?"

"You mean Dawn? Left town with a guy with his own tractor-trailer. Haven't heard from her since." Crystal showed no signs of self-consciousness about sitting in her underwear while she talked with a virtual stranger.

"Hey, Crystal, why don't you get dressed," Sterling suggested.

"Nothin' showin' more than a bikini would," she protested.

"Just get dressed." Sterling was now zipping up his own pants.

"You're the gentleman, aren't you?" With some awkward stretching and tugging, Crystal put her sweater and slacks back on. As she dressed, I noticed that she had with her a suitcase and a little toy dog with a radio installed in its stomach.

I grabbed Sterling by the arm and pulled him aside. "What gives? She looks like she's moving in."

"She's low on money and needs a place. She'll stay in my room...out of the way."

"You never asked me about this."

"How could I? You weren't here."

"Well, I'm here now."

"If you think that I should pay a bigger share of the rent because Crystal is staying in my room, fine."

"Forget it. I don't care about the rent."

I marched into my room, closed the door, and stewed in my own petty juices. I knew that there might be some relationship between Crystal's moving in and my spending time with Minnie but I was still angry. There was something in this latest move that gave me the feeling that, despite appearances to the contrary, Sterling was using Crystal more than she was using him. I had to get out of there. I felt physical relief as I walked out of the apartment and headed back to Minnie's.

When Minnie answered the knock on her door, she stepped back in surprise. I immediately began to tell her about the new situation with Sterling and Crystal. Minnie was having trouble following me.

"You left here two hours ago and now you're back telling me something about Sterling and a woman he picked up in a bar. This business with Sterling is not a reason to want to spend the night with me. Forget about Sterling!"

"I made a mistake walking out like I did. I'm sorry. I'm really sorry for acting like such a fool...I don't know...I just kind of panicked I'm sorry."

"You're repeating yourself. Both of us agree that you acted like a fool. Now either stay here or go back to your apartment."

I walked into her living room and started going around in little circles as if I were a dog trying to find a comfortable place to lie down.

"You've got to calm down. Have you decided to stay because you want to be with me?"

"Yes."

"Then follow me." She motioned in the direction of the bedroom.

In the bedroom, Minnie picked up a brush from the bureau and began combing her hair with natural, instinctive motions, her head tilted to the side, her brushstrokes knowing, sensual, like a cat grooming herself with her tongue. "Tell me a little more about this woman Sterling brought back with him."

"There's not much to tell because I don't know anything about her except that she's kind of a drifter with barely two nickels to rub together."

"Well, I'm sure that he can look out for himself and if he can't, I'm not sure it's any of your business." She sat on the edge of her bed. "Do what you have to do to get ready. I'm going to read for a few minutes, but then I'm turning out the light."

I went to the bathroom and washed my mouth out

and spent a few seconds evaluating my appearance. When I returned to the bedroom, Minnie had already switched off the light. I slipped under the covers next to her. She turned and put her head on my shoulder. She quickly fell asleep. I stayed awake with an acute awareness of everything around me, listening to an unfamiliar sound, close to my head, as if my pillow were pulsating. It was the sound of my own blood flowing through an artery in my ear.

* * *

In the morning, I went back to my apartment to connect with Sterling. He was not waiting for me, so I had to go into the building and yell at him to get up. Crystal ignored it all by pulling the top sheet over her head. Sterling mumbled and grumbled but eventually was able to get himself ready.

"Are you missing your wallet?" I finally asked to break the silence in the car as we headed to work. "Or did she let you keep it?"

"Don't be a wiseass. She's probably more honest than half the people I know."

"Is she staying?" I asked.

"Yes ... and that's OK by me. A woman with no regrets, no excuses, no hang-ups."

"And no money. Be careful. She may try to use you like an ATM."

"If that happens, don't worry. You won't lose a dime."

CHAPTER ELEVEN

Crystal did not leave. In fact, she made a limited commitment to stay by trying to clean up the apartment. The first thing she attended to was the dirt around the sink drain in the bathroom. Then she cleaned up the dust balls in the corners of the kitchen and the living room. She also tried to decorate. A small poster of a stylized geisha ended up on the wall. I went back and forth between giving her credit for her effort to improve the dump and dismissing her as an ingratiating opportunist. To the extent that Sterling noticed, he was impressed. He always showed his appreciation in the same way: a trip to Ray's Oasis.

Sterling did not say anything about my spending nights at Minnie's except to tell me, in a put-upon tone, that he was willing to pick me up in the morning if I would kick in more for gas. I never actually moved out of my apartment and into Minnie's. I did bring over some clothes and some personal items, but most of my things I left where they were. Minnie did not encourage me to do it differently. "This is still my apartment, not yours," she said. "I'm happy you're here, but don't be thinking that you own the place."

In fact, I was uncomfortable most of the time, wherever I was. Part of it was attributable to my sense of being swept downstream in Minnie's current without making any effort to find dry ground. And part of it was attributable to working as a piledriver. I felt as if things were happening to me before I really knew why other than that I was physically present when certain circumstances came together.

When I had decided to join the piledriver apprenticeship program, I had no real notion of giving up anything permanently because everything seemed recoverable at some later date. Even time seemed as if it could be returned to me if I asked for it. But now I was beginning to measure days with finer and finer calculations. No amount of posturing decisiveness, no amount of self-congratulatory rebellion could overcome my increasing concern about the need to get a handle on things.

* * *

Of course, one of the new circumstances that I would have to get a handle on was working for Elbell Construction Company. Ever since my conversation with Ellis about Elbell, the company had been in the back of my mind and sometimes in the front. Sterling also seemed nervous about the prospect as we drove to the new work site. He jabbered about how Crystal was "OK by him" almost as if he were trying to distract himself from what was waiting for us on the job.

Despite Ellis' warnings, I was not prepared for the Elbell site. The yard, which was crammed in between an excavation and an office building, was surprisingly small. However, since most of the work was being done underground, the yard did not really reflect the true size of the project.

What there was of a yard was total chaos. Steel beams of all sizes were jammed together in massive piles near the trailers. Reinforcing rods, form lumber, junction boxes, electric cables, welding tanks, tires, chains, broken signs were scattered along the fences and in between the trailers. Cranes, compressors, and forklifts blocked the few narrow pathways through the piles of materials. It took us a few minutes just to figure out how to get to the piledrivers' trailer. As we approached it, Sterling and I looked at each other as if to say: "We are not ready for this."

When we finally made it, we saw a weird guy standing next to the trailer door. He had on a hard hat and work shoes but did not look like he belonged on the job. All of his pockets were stuffed with papers, some in envelopes, some held together with paper clips, some folded into tiny rectangles with dirty edges. A walking file cabinet. His gray eyes had an off-center, wall-eyed aspect that made it impossible to look at him directly. Dirty ringlets of slate-colored hair stuck out from the bottom of his hardhat. His pants carried stains that could have come from recent or maybe not so recent meals. He started talking to us as soon as we were within range.

"Doctors tried to tell me it was degenerate arthritis or something like that. The hell it was. Ain't no way a man can take what I did and still use his hands. Lucky to be alive. I wrote to my Congressman. Told him it was nothin' but a kangaroo court. Here look at this. Can you believe it?" His raspy voice percolated through saliva, which made me wish that he would swallow before continuing.

The man pulled one of the paper rectangles from his belt and carefully unfolded it. The document was so old and had been folded and unfolded so many times that words were missing along the creases.

"There it is in black and white. Read it for yourself. Not a word about the three weeks I was in the hospital."

I could not make head or tail of what the guy was driving at.

"Read it for yourself. Doctors never even took another set of X-rays like I asked 'em. My wife said she was going back to Akron to live with her sister."

Ellis arrived at the trailer and the man seemed to recognize him. "Hey, remember the subway job? Sunday overtime for two months. Best money I ever made."

"How ya doin', Frankie?" Ellis answered.

"I'm waitin' on my appeal."

"Still at it, huh?"

"Gonna talk to a new lawyer tomorrow."

"Comin' back to work?"

"Can't. I get blackouts. Here look at this." Frankie reached into one of his envelopes and pulled out another worn paper. "This doctor ain't even from America. Look at his name."

"You got a point there, Frankie." Ellis took him by the arm and steered him away from the trailer toward the gate. "You better be headin' down to the Department of Labor to be checkin' on things."

"Yeah. I got to check on things." Frankie continued to talk as Ellis walked with him.

"What's the story with him?" I asked Ellis when he returned.

"Light's on, but nobody's home." Ellis twirled his finger next to his temple. "Injured on the job years ago. Never been the same since. Stopped workin' after the accident. His comp money ran out. Now he just hangs out, talkin' about the case. Every once in a while, he shows up on some job with all his papers. He gets on the site because he always wears a hard hat. Usually, someone recognizes him pretty quickly and escorts him off the job. We just try to keep him out of trouble."

"You talkin' about Frankie?" Carl asked after he arrived in the middle of Ellis' answer.

"Yes."

"I figured as much by what you were sayin'. Sad story."

"What happened when he got hurt?" I asked.

"It was a tough job," Ellis said with a pained expression on his face. "Lots of foundation work. Wait 'til you have to underpin a building. Workin' on your hands and knees, crawlin' around like a mole. A piece of steel hit him in the head. Knocked off his hard hat and his glasses, knocked out the light he was workin' with. There he was in the dark, semi-conscious, virtually blind, blood running from his head like it was some kind of leaky pipe."

"We're gonna be crawlin' around on this job too," Carl said. "The yard here is just like everybody said it was. A fuckin' disaster. And it'll be even worse underground."

"Like Lloyd said, it's a special situation, because they ain't got any space to work with. Everything is jammed in between buildings. What are they gonna do?" Ellis spoke with little conviction.

Carl still looked concerned. "No one was injured on the 16th Street job or on the Marvin Towers job or on the hotel job, right?"

"Right."

"Yeah, that's what I thought. The odds are gettin' bad. Last three jobs, nothin's happened. Odds say that somethin' bad is waitin' out there."

Early, who had just walked up to us, shook his head in agreement. "Luck's got a lot to do with it."

Malcolm was of a similar mind. "I seen the best crane operator in the business boom up too fast and knock a man into a hole. It's a crapshoot. When your time is up, ain't nothing you can do about it."

"These accidents you're talkin' about, they didn't just happen," I said in a challenging voice which took everyone, myself included, a little by surprise. "Every one of them probably could have been prevented by somebody."

Carl looked at me indulgently. "I ain't so dumb I can't figure out that when people fuck up, somebody can get hurt. But when you been around construction, you understand about the odds. Or take the army. Why does the fifth guy in the column step on the mine after four other guys walk right past it? It's just because the man's number was up."

* * *

It took me a while to grasp the dimensions of the project. Elbell and its subcontractors were building a major pumping station in the city's main water tunnel. The underground structure was to be nearly 300 feet long. The construction process, which called "cut and cover," was simple in its basic conception. The first step was to close the street and then open a massive excavation into which a steel structure would be erected. The steel skeleton was intended to provide support for the retaining walls and for a temporary street to be built out of heavy-wooden mats above the excavation. This temporary street would permit city traffic to move over the hole while the station was being built below. When the station was completed, it would be covered on the outside with waterproofing material and then dirt up to the street level. In the process, much of the steel skeleton would be removed. Then the permanent street would be reconstructed over the completed dome and traffic would return to normal. The piledrivers' main assignment was to install and then remove the steel bracing and skeleton. By the time that our crew arrived on the site, most of the bracing and skeleton had already been installed. Our assignment was to complete the installation and to begin the process of removing steel where possible.

It was a tricky job. To begin with, the steel was much bigger than anything the crew had handled since Sterling and I had been working with them. The steel supporting the temporary street consisted of multi-ton H-beams, 35 feet long. The piles, the whalers, everything was bigger. Then there were the tight spaces of the excavation itself. As Ellis said, "More goes on under most city streets than on top of them." Foundation piles, water pipes, sewer lines, gas lines, electrical cables, air shafts, telephone conduits all run underground and get in the way. Same for equipment and materials. Since the excavation was covered, except for comparatively small openings through which steel and materials were being lifted, no natural light was available in most areas. I would have to stay on my toes.

Lloyd showed up and told everyone to get into the trailer. The inside of the trailer was a dump too. Candy wrappers and paper coffee cups overflowed a bin in the corner. Only one of the light sockets had a bulb in it.

Lloyd could see the look of alarm on our faces. "The project manager says they need a bigger yard, but there's no more space so they're doing the best they can."

"Their best is the worst." Malcolm blurted out.

"This isn't exactly what you would call your average construction job, so we've got to deal with it. Now listen up; I've got a few things to tell you."

"Tell us what?" Ellis asked with a little agitation in his voice.

"First of all, Crispin told me that Drager is going to be coming back in a few days. Crispin said that he tried to find a new project for him but came up dry. So he wants all of us to cut him some slack."

I let out a little gasp. I had nurtured the hope, increasingly so as the days passed, that Drager would never appear on the job again, that he would relocate to Nevada or some other place where he could start over. But that hope always ended up going down a narrow alley that was blocked by a brick wall. Now I had to confront the fact that he was actually coming back.

Ellis looked up at the ceiling. "Everybody knows that Crispin had Drager put away somewhere before he got into more trouble. Now just because some guy in a white coat says that he's all fixed don't mean that he is. No one ever talked to me about him coming back here."

Lloyd shook his head, "Ellis, none of us knows the whole story about Drager and none of us can say how he's really doin'. I'm just sayin' that Don wants us to do what we can to stay out of his way and give things a chance to run their course."

"Well, Crispin would say something like that because he doesn't have to work with him."

"Look, we've got to tolerate him ... at least until he fucks up so bad that even Crispin can't save his ass."

"So what else you got to tell us?" Carl asked.

Lloyd pressed his lips together and then exhaled. "I won't be working with you as foreman anymore."

We just looked at him.

"No, I haven't been fired. Kind of the opposite. Elbell is giving me a job as a superintendent."

We still just looked at him.

"Don't stare at me like that. I haven't died."

Finally, Ellis offered his hand in congratulation. Then in a joyless procession, the rest of us followed his lead.

"So what's going to happen to us now?" Ellis said.

"You'll get a new foreman, but I'll still be around."

"Who's gonna be the new foreman?" Ellis asked.

"Clyde Bender, the project manager, has picked him. He's gonna bring the new guy over here so you can meet him. I'll go get 'em and be back in a few minutes."

* * *

Shell shock. That is what everyone looked like he was suffering from. Lloyd was essential to maintaining the competence and equilibrium of the crew. He knew his piledriving. He had a crafty way of not over-supervising the veterans and of containing the errors and impulses of everybody else. He could control Drager. Particularly on a project like the Elbell job, we needed a good foreman. Like a stain being soaked up, uneasiness about Lloyd's move spread through the crew as we stood in the trailer waiting to meet Clyde Bender and the new man. For different reasons, some individual, the men examined and reexamined the situation. Ellis got bluer as the minutes wore on.

"Ellis, you thinking about the foreman's job?" I finally asked.

"Never get a damn break," he answered bleakly. "I ain't gettin' any younger. I guess my time's come and gone and I'll be doin' the same thing forever. If I didn't have a wife and kids, I might say 'fuck it'. You get to a point where you feel you're due."

Carl shook his head. "I'm due too," he said. "You ain't got any special claim on it."

"I ain't sayin' that I do. But neither does the guy that Lloyd is gonna bring over here. Nobody even asked if I was interested. Never thought of me. Never thought of you either. How does that make you feel?"

Carl did not respond but simply bent over and tucked in his shirt. I tried to think of something positive to say.

Clyde Bender and the new foreman rumbled into the trailer before I could offer any consolation. Bender was a small man with a red face who looked to be furious about something. His iron eyes would have conveyed the same message except that they were not clearly visible through his glasses, which were covered with fingerprints — the result of his apparent practice of picking up his glasses by the lenses. Never mind the homilies; he was a book you could judge by the cover. The man looked angry and was.

Bender introduced himself and began talking bluntly to us. "Not an easy job here, so I don't want any shit from you guys." He spoke as if he had reason to believe that we already had complaints. "You work, we get along. You stand around with a thumb up your butt, we got problems." He stopped to blow his nose using only one hand to hold his handkerchief. "I know that some of you might not like the way I run things, but just remember that after you guys move on to another job, I'll still be working for Elbell, and if this one turns into a piece of shit, I'm gonna pay for it, not you. You screw up, you're takin' money out of my pocket."

Clyde pushed his glasses up higher on his nose. "This here's D.T. Hadden. He's gonna be your new foreman. He just got done workin' on the Fairhaven Plaza job. Why don't y'all give him your names."

We did and then stood back a pace to take measure of the man. I disliked him simply because of his face. It was almost reptilian. The corners of his mouth stretched with the horizontal movement of his jaw as he worked on his gum. He chewed like a lizard. As he looked over the crew, his small eyes focused with the shallow intensity of a creature that was hunting, not thinking. Here, in my opinion, was a small-time predator. "Lizard," I would call him.

"D.T.'s worked with me before so he knows what I want." Clyde went on. "He might tell you to do things a little different than you was doin' them before but there's no use belly-aching because that's the way it's gonna be." Clyde took off his glasses and rubbed the lenses between his thumb and index finger. "We're gonna be takin' out some H beams this week. They have to be out by Friday." Clyde put his glasses back on. "OK, D.T., now they're yours."

Clyde left and Hadden positioned himself to say something to the crew. "I may be wrong, but I think that I worked on a job with a couple of you guys a few years back. An underground parking garage in Arlington. No problems. In and out."

No one responded.

"Ah ... As I said, I might be wrong. Now this here job has got problems and I understand from Clyde that it's behind schedule, so we're gonna feel the pressure. I'll be lookin' to you guys to help me out. I think that we can work together."

No one responded.

"Ah ... ah ... well, Clyde told you he's got his ways of doin' things and that's pretty much the way it's gonna be done."

Malcolm stuffed both of his hands into his back pockets. "I thought you just said that we were gonna work together and, and then you're tellin' us that it's Clyde's way or the highway."

"Don't be tryin' to catch me up on my words."

"Yeah, I remember you," Ellis said with a flash of recognition in his voice. "Didn't you burn a hole in your shoe on the Arlington job? I wouldn't be bringin' that job up if I were you."

"I ain't here to argue with you guys."

Over Lizard's shoulder, I could see Frankie open the door to the trailer. He was talking as he walked in. Lizard turned around to see where the disarranged words were coming from. "Who in the hell is . . ."

Ellis stepped forward. "He comes around from time to time. He's harmless. We'll take care of him."

Frankie started talking to Ellis. "Hey, you finally gonna pay some attention to what I been sayin'. I was on TV. I stood right in front of the camera and showed 'em what the doctor said and everything. Congress could have done something if they'd wanted to."

"You probably got a point there, Frankie. Where should we look for you on TV?"

Frankie launched into a long statement using words that were not in the dictionary. As far as I could make out, the TV appearance in question was on a security camera in an all-night convenience store. Frankie turned to make his exit and then looked at Hadden. "You're new with these guys, right?" Without waiting for an answer, Frankie turned to the crew, "Watch him. He don't look too bright to me."

Hadden ignored Frankie's parting shot and started talking again. The assignment was to take out some big steel beams by cutting them into two sections and then lifting each section out separately. Tight work. Really heavy work. Lots of chances to fuck up. Not a good job for someone like Lizard to be learning on.

As Hadden mumbled through his description of the work, he seemed simply to be repeating word for word what he had been told. Lloyd would have added his own comments about special precautions to be taken, about special techniques to be utilized based on his experience in the trade. He would have asked us if we had any questions to make sure that all of us were on the same page. He would have encouraged Ellis, Carl, or Malcolm to share anything from their experience which they thought might be useful. He would make us feel prepared.

Listening to Lizard's thin, rote statements, I feared that he didn't know enough to say anything more. The swallowed words, the nervous look in his eyes told me that he was overmatched by this project.

Although Lizard acknowledged that Sterling and I

were apprentices, he was uncertain about what type of assignment to give us. At first, he indicated that we should stay out of the hole and work in the yard. Then he changed his mind and said that since there were torches available, we should go underground and do some burning work to remove some small braces. I straightened my posture as I thought about questioning whether that was a good idea since working down in the hole, Sterling and I could get into trouble without anyone seeing what was happening. Carl noticed the shift in my back and glanced at me. His look, even though it was merely quizzical, stopped me and I said nothing. After all, there would have been no point to it since Lizard was not about to take any direction from me and probably would tell me that if I was afraid to do such a simple job, I should forget about piledriving and look for another line of work.

* * *

To get to our work area, Ellis, Malcolm, Sterling, and I had to climb down a series of ladders into a dark, cavernous world, which, with dimly-seen construction workers as lost souls, resembled some vaulted den in the afterlife. The darkness grew deeper and the air became denser with the smell of dirt, oil, and sweat as we climbed over the struts and piles to find our assigned location. When we found it on some steel braces and scaffolding, we were grateful for the few splinters of sunlight that came through cracks in the wooden street decking.

"Shit, we can't work in here unless we get some

lights or a street mat pulled," Ellis said to Lizard, who had followed us down into the hole. "I can't even see where the damn whalers are bolted to the wall." Hadden did not argue the point and left to find Clyde Bender. He returned very quickly.

"You're back in a hurry," Ellis said in a confrontational voice.

"The street mat stays down. They say they can't take it up without rerouting street traffic and that's too much of a hassle. You'll have to make do."

"It's too dangerous," Ellis protested.

"Don't be givin' me shit because I'm new. You want Clyde to come down here, I'll call him."

"No point in that."

"So get to work."

The light from our torches, while barely adequate for the work, gave us something new to worry about. Revealed below us was a vast junk pile of construction debris. It was almost as big as the mess in the yard. Broken ladders, stripped lumber, dented scaffolds, dirty clouds of plastic waterproofing material, packing paper, sandwich wrappers, and a few rats poking through things.

"God Almighty," Ellis exhaled. "They ain't taken nothin' out of here since the first day they been workin'. Probably some bodies in that stuff."

"You see those rats?" I asked nervously.

"Forget the rodents! What do you think is going to happen to that junk when our slag hits it? This place will go up in flames and us with it."

When Lizard came over to see what we were doing, Ellis got in his face about the junk in the hole. "Why is all that stuff still in here?"

"They're gonna take it out all at once. It's more efficient that way. Get all the right equipment. Get a full-time crew of laborers. Do it when it won't slow down our work. Makes sense."

"But the stuff's dangerous."

"It ain't blocking anything, so calm down."

"Why haven't the safety inspectors done something?" I asked.

"They wrote up Elbell for the junk, but I told you it ain't exactly a big hazard, so why don't you shut up, do your job, and don't forget that you're a punk."

When the crew broke for lunch, everyone had a bad stomach. Although no one said much, everyone seemed to be thinking that we would more than earn our money here.

Eventually, Ellis gave notice to what I suspected and feared was on his mind when he talked with me at the open bar after we finished the 16th Street job. "This place is gonna kill somebody."

"Don't be talkin' like that," Malcolm objected.

"I ain't sayin' it's gonna be one of us." Ellis cushioned his jaw in the palm of his hand. "My teeth hurt."

"So what does that mean?" Carl asked.

"It means my teeth hurt. I just told you that."

* * *

Behind their backs, Clyde Bender and Lizard kept getting fuck-you fingers, but no one said anything to them face-to-face. We did the work and grumbled. At the end of the day, I suggested that the crew take Lloyd for a beer to show our appreciation for his good work as our foreman. Everyone quickly agreed, but Lloyd turned down the invitation. He seemed glum about the whole thing as if he were worried that he was in danger of rising up too high in the world. "Never seen nobody so in his cups about makin' more money," Ellis said.

The day's events had put me in a glum mood too. The fact that Lizard and Clyde Bender were now running the show, the fact that the Elbell site was a hell hole, the fact that Drager would be coming back all conspired to make me feel suddenly defenseless.

* * *

My deteriorating mood followed me off the job. I was bad company when I took Minnie out to eat at a place which was done up in a nautical theme with portholes for windows and "Buoys" and "Gulls" restrooms. When she commented that she thought that the decor was "cute", I responded sarcastically that it was hokey.

Her eyes flashed. "No reason to use that tone with me!"

"I'm sorry."

She took a sip from her water glass. "I think that it's time that you told Lloyd about me. I also think that it's time that you meet my family."

I looked at her blankly. "Meet your family?"

"Come over to my parents' place for dinner. For a few hours. It's no big thing. Why are you looking at me like that?"

"Like what?"

"Like what I am talking about is bizarre. Did you

really think that you were going to be some type of secret kept in a dark closet?"

"I get that I should tell Lloyd. But meeting the rest of your family? Why does it have to happen now?"

"Because we're seeing each other."

"You just kind of caught me by surprise." I looked at the menu as an excuse not to continue talking. Finally, after taking as long as I could reasonably dedicate to selecting the flounder special, I looked up at Minnie. "I suppose you already heard about Lloyd's promotion."

"I have and I'm proud of him. He's worked long and hard for this and now he's gone much further than my father ever did."

"You seem happier about it than he is."

"It's Elbell. He wishes that it had been a better company that made him the first offer. At least that's what I think. I don't really know for sure because he doesn't talk to me much about these things."

"He doesn't say much to me either."

"No surprise, you being a college guy and all"

"Why would that make a difference?"

"Bad associations. Goes back to when he was hooked up with Kelsey. I never liked her because I thought that she had ambitions bigger than Lloyd and I was right. While he worked construction, she went to college and he helped her pay for the tuition. He wanted to get married but she kept delaying things. 'I need to get my degree first,' she would always say. He stands by her through all of those years, shelling out dollars, and then just before she's ready to graduate, she tells him that he should not attend the graduation ceremony. When he asks her why, she says that she's done with him. It turned out that she had started seeing a guy she had met in one of her classes. She thinks she treated Lloyd fairly because she paid back the tuition."

The waitress sauntered up to our table to find out what we wanted to eat. I ordered and then withdrew deeper into my bad mood. Minnie let me stay there. Neither one of us finished our meals after they were delivered; we ate slowly and then just pushed the food around on our plates.

"Do you want to talk about what's bothering you?" Minnie asked after the waitress dropped the check by my water glass.

"You don't need to hear it," I said without taking my eyes off my plate.

"Maybe I do."

"Nothing you can do about most of it anyway."

"Probably true but talk to me anyway."

"You already know that we're working at a new site. The company that is running things...the company that promoted Lloyd....is screwed up...not because they promoted Lloyd...that made sense...but because of how sloppy they seem to be. The job is a mess. A bigger mess than Lloyd can deal with. And our new foreman acts as if he is in way over his head. He certainly can't match up with Lloyd. So it's like I'm just hanging out there waiting for something ugly to happen. And if you add to that the likelihood that this new foreman won't be able to teach me anything about the trade, I beginning to feel that it's time for me to move on." I knew that it would not be a good idea to tell her about Drager. I picked up the check abruptly, almost rudely. "Ready to go?"

For the first few steps out of the cafe door, I walked

faster than Minnie did and put some distance between us. Then I stopped and let her catch up under the cafe's buzzing neon sign.

Her eyes were brimming and turning red. I could see her breath come in gulps. "I told you that it has nothing to do with you," I said as I brushed a tear away from the corner of her eye. "It's been a long day."

"So are you going to talk to Lloyd about us?" she asked after exhaling unevenly.

"I told you that I would."

CHAPTER TWELVE

The next morning, Sterling looked slack and unfocused on our way to work. At times, he appeared to have only one eye open.

"You shouldn't be driving," I finally said. "Pull over."

He did and then leaned back against the headrest. "I'll bet but you f-f-five bucks you can't get me to go to work this morning." He closed both eyes. "You lose."

"You're not going?"

"Hey, last night I was outta control. Now just the thought of going back to Elbell makes me want to puke. Take the keys. Drive me back to the apartment and then drive yourself to work. Tell Elbell I'm sick."

"I'm not telling them anything. You've got to call in yourself."

"OK. OK. Just drive me home."

I delivered Sterling back to the apartment and watched from the car as he stumbled into the building. As I drove to the job by myself, I felt even weirder about how things were playing out.

When I walked into the piledrivers' trailer, I found the crew to be a pack of snarling dogs. Carl said that he hated the townhouse that he was renting because all of the doors were hollow and his son had already put his foot through one. When Early was asked how he was doing, he said "aw right" but then went on to complain that his girlfriend Velveeta was always off doing something for her kids and hardly had any time for him.

"Where's Nesko?" Carl asked.

"Out sick," I answered.

"You mean he's got a hangover."

"Basically. But there's nothing I can do about it."

The door to the trailer swung open. Lizard walked in. "Hey, anybody seen this guy Drager? Bender told me that he's supposed to report here today."

I immediately felt a little shaky and sat down on a bench. I had known that this day would eventually arrive but nevertheless was unprepared for it. My mind began to race as it went through unanswered questions which had been raised many times before. How would I defend myself if he went after me again? Maybe I should use some type of weapon, an iron bar, a 2x4, anything to knock him silly. But what good would it do if I didn't kill him in the process, because, if left alive, he would keep trying to seek his revenge? Maybe if I stayed out of his way, watched where he was, watched where I was, never let him get a shot at me, things would blow over. I'd tried to convince myself once again that maybe he had turned over a new leaf.

"Drager?" Lizard repeated. "Any of you seen him?"

"No," Malcolm replied. "You know anything about him? He's a head case."

Lizard pulled on his ear. "I've heard a few stories, but it ain't no business of mine what his problems are. That's for Crispin and Bender to handle. Should be easy for them if he don't show up today."

Before I could latch onto the hope that Drager had skipped out, I heard the sound of heavy feet on the steps to the trailer and turned, along with everyone else, towards the door. Drager walked in slowly and silently. He looked pale and drawn, as if gravity were pulling down the skin on his face. His eyes had no whites, just red patches. His mouth did not close right. He reminded me of an abandoned, out-of-plumb house with sagging beams, broken windows, doors ajar. All of us in the trailer, even Lizard, moved away from him as if we were afraid of being buried in the rubble when he came down.

I wondered what kind of treatment he had received if this were the outcome. Maybe the goal had been to simply subdue him rather than to reform him. But by apparently attempting to drain him of his viciousness, they had also drained him of much of his personality. I didn't know what I was looking at.

Carl had told me more stories about Drager, which had come his way over the years, and which served only to further confuse me. About how Drager had hated his father not only because of the beatings but also because the man had been so petty. To hear tell it, there was no predicting what would set him off. A television on the wrong channel, a bit of mashed potatoes left on the edge of a plate, a slight delay in getting him a beer when he demanded one, not calling him "Sir" when he expected it, and he would pound on his oldest son. In the end, the only defense had been for the son to become equally volatile so that his father would have to fear him too. In the first fight, both of them suffered broken noses. And now, I had broken Drager's nose for the second time, who knows, maybe even the third, fourth, or fifth.

As I looked at Drager sagging against a locker in the trailer, I wanted to give him the benefit of every one of my doubts, but could not do it. I could not rid myself of the suspicion that residing somewhere in his psyche, perhaps temporarily suppressed, was something that could be called, with no exaggeration, evil. A cruel, dim-witted urge to maim that gave no consideration to the consequences. The brutality of a terrorist without a cause.

Finally, Drager looked up at Lizard. "You the new man in charge?" he asked in a drawl which sounded medicated.

"Yeah, I been wonderin' when you were gonna show up."

"Well, I'm here."

"OK. Then let's get goin'." Lizard was still eyeing Drager. "You can stay up top for today. Why don't you work with the rigging when the steel comes up. I'll stay up top too. The rest of you are goin' to have to work down in the hole."

I thought that I saw Drager sneak a look at me. His eyes started to fidget and his nostrils flared, but then he quickly looked away. I felt sick to my stomach.

"OK, let's hustle up," Lizard said impatiently.

I left the trailer to get some fresh air and to try to calm down by reminding myself that Drager would not be down in the hole with me.

* * *

An hour into the day, Carl and Malcolm got into an argument with Lizard as to how to move steel so that it could be lifted out of the hole through one of the openings in the street mats. They kept telling Lizard to use a snatch block to redirect the crane line horizontally so that the steel could be pulled into position directly beneath the opening and then lifted vertically. But Lizard did not want to go through the trouble of getting and setting up the snatch block and wanted us to direct the steel by hand. There was a similar argument in the afternoon.

Even though Lizard was obviously showing bad judgment, I was not unhappy with his decision, since it required that I help out with moving the steel. This assignment gave me a break from burning and a feeling of rough equality with other piledrivers for a few hours because during that brief time we were all doing basically the same bull work. But eventually, I was reassigned back to a cramped intersection of braces where I spent the rest of the day crouching with a torch in my hand, making small cuts and thinking about my current circumstances.

When I was not obsessing about Drager, I tried to think about the shower that I would take after work. That was the only way I was able to stand the dirt all around me. It was everywhere down in the hole. On the beams, on the tools, on my clothes, on my skin, on my teeth. The few thin shafts of light that slipped through the street mats down into the excavation only emphasized how bad things were. Caught by the light were drifting clouds of smoke and suspended dust. I worried that there would come a day when I would no longer be able to get clean anymore and that the skin on my hands and arms would end up with the texture of sandpaper.

And when I was not worrying about how the grit from the job would become embedded in me, I wrung my hands over how to tell Lloyd that I was seeing his sister. I had promised Minnie that I would do it, so there could be no backing away. Postponing telling Lloyd did not seem to offer much other than multiplying the days during which I would be anxious about not having done what needed to be done.

Over the course of the workday, I inched my way closer and closer to the conclusion that I should just get it over with, do it before I left the job site. Sterling was not with me so I could seek out Lloyd without keeping Sterling waiting or having to explain to him what I was doing.

But when quitting time actually arrived, I was having second thoughts, if for no other reason than I had had enough for one day. Finally, after making sure that Drager was no longer around, I forced myself to head in the direction of the superintendent's trailer.

When I stepped into the trailer, Lloyd was the first person I saw. He stood up from behind a metal desk. "Travers, you looking for me?"

"You got a moment?"

"What's up?"

There was another supervisor in the trailer which made the situation a little awkward.

"Maybe we should step outside."

We exited the trailer and then took a few steps to the side of the door. "OK, now you've got me outside," Lloyd said with some impatience beginning to show in his voice. "What's this all about?"

"I wanted you to know that I'm seeing Minnie."

Lloyd's head snapped forward. "My sister?"

"Yeah."

"How did this get started?"

"I met her at Arlene's."

"How did you know that she worked at Arlene's?"

"Somebody on the crew told me."

"And you went there to meet her?"

"Correct."

"How serious is this?"

"I'm not sure how to answer that."

"I'm not going to vouch for you if that's what you're looking for." Without saying another word, Lloyd turned his back on me and went back to the trailer.

I felt a little silly standing there by myself. I waited for what seemed like a few minutes with the stupid expectation that Lloyd might come back out of the trailer to talk things over. When he didn't, I walked off the job, weighted down with the certain conclusion that the conversation with Lloyd had not gone well.

* * *

When I entered the apartment, I heard the shower running in the bathroom. The dense air smelled like a wet dog. I walked toward the bathroom and saw that more empty beer cans had been tossed in the direction of the previous accumulation along with an empty bourbon bottle. Entering the apartment now was like going into a carnival House of Mirrors; you never knew what distortions were going to be on the inside.

In the bathroom, I found Sterling passed out in the tub. I turned off the water and tried to get him on his feet, found the job to be impossible, and then turned the shower back on, this time with only cold water running. He twitched and woke up.

"Sterling, where's Crystal?"

"Look for her in the bedroom."

I found her in the bedroom, half in and half out of

bed. When I helped her to get her legs all the way onto the mattress, she looked as if she were genuinely embarrassed. "I'm sorry about this. I really am. I don't want anybody to see me like this."

With good reason. She looked catastrophically bad. Her hair was tangled and out of place, some of it falling forward into her face. Her makeup was smudged on her pallid skin as if it had been applied with a dirty pencil eraser. Her eyes were off-center and filmy. "Where's Sterling?" she asked.

"He's putting himself back together in the bathroom. I found him passed out in the bathtub with the shower still running. He could have slipped and cracked his head open. If he'd fallen a certain way, he might have even drowned. You could have cracked your head open too."

"I'm not going to argue with you. I know it's wrong." Crystal started to cry. I got her a tissue. She thanked me and then dabbed her eyes. "You won't see me like this again," she said.

Sterling shuffled into the bedroom. He had dried some of himself off, put on his clothes, and combed some of his hair. He sat on the bed next to Crystal and put his arm around her. She put her head on his shoulder and repeated what she had said to me. "You won't see me like this again." She dabbed her eyes with another tissue.

Sterling squeezed her shoulder. "Hey, it takes two."

"Then you've got to help me. We've got to help each other."

Crystal seemed to be truly disappointed in herself, truly pleading for assistance. I felt that I had already seen and heard too much.

"Are you two going to be OK now?" I asked.

Both of them looked up at me as if they were surprised that I was still there. "We'll be fine," Sterling said.

I left them sitting on the edge of the bed looking exhausted and totally dependent on each other.

* * *

When I arrived at Minnie's, she gestured for me to get cleaned up. Then I found myself standing in her bathroom trying to figure out where to put my dirty clothes. Everything was so pristine and decorated that there was really no good place. Even the water tank behind the toilet was dressed up with a little skirt and ruffle. I piled my clothes on the floor next to the sink. When some caked dirt fell off my pants, I immediately picked it up and put it in the wastebasket.

After my shower, I wiped the tub down so that it would be as clean as when I had started. The room demanded this care.

I asked through the door for a fresh shirt and pair of pants, which by now, I had started keeping at Minnie's. She handed the clothes to me through the cracked door and after a few minutes, I walked out of the bathroom feeling presentable.

"I told Lloyd about us," I said when Minnie handed me a beer.

Minnie hesitated. "How did he react?" she finally asked.

"He seemed upset."

"Did he say anything?"

"That he wouldn't vouch for me. Then he just walked

away and left me standing there."

"As I said before, it's my business, not his, who I go out with."

"You think that he is just going to stay on the sidelines and not do anything?"

"The dinner at my parents is coming up and he is supposed to be there. I can't believe that he would mess that up. But if I'm headed for trouble with him, so be it."

"But if I'm headed for trouble with him, I may be out of a job."

"The cat's out of the bag so just hope for the best."

"I am, but I still have to ask you whether it's a good idea to have me come to that dinner at your parents' house. It's not just Lloyd. A lot of people are going to be there and I don't know if I'd feel..."

"Comfortable being 'my man'?" she asked before I could complete my sentence.

That was exactly the problem. It was not that I was embarrassed to be seen with her; I wasn't. It was that when Minnie's family saw her with me, when she presented herself with me to them, some of them might develop some big expectations and others might develop some big misgivings. In either case, they would talk and eventually complicate things.

"Do you think it's a good idea for me to meet so many people at once?"

"Yes," she answered emphatically.

She adjusted a ring that she wore on her thumb. I felt disadvantaged in her presence despite the privileges that had accompanied my earlier life and the struggles that had accompanied hers. Now she was self-propelled because she hadn't depended on others the way I had. I admired her for trying to get beyond her circumstances without denouncing them. Her radiant tenacity had an almost physical quality to it. I always kept coming back to her eyes. They not only collected light, they multiplied it.

"Were you seeing somebody else when I first met you?" I asked. "Don't take this the wrong way, but I was a little surprised that you were willing ... available to go out with me."

"Yes, I had to make room for you. But I was ready to make a change. You came along at a good time. The fruit was ready to be harvested so to speak." She tossed her head back in a laugh, momentarily amused by her own candor.

"I can't remember a time when I wasn't seeing somebody, but every relationship had a flaw," she continued. "Different reasons for different guys. Sometimes it was simple things that I just couldn't get out of my mind. For one guy, it was his way of eating. Kind of swallowed without chewing. Finished a meal in a few minutes and then threw down a couple of Tums for heartburn. I know it sounds foolish to focus on something like that, but I did. And then there was Jack Turley who was always coming back to me with a swollen lip or cut-up knuckle because he had been brawling in a parking lot next to a bar. Came back to my place expecting me to admire him just because he had been hurt in a fight and then to patch him up. And then there was Gene Calistro....no, you've heard enough. Anyway, when you came along - I told you this - I could tell right away things were going to be different."

Minnie's cell phone rang. It was her mother. Minnie gestured to me in a way that said that she was going to be a few minutes. Then she walked into her bedroom and closed the door.

When she came out, she looked a little agitated. "My mother wants me to come over to her place tonight. Wants to talk about you. No surprise: Lloyd told her about you. At least for once, we won't be talking about my father's shortcomings. I'll go but don't worry; she's not going to change my mind on anything."

"I'll stay at my place tonight."

On my way back to my apartment, I mulled over the fact that neither my mother nor my father had called me in weeks. I knew that they were going through a difficult time and probably did not want to discuss the gory details with me. Nevertheless, I was disappointed that they displayed so little curiosity about how I was doing. Of course, they had seen very little interest from me in their lives, so maybe they were just sinking to my level. But, in my own defense, I have to say that I called them on the prior Sunday night but only got voicemail.

* * *

Sterling and Crystal were surprised by my return but did not ask any questions. We talked briefly and then I excused myself and went to bed, not out of any consideration for them but because I had to get up early the next morning to go to work. In fact, I was amazed that I had been able to adjust my sleeping pattern to the construction workday. It was still something of a struggle but apparently not as big of one as was being experienced by Sterling. I anticipated that in the morning I would have to argue with him while he was lying in bed with Crystal with their naked limbs all tangled up, and she would not be much help in the process.

But when I got up, Crystal was already out of bed, making coffee. After she awakened Sterling, she came back to the kitchen to pour me a cup and offer me a donut on a paper napkin. "I'm sorry about the other night. Really sorry."

When I thanked her for the coffee and the donut, she said that she didn't mind getting up because it was the first time in months that she had had a reason to do so. "You know, Henry, the worst part about sleeping 'til noon is being able to do it. Didn't make a damn bit of difference to anybody whether I got up at 7:00 or noon or even whether I got up at all. I ain't gonna lie and tell you that I won't go back to bed after you and Sterling go to work. But it won't be 'til noon. I'm even thinkin' about lookin' for a job."

"What kind of job?" I asked as the two of us leaned against appliances in the small kitchen.

"I could do office work," she said. "I finished high school you know. I'm good on the phone and good with strangers. I was a receptionist once. I could go back to that type of thing."

"If you liked the work, why did you leave?"

"I was fired by the boss' wife if you know what I mean. I was about to call off the relationship anyway. He kept telling me the same stories about how he blocked a punt in a high school football game. In bed, he was kind of a blocked punt himself."

Her eyes danced for a second. She seemed to be smiling at herself. At that moment, she looked alert, intelligent, aware of her shortcomings and of how to overcome them. There was nothing definite in any of this, just a suggestion of something promising. "You're really going to look for a job?" I asked.

"Maybe not today. But soon though."

"What did you do after that receptionist's job?" To my surprise, I was really interested in what she was saying.

"I got turned down for new jobs once they found out about me being fired. I couldn't get anything, no matter how hard I looked. Well, maybe I could have looked harder. Well, anyway, I moved in with Dawn. She had a job then. And an apartment. I did some waitressing. A week here. Two weeks there. Some of those places were pretty touchy about my being late now and then, so I moved on. Then a gentleman acquaintance would come along or not. I'm not real proud of everything I've done, but I've got by and now I'm lookin' to do better."

Crystal smiled. Her teeth were white and obviously cared for, but overlapping. I concluded that she would have had orthodonture if she could have afforded it.

* * *

When Lloyd saw me coming onto the job, he didn't say a word but just kept on walking. His apparent indifference was so complete that it did not even qualify as a cold shoulder. On the positive side, I interpreted this as an indication that he was not going to fire me. By the time that Sterling and I made it to the piledrivers' trailer, everybody else was already there. I weaved my way through the crew to a bench as far away from Drager as possible.

Ellis Harper kicked his locker door shut with a metallic bang and then slumped down on the bench next to me. As he leaned over to put his elbows on his knees, his face seemed to sag forward with the weight of his frustration. "My son don't give a shit about what I do to put bread on the table. Why am I puttin' up with this shit work if he doesn't show me some respect? And my teeth are killin' me."

"Don't be takin' it so hard," Carl responded quickly. "Ain't none of us haven't had the same problem at one time or another."

"Well, I just about lost it last night," Ellis said with his elbows no longer on his knees. "My older one gets fired from his part-time job with one of them lawn care companies because he didn't show up and never called in. Now he wants me to help him pay the insurance on his car and I say 'no,' and he goes after me. Yellin' mostly. But I grabbed him by the shirt and put him against the wall. I came within an inch of smackin' him."

Suddenly, Drager stepped forward from his corner retreat. "You should leave him be," he said.

"I didn't hit him," Ellis answered sharply. "I said that I almost did."

Drager turned his back to Ellis and went back to his corner.

That was it. A small flash of something surprising from Drager. Why had he said what he did? Did it indicate that he had some emotional depth which I had overlooked? I was not willing to go there, because it felt as if that would compromise my vigilance.

At the lunch break, I began to feel guilty about this as I watched Drager eating alone. I considered approaching him to see if I could have a conversation with him. Clear the air. Offer an olive branch. Try to figure him out. I stood up from where I was sitting with Sterling and looked in Drager's direction. He was already staring at me with that same malicious opaqueness that I had seen when I first met him and that discouraged any hope of a civil word between us. I sat back down.

"You were thinking about talking to Drager, weren't you?" Sterling asked. "You thought that because he said something to Ellis about leaving his son alone, you could connect with him?"

"Yeah."

Sterling opened up a bag of chips. "I know you told me how Drager's father used to kick the shit out of him. At least he had some interaction with the man." Sterling pulled some chips out of the bag. "Probably shouldn't be eatin' this crap. Crystal says I should lose some weight and that she'll go on a diet with me. She might have a point." Sterling crumpled the bag between his hands, crushing the uneaten chips. "My old man probably had his reasons for leaving, but what difference does it make? He left."

"So when's the last time you heard from him?" I asked.

"Seven years ago he sent me a note with an artsy picture from some museum. He always wanted to be a painter. I guess that's OK so long as you don't have a wife and a kid. I've still got the picture and the note he wrote."

"You serious?"

"I carry the note in my wallet."

Sterling reached into his hip pocket, pulled out a black leather billfold, fingered through a few bills, then removed a small gray piece of paper and handed it to me. I unfolded and read the faded words: "Sterling, I'm sorry. Your mother said that I should not return unless I was going to stay. She told me that she was not some type of experiment. I don't blame her. Life is full of some pretty miserable outcomes, so I guess what you end up doing depends mostly on what you're afraid of. Maybe, someday you'll understand. Harold Nesko, your father."

"Did you ever talk to him about this?"

"Pretty difficult....never saw him again."

"Did you write him back?"

"I was in high school when I got this and wasn't much for writing letters. Eventually, I made the effort, but three weeks after I mailed the letter, it came back to me with a label on it "Undeliverable. No forwarding address."

"What did you say to him in the letter?"

"I ripped it up and I can't remember the details now. The gist of what I do remember was to tell him that it meant a lot that he wrote to me even if it was only a note; that it meant a lot that he seemed to be trying to be honest about himself; that I wanted to follow-up with him in person....it could be at a diner, nothing fancy; that I wanted to have a father even if he didn't have all of his shit together. It didn't make any difference because he never got the letter."

"Did he ever write to you again?"

"No. And my mother refused to try to track him down." After I handed the note back to Sterling, he refolded it and returned it to his wallet, "I don't know why I carry this damn thing around with me. I've gotten this far without Harold Nesko in my life so what's the point of being reminded of him." Sterling shook his head. "I keep telling myself that if he had been the real deal, he would have stayed with his family and suffered with us." Sterling paused again. "But how does anybody know how to do anything, including being a father... really know ... until they've already done it?"

I was tempted to tell Sterling about my difficulties with my own father but said nothing. Initially, my silence felt like emotional weakness. But then it felt like something quite different: my sense, however tentative, that I was not qualified to judge my father because I was missing necessary information. What if Sterling was right? What if my father hadn't figured how to be a father until it was too late?" Sterling seemed grateful that I stayed quiet, as if he did not want to pursue this topic any further. The two of us just sat in the warm air, relieved to be out of the hole.

* * *

It was not long before Lizard got all of us on our feet to go back to work. My feet felt particularly heavy as I made my way underground. The air in the hole was thick. About an hour into the afternoon, a pounding rainstorm hit up top and water ran through the street mats. Little falls came down on us, turning dirt into mud and making every surface treacherous. I was getting soaked and didn't mind it because the water was cool. But I and everyone else on the crew complained to Lizard about the footing. All of us slowed down what we were doing to protect ourselves. Finally, Lizard told us that Elbell had shut the job down and we could go home.

I climbed out of the hole and looked up at a filthy sky of stratus clouds. The rain was still coming down and I tilted my face into it and welcomed this weather.

Since I was soaked and was off early, I went back to the apartment with Sterling. When we arrived, Crystal was pressed into a pile of pillows which she and Sterling had recently acquired for the living room. She was eating microwave popcorn out of the bag and watching television. Although she hit the mute button on the remote when Sterling and I walked through the door, she did not get up. "You boys are home early. Was it the weather?"

"Even Elbell won't work people on a day like this," Sterling answered.

"I don't think that the Union contract lets them do it," I said. "Otherwise, they probably would."

Crystal rolled to the side to free herself from the pillows and then, one knee at a time, she managed to stand up. "Well, I've got my exercise for the day. Sterling, we need to do some shopping. I'm thinkin' about doin' some cookin'. We've had enough take-out pizza. You deserve better."

Sterling welcomed the expedition and quickly dropped his wet, dirty work clothes on the bathroom floor, showered, and pulled on a new T-shirt and a pair of jeans. "Be sure to lock up when you go to Minnie's," he said when he escorted Crystal out the door.

After they left I paced around the apartment with the restlessness of a zoo animal. I wondered how Minnie's evening with her mother had gone. I checked the time to see how long it would be before she got off work. Another three hours.

I walked into Sterling's bedroom. I felt a little self-conscious about intruding into his personal space, but did not give it more thought because the door had been open and I was not going to pull out any drawers.

Crystal's dog radio was sitting on the bureau next to a paperweight in the shape of the Empire State Building, several pairs of earrings, a take-out menu from a pizza restaurant, and scattered coins. The bed was made although not with tight corners. With the exception of a few magazines lying about, the floor was picked up and orderly. Crystal had brought Sterling a long way.

To the side of the bed, just above a nightstand, anchored to the wall with a thumbtack was a small card showing a colorful painting. I concluded that this was the artsy picture Sterling's father had sent to him. I read the fine print along the bottom margin. It said: "Self-portrait of the artist, Paul Gauguin, 1889."

The painting showed the head of a man against a deep yellow and red background. Crossing the lower left corner of the picture were dark green lines that gave the impression of branches. Behind the man's head, two apples hung from a twig. The rest of the painting confused me. The man's face was drawn and angular with a distorted, aquiline nose. Framed by arching thin eyebrows, his eyes were narrow and strange. In his hand, the man held, as if he were smoking it, a small snake. The portrait suggested casual malevolence. And yet, above the man's head, there was, quite distinctly, a halo.

For some reason, I thought that the painting was trying to tell me something. I wondered how the artist had come to such contradictory views of himself. Then my mind skipped to the note from Sterling's father and why I even cared about the answer. My thoughts were becoming urgent and repetitious. I checked the time again to see how long it would be before Minnie got off from work.

I retreated to my room, took off my shirt and pants, and flopped down on the bed. I closed my eyes but they popped open again. Something flashed in my head like sunlight momentarily reflected off a passerby's watch dial. At that moment, I felt a bewildering sympathy for my own father. Maybe his pursuit of money and ultimate slide into deep leisure were a response to the dependencies and stupidities of working for others. That in the end, he had simply decided to stop and smell the roses and thereafter to continue smelling them. Life was too large and too complicated to do much about it, so you might as well enjoy what you can while you can.

But to continue to smell the roses you need money and unless you inherit it, how do you get it without working your ass off? And then even if you have it, however, you got it, and, as my father said, you can get "people to cater to you", who is to say that you wouldn't end up either restless or listless, take your pick. There has to be something higher or even lower to aim for than being really comfortable. Sterling's big point had always been that if you are going to do anything important in life, you had to have illusions, convince yourself to believe your own bullshit. My problem was that I could never come up with the bullshit. As hard as I tried, some moment of discouraging honesty always got in the way and I was left with my insecurities, uncertainties, and self-criticisms. Maybe Sterling's dad was right: What you end up doing depends mostly on what you are afraid of.

* * *

Hanging out in my apartment was not going well. Finally, I decided that I would make my way to Arlene's to pick up Minnie when she got off work. She was surprised and happy to see me. "To what do I owe the honor?" she asked with mock formality.

"They shut down the job early because of the rain, so I thought that I would come here and escort you back to your place."

"Impressive."

"How did it go with your mother last night?" I asked perhaps a little too quickly.

"Pretty much as I expected it would. She started asking me all of these questions about you. How did you get into piledriving? Where did your parents live? Where did their money come from? Where were you living now? Did I know what I was doing getting into a relationship with you? Lloyd said that he didn't know much about you but had his doubts."

"Doubts? Based on what?"

"On his conclusion that you're kind of passing through, so to speak."

"So Lloyd thinks that he has me all figured out even though he hasn't talked with me for more than two minutes about anything other than piledriving?"

"Don't get yourself all agitated. I put my foot down. I told her that she should trust me to not give myself away to a bum. Eventually, she backed off, but it's probably only a matter of time before she takes another shot. Regardless, the bottom line hasn't changed: the dinner with my family is still on and my mother expects that you will be there with me. Like it or not, my family is just going to have to adjust to what I am doing with my life. And you're going to have to do the same thing."

CHAPTER THIRTEEN

Crystal seemed to be adjusting to her new situation, maybe even to the point of acquiring routine domestic responsibility. She wanted to be useful to Sterling. She wanted to justify her own existence and, in that regard, she and I were very much alike.

Sterling seemed to understand what was behind Crystal's efforts to tidy up the apartment and herself. He expressed his appreciation for her little changes and encouraged her to do more. He called her "sweet thing" as in: "You may be the first person, sweet thing, who will convince me to buy a vacuum cleaner."

Crystal was on the edge of discovering ambition. It was not only her talk about finding a job. It was also an attitude about what she found acceptable. Conning drinks at Ray's Oasis seemed beneath her now. She was no longer cheap, although she still might be a bargain.

To be sure, her path to self-improvement was not a straight one. She and Sterling were still getting hammered, which, for me, usually meant dealing with the aftermath of their late night sessions at Ray's. My exchange with Sterling was always basically the same as I tried to convince him that he had to go to work.

"Not so fast ... uh ... slow," I would say. "You can't not show up just because you don't feel like it."

"Says who? I've been doin' my job; I'm entitled to a few days off."

"Says Lizard. Says Clyde Bender."

"I've got half a mind to tell them to fuck themselves."

"Well, you're right about the 'half a mind' part. Now get dressed."

* * *

"We're gonna be short again," Lizard announced after he finally collected us together in the trailer. "Ellis is out. Something about getting dentures. I'm gettin' sick and tired of workin' short-handed."

We were assigned to a new work area in a bay over big piles of discarded waterproofing materials. "You could set that stuff off just by rubbin' your socks together," Malcolm said to Lizard, but Lizard pretended not to hear.

Drager looked at me and mouthed something I could not understand. I thought I was hallucinating. I turned my head to see if anyone else in the trailer had seen what I thought I had seen. No one seemed to be paying attention. I looked back at Drager. He was rearranging something in his pocket and did not make eye contact with me. As I watched him ... I had to ... I almost had the feeling that he was actually suffering at that moment from not being able to fully utilize his true talent ... everybody has to be good at something ... for being a vicious son of a bitch.

He looked up at me. "You shoulda left before I came back," he said clearly and then turned away.

"Did you hear that?" I whispered to Sterling who was sitting next to me.

"Hear what?" he answered in full volume.

"Hear Drager threaten me."

"No," Sterling answered in a lower voice. "But it wouldn't surprise me if he did."

"Did you see anything different in him?"

"I try not to look at him."

Lizard pointed to the door. "We're gonna start with everyone down in the hole. We'll move things around in the afternoon. Let's see how much we can get done."

I wanted to stop him and say something about Drager but the men were already moving out of the trailer. I was still sitting on the bench as they filed by. There was an expanding hollow feeling in my stomach.

"You comin'?" Sterling asked when the two of us were the last ones inside.

I stood up slowly and followed Sterling out the door.

* * *

The work location was difficult to reach. It was adjacent to a complex series of whalers and oddly-placed beams. I picked my way carefully over the steel, since, as usual, the lighting was poor; the beams were covered with dirt and rust. I could not see Drager since he had gone down into the hole ahead of everyone else.

As I moved over one beam, I saw a pigeon sitting on an adjacent whaler. One of the bird's wings hung limply at its side. The creature must have flown in through an opening in the mats, run into something, and then could not make it back out. "Birds of a feather flock together," I thought to myself.

I inched my way in its direction in hopes of gathering it in and taking it with me. This frightened, banged up bird needed my help and I wanted to give it. I reached in the pigeon's direction. My sudden movement startled it and it stepped off the steel into the air and tried to fly.

The damaged wing would not work. The bird struggled in a hopeless spiral and disappeared from my sight.

I drew back, sat on the whaler near the soil wall, and tried to gather myself. Sweat poured off my face. The hollow feeling in my gut was turning into nausea. I looked in all directions to see if Drager was near me.

Slowly, ever so slowly, I found my torch cables and set up myself to cut some small pieces of steel away from an H-beam.

I started my burning work, being careful to watch the slag so that it would not fall onto the pile of junk below me, positioning the flame at a slightly greater distance from the steel than normal and then moving the torch at a deliberate pace. After a while, I noticed that I was shaking. The sight of that damn pigeon came back to me. I stopped burning for a second.

I smelled something other than the fumes from the burning steel. Something seemed wrong. I turned off my torch, flipped up my shield, and saw that black smoke was snaking from the trash below me. There was a fire in the excavation. I had to get out of there. I took off my shield and started to make my way out of the hole.

Then I heard Carl scream. I recognized his voice immediately and stopped in my tracks. He screamed again, but I could not understand what he said. The smoke had begun to surround me and I started to panic. Carl yelled again. It was a plea for help. I moved towards his voice through the smoke.

Trembling, I picked my way to the front of a big I-beam. On the other side of the beam, I could see his legs hanging down.

"Carl, it's me, Harry," I coughed out.

"I'm stuck!"

I climbed on top of the beam and tried to get a hold under his arms, but could not move him. He was trapped between an angle brace and the I-beam with his belly acting as the wedge that locked him in place. I tried to lift him again. The smoke was now pouring over us like a dirty wave.

"Pull on me again!" he yelled.

"I'm not strong enough!"

"Then get the fuck outta here!"

I hesitated but then took a step away from him. Before I could take another step, I saw a figure coming at me. It was Drager. In a few seconds, we were face to face.

"Carl's trapped in some steel!" I yelled before Drager could say or do anything.

"Shut up and help me get him out of there!" he yelled back.

Drager climbed up next to Carl and got on one of Carl's arms and I got on the other. "Ready, pull!" Drager shouted.

Carl screamed in pain and came free. His stomach was covered with awful black holes and gave off a smell of burnt flesh.

We could see that the fire had broken out into dirty orange flames and was advancing along the bottom of the hole. The only way out was to stay close to the excavation wall where there was still some air and try to make it to a ladder below an opening in the mats. Drager moved out first, keeping his hand along the wall for support and direction. Carl held onto Drager's belt from behind. I brought up the rear.

The flames grew with the rush of air in the tunnel

and were nearing the base of the ladder. I could feel the heat surrounding me. Carl doubled up with the pain in his stomach and pulled Drager to a stop. Drager turned and yanked Carl up straight.

We moved forward and when Carl bent over again we straightened him up again and pushed and pulled him where we wanted him to go. The ladder was in reach. We helped Carl over the last beam in our path and pushed him to the base. He grabbed the ladder and with difficulty started to climb. Drager and I were right behind him. We were climbing in the smoke blowing past us on its way out of the excavation. My eyes smarted and my lungs ached. Carl reached the landing at the halfway point. A can of something exploded and sent metal and wood splinters flying. He fell down onto his knees. We grabbed him under the arms and picked him up. He looked dazed. "Climb, Carl!" He started again. I looked up and saw Malcolm and Sterling reaching down to help us.

When we got up to the street level, Lloyd and Lizard took Carl from us. Sterling embraced me, but I just left my arms hanging at my side. Through the fatigue, I felt a deep relief that I had been tested and did not fail, then a shivering realization that I could have died down in that hole.

"You're shaking like a leaf," Sterling said as he peeled off his shirt. "Here. Put this around you."

I waved him off. "Is Carl OK?"

"He's over with Lloyd and Lizard. I'll go find out and be right back."

Sterling walked away to check on Carl and left me to my wheezing and coughing. I dropped my head to make it easier on my lungs. I thought about what Drager had done to save Carl and felt both guilt and frustration in my acknowledgment that Drager could change shapes. I needed to have him in focus so that I knew how dangerous he was, but now the lines were increasingly blurry.

From my bent position, I saw a soda can held in front of my face. I looked up and there was Drager standing in front of me with a frozen, unnatural expression as if it had been painted on his face. "Don't be thinkin' you're some kind of hero." His odd expression did not change. "You were in the right place at the right time," he continued, not giving me a chance to say anything. "Nothin' more to it than that. You ain't nothin' but a fuckin' tourist on this job."

I was taken back. I had hoped that what we had just been through would cause him to see me in a different light. "There's no reason for you to talk to me like this," I finally responded weakly. "I'm only trying to hold down this job."

"You're worse than a tourist. You're a fuckin' trespasser. You come into my territory and treat me like I'm a shit head."

"What are you talking about?"

"Fuck you. You think that I'm gonna forget that you broke my nose. This thing with Carl don't change nothin' between us." He raised the soda can to his mouth, drank it dry, threw the empty can at my feet, and walked away.

I did not move. I tried to take a deep breath but my cough hitched me up. I felt drained not only by my effort and fear down in the hole but also by my recognition that Drager had built around himself a fortress of hatred for me. Whatever difficulties in his life had caused him to construct these bitter walls made no difference now; the walls were too high for me to scale.

Sterling returned. "Looks like Carl got burned pretty bad on his stomach. Says that he slipped trying to get out when the fire started. He got stuck under the beam and then his slag came right back on him. There was nothing he could do except clench his teeth and take it. Says that you and Drager pulled him out."

I looked back at the opening in the street mats through which I had made my escape. Black smoke was squeezing out of the hole and then expanding into the air. If Carl or any of the rest of us had still been underground, he would be a dead man. I shivered again with the fearful recognition of how small the margin was between my being up top talking to Sterling and my lying down below with soot in my lifeless lungs.

"You sure you're OK?" Sterling asked.

The sirens of the arriving fire trucks, police cars, and ambulance cut off any further conversation. The emergency personnel jumped out of their vehicles and put their training to work. Hoses were pulled from trucks and attached to hydrants, traffic was diverted, air packs were assembled.

Some paramedics were attending to Carl. They eased him onto a stretcher and then rolled him to the back of their van. One of the EMTs came over to ask me if I had breathed in too much smoke and wanted to be taken to the emergency room. I said, "No thanks." I wasn't feeling tip-top, but I didn't think that sitting in a hospital waiting room would do much to help me.

After the EMT left, Clyde Bender came up to us. "You guys see how it started?" he asked in an angry tone which suggested that he was looking for a piledriver to blame.

"No. All I saw was smoke and trash burning."

"Same as him," Sterling added.

"You piledrivers been complaining about trash ever since you got here. So somebody figures he's going to make me look bad and starts a fire."

Clyde could be right, I thought to myself. And Drager would be the type of guy to do something like that. Not to make Clyde look bad but to scare the shit out of me. He hadn't figured on Carl getting stuck in the steel.

Clyde turned and looked at the smoke billowing out of the hole. "Another day shot to hell. Not that anyone else around here cares. D.T. will tell you when to punch out." Not a word about what I had done to get Carl out of the hole. I felt ashamed that I was looking for his praise.

CHAPTER FOURTEEN

I was still coughing as Sterling and I drove away from the job site. I rethought my decision not to go to the hospital since I was feeling poorly and I had no desire to return to the dingy confines of the apartment, but I said nothing.

Amazingly, the apartment looked almost bright when we arrived. Crystal had done the necessary work, creating the appearance that people actually lived, rather than just passed out, in the place. Crystal also looked a damn sight better. She had washed and set her hair, done her nails with some precision, put on only slightly too much blusher, and selected a shrewdly loose-fitting, red, green, and yellow flower print dress for herself.

The only obvious problem with her presentation was her plucked eyebrows, which she had attempted to improve with pencil, unfortunately straying off her natural eyebrow line. With her penciled handiwork wandering down her temple, she had created a rather daring science-fiction look. Regardless, her grooming had helped her to regain some of the years she had lost with Sterling in previous days.

Sterling told Crystal about the fire and what I had done. She listened with the same concentration she usually reserved for watching television. When Sterling described what his stomach looked like, she put a hand over her mouth. Her concern for Carl, for Sterling, for all of us, seemed genuine.

When Sterling finished, she turned to me and gave me a hug. "That was a brave thing you did," she said.

Her words meant a lot to me. I had wanted to hear them. The fact that they came from Crystal did not lessen their value. But I also felt that they were undeserved. I had been scared shitless and had taken a step to abandon Carl when Drager appeared. Drager was not far off the mark to say that I just happened to be there to help him pull Carl free. At least I had done something to save him. And now I felt nervous relief that I had done so and that I had survived.

"Why don't you invite Minnie to join us this evening and we'll have a spaghetti dinner," Crystal said. "I've got all the fixings. Although it might be a good idea to ask her to bring some more beer." Reluctant to introduce Minnie to her and Sterling, I hesitated.

"Come on, Harry, it's not a big deal. Just call her," Sterling insisted.

"I guess we could do it. Give me a minute to talk to her."

Minnie answered the phone quickly and said "yes" that she would come even before I had fully explained the invitation. She sounded happy that for once an evening would not just be the two of us. I didn't tell her about the fire.

I returned to the living room where Crystal and Sterling were waiting to hear Minnie's answer. "She'll come."

* * *

Minnie arrived at the apartment with the beer and her own effervescence. Her pleasure at being invited was obvious as she greeted Crystal and Sterling, who responded in kind.

"Aren't you proud of Harry for what he did in the fire?" Crystal asked as soon as the initial pleasantries were completed.

"What fire?"

"There was a fire today at work," I answered in a low-key way.

"What did you have to do with the fire?"

"Harry and another guy saved a man on our crew," Sterling answered and then went on to explain what we had done.

Minnie listened without interrupting him. When he finished, she looked at me and said, "I am proud of you," and then embraced me. It was the most I could hope for.

When Minnie drew back from me she asked, "How did it get started?"

"The head man for Elbell thinks that someone on the crew set it. He might be right but I don't see how he'll ever prove it."

"Why would someone do something like that?" Minnie asked.

"Clyde thinks that it was done to make him look bad. The fire was in a big trash pile that Elbell had let build up. Piledrivers had complained about it being a hazard and this fire proved it."

I thought again about the possibility that Drager started the blaze. He didn't have to be a killer to have done it; he could have been just trying to show me that things can happen. How could he know that Carl would get stuck in the beams? But if I said anything to Minnie about Drager, the conversation could go in a direction I wanted to avoid.

"I don't think that anyone had to set the fire," I continued. "It could have happened by accident pretty easily."

I could see the concern on Minnie's face. "Don't be thinking you've got to be a hero all the time," she said.

"Believe me, I was not looking for the opportunity."

"Is anybody hungry?" Crystal interjected. "Everything is ready for us to sit down and eat."

I was impressed, even a little touched, by Crystal's straightforward efforts to set a good table. Things were pleasantly ordered despite the fact that none of the place settings matched. The various sizes of the silverware reflected the variety of eateries from which it had been lifted. But the drinking glasses were fairly consistent, since most of them had been picked up from a curbside giveaway.

As we sat down on the floor in the living room, Sterling handed out beers and then opened a can for himself as if he were pulling the pin on a grenade.

Crystal served spaghetti with a tomato and hamburger sauce. There were two empty Ragu jars in the kitchen, but Sterling wanted to compliment Crystal anyway. He raised his can of beer. "To the cook," he toasted.

"To the cook," Minnie and I repeated.

Crystal beamed with evident delight at being the hostess.

"You have any family around here?" Minnie asked Crystal.

"Not a soul," Crystal answered. "My father died when I was in junior high school. Don't go feeling sorry for me because he just sat in his chair every night and drank beer until he got nasty. Would tell us, whenever we were stupid enough to go near him, that we were wasting his money, keeping him at a bad job. Can't remember him saying anything nice to anybody even on holidays. When he cashed in his chips, I didn't even cry. I cry now thinkin' about not cryin' then. And my momma ain't been right in the head for several years. She keeps calling me Charice. That's my sister's name."

"What about Charise?" Minnie asked.

"Married to a real nice guy in San Diego, who's got a stump grinding business. We aren't close because I kind of embarrass her. Oh, I guess I have to admit that she bores me too. Always watches her P's and Q's, never drinks, always has sunglasses on the top of her head ... gets on my nerves." There was not a hint of bitterness or self-pity in her voice. "She gave me a big lecture when I told her I was looking for a man who'll keep me in beer and cigarettes."

I looked over to Sterling to see if he would react to Crystal's social aspirations. I didn't see a twitch. He just looked at her for a few seconds and then smiled.

Crystal smiled back at him. "I suppose I deserved that lecture," she continued. "I go back and forth about my sister. I've asked her for money once... it wasn't that much ... but she said 'no' and that I would have to support myself. She was right, of course. I'm sorry...I'm getting a little worked up. Minnie, what about you? I mean your family. What about your family?"

"They're all in the area, getting in each other's way. I've been lectured a few times myself."

Crystal turned her head in my direction and I could see that she was preparing to ask me about my family, but Minnie kept on talking. "I know that this is a little off track, but I meant to ask earlier what happened to the guy Harry rescued. I don't know his name."

"Carl Baltimore," Sterling said.

"Was Carl hurt badly? What happened to him?"

"He got some pretty nasty burns on his stomach. They weren't from the fire. They were from molten steel dripping on him where he was stuck in the steel. The paramedics took him away in an ambulance."

Sterling tilted his beer can to his mouth as if he were pouring the brew directly into his stomach without swallowing. Then he snapped his head forward and banged the can on the table. "This meeting is hereby called to order. The chair has a proposal. I move that we go see Carl in the hospital."

"I second the motion," Minnie said before I could say anything.

"I third it," Crystal chimed in. "And let's take him a gift."

"The motion carries," Sterling declared. "The chair proposes that the gift be expensive toilet paper -- the thick kind. That's what he says he likes."

"Second," came from Minnie.

"Third," from Crystal again.

"Hearing no objection, the motion is adopted."

* * *

The idea was invested with the energy, seriousness of purpose, and high expectations reserved for pranks. We all piled into Sterling's car and headed off to find someplace that sold toilet paper. In the lucky store that got our business, we stood around squeezing rolls and debating the merits of various brands. Sterling and Crystal continued to promote most of this nonsense. They were strangely appealing. Two playful beagles nipping at each other's ears.

When we arrived at the hospital, a nurse on Carl's floor said that not all of us could go into his room at once. Minnie stepped forward to argue our case and the nurse relented. Then we paraded into Carl's room with 24 rolls of the best two-ply. Carl's family stood by his bedside. They squeezed together in a tight semicircle to make room for us.

Carl told them who we were and then laughed as much as the pain in his stomach would let him when he saw the toilet paper. "I'd like y'all to meet my wife Barbara." Mrs. Baltimore, a fireplug of a woman with graying hair and slightly crossed eyes nodded in our direction with the easy warmth of someone who enjoys organizing pot luck suppers. Carl then introduced his son, a fireplug of a young man with an ear stud, and his daughter, a fireplug of a young girl who smiled sheepishly and tried to make herself smaller.

Carl adjusted his position in bed and looked at Minnie and Crystal. "I don't believe that I've had the pleasure of meeting the two ladies."

Crystal winked at him and blew him a kiss. "I knew you'd say that with your wife here. No. Seriously, Mrs. Baltimore, seriously, I've never met your husband before. My name's Crystal and I'm with Sterling."

"And I'm Minnie. I'm a friend of Harry. We don't mean to intrude..."

"Don't worry about it," Carl said. "I'm glad y'all came down here because I didn't get a good chance to thank

Harry for what he did for me. I've told my family all about it. We're real grateful. I mean it."

Carl's sincerity quieted everyone down and caused some shuffling of feet. As I looked at Carl and his family, I became choked up, not because there was anything pitiful about them, but because they suggested a simple integrity. Mrs. Baltimore stood at the edge of Carl's bed with her arm behind his pillow. It was as if she were trying not only to comfort him but also to say, "He's mine and I'm staying with him; I vowed 'in sickness and in health' and I keep my promises."

* * *

Sterling and Crystal walked a few paces ahead of the rest of us on the way out of the hospital. When we reached the parking lot, they gathered us around them. "We have an announcement to make. We've decided to get married."

"Is this some sort of joke?"

"No more than any other marriage," Sterling threw back at me.

"Are we talkin' Holy Estate here? With a real ceremony ... a license ... blood tests?"

"The works," Sterling said without hesitation.

"But you hardly know each other."

"That's the beauty of it!"

"When did you decide to do this?"

"A few minutes ago. Crystal and I agreed that we like what we saw with Carl and his wife. She was standing by him. It was beautiful."

"You're not making any sense."

"Yes, he is," Minnie interjected. "It was beautiful."

"I mean not making any sense by deciding to get married on the spur of the moment like this," I responded with increasing strain in my voice.

"I'm a man of action," Sterling answered.

"Is this some sort of joke?" I repeated. "You can't be serious."

Minnie pulled on my arm. "You've said enough."

* * *

Back in Minnie's apartment, I prepared for bed without talking. I was still dumbfounded by Sterling's clownish announcement. Confused thoughts ran across my mind like a cycling screen saver.

"Stop stewing about Sterling and Crystal," Minnie said.

"They can't go through with it. They're virtual strangers to each other. Sterling's talking this way because he's all twisted up about his family, such as it is. Either that or this really is just some sort of stunt. Like: 'Hey. you'll never be able to top this one!' The whole thing is ridiculous."

"I believe him when he said that they wanted to have what the Baltimores seem to have. It was beautiful ... admit it."

"But they're just one couple. Look at all the bad marriages."

"You don't even have to look at the bad ones; just look at the so-so ones. Oh, I'm sure my mother would take care of my dad if he got hurt like Carl did ... it's not that. I just don't know if they really have much to do with each other ... day-to-day, I mean."

"I can remember only one time that my father had a health problem ... an irregular heartbeat ... and my mother blamed him for it. Said that he didn't take care of himself, and then she told him to increase his life insurance."

"When you come to dinner at my folks' house, see whether they even look at each other."

"I know what you're talking about. I've seen it with my parents. But it sounds as if you are kind of agreeing with me."

"No. I was only referring to my parents' marriage. OK, maybe I agree with you that many marriages are far from perfect. But that is not exactly news. What I am saying is that Sterling and Crystal might be a good match. We don't know. Besides, I just like the sound of it. 'Let's bring out the sterling and the crystal; it's a special occasion. We can talk about my parents' marriage, if you want to, after you see them for yourself."

"I'm still not comfortable about going to this dinner."

"You're invited as my friend, nothing else. Sonny is going to be bringing his girlfriend, and if my mother is in her usual mood, she'll focus on him, not me, not you, not Lloyd, not my dad. On Sonny because he's her 'troubled soul' as she calls him. So she babies him. He quit his job to day-trade on the stock market, and within a week she loaned him some money. He would say that she invested it with him."

"Am I the first guy you've brought home?"

"Are you crazy? Of course not!"

"Who was the last one?"

"Gene. I was seeing him when you called me, so I had to excuse myself from that situation. I was not going to play him off against you or the other way around, because I had already made up my mind."

"Just because you had seen me once?"

"That's right and don't tell me that you felt any differently. I don't see why you'd care, but he talked too much about his divorce. Wanted me to take his side on every issue. I feel bad that I let him spend money on me even after I knew that I was not about to fall in love with him, but I never lied to him."

"Well, Crystal might do something like that to Sterling."

"There's more going on with them. They need each other." Minnie took my hands in hers. "And, as a matter of fact, you need somebody yourself and now I'm here."

She was right. And she was right that there was something beautiful about the Baltimores. And she was right that Sterling may have been totally sincere in his recognition of that beauty. In fact, given Sterling's contrary nature, he may have regarded making a lifetime commitment...a real lifetime commitment to another person as being so unlikely in a world that emphasizes commitment to yourself that he had to do it.

CHAPTER FIFTEEN

A week after the fire, Ellis returned to work. As soon as he stepped into the piledrivers' trailer, he flashed his new $600 smile. There was no doubt that his new set of choppers had given him fresh confidence as well as a slight whistle when he talked. I liked them because they were better than what had been there before, but I couldn't help thinking that the dentures were so white, so regular, so tightly arranged that they had no business being in Ellis' mouth.

As he described it, getting the new teeth had almost been a rite of passage. "My dad's been wearin' false teeth for years. Said that his real ones were always givin' him trouble, so he got rid of 'em and was real proud when he got his new ones. Made him feel successful. When I told him that I got new teeth, he shook my hand."

"They be aw right," Early said with admiration.

"Thanks, Early."

Drager, who was sitting in the corner of the trailer, raised his head. "Ellis, see these teeth," he said pointing to his front row. "I don't take 'em out at night."

"Why are you dealing me that shit?" Ellis asked with surprise in his voice.

"Someday you're gonna respect me."

"What does this have to do with respectin' you?"

"You ain't getting' my point."

"Which is?"

"Which is that if you're so fuckin' stupid you can't figure it for yourself, I ain't tellin' you." The trailer fell

166

silent. Drager stood up and with his weirdly lined face and odd color appeared to me as if he were a large fungus.

Ellis looked away from Drager. I admired his restraint. At that moment, he seemed completely adult to me. I was glad that he had returned to the crew. No denying that he complained about things. But he usually had his reasons, and when it came time to stop complaining, he usually did. He seemed to manage the fine line between resignation and the ability to do what had to be done.

Drager slid along the wall and then through the trailer door. After Drager left, Ellis turned to the rest of us. "I heard all about the fire. Is it true that Drager helped Carl to get out of the hole?"

Malcolm rotated his shoulder as if to work out a kink. "Confirmed."

"If he could do that, then why he is actin' like such an asshole now? I don't get it."

"None of us do. He's just twisted."

"Anything change after the fire?"

"After they put the damn thing out, the place was crawlin' with government people," Malcolm continued. "I heard that they're gonna slap some fines on Elbell. Bender keeps sayin' that one of us set him up and torched the stuff in the hole. And that now the job is even further behind."

"So did Clyde actually clean things up?" Ellis asked.

"They took out four truckloads of junk and then stopped. Bender said that they didn't have to do more right then since the stuff wasn't in the way and if we paid attention, there would be no problem. That's his answer to everything: be careful and there should be no problem."

"But it sounds like Carl or maybe somebody else could've died in the fire."

"Clyde says that was a fluke, Didn't have nothin' to do with the junk. It had to do with Carl bein' too fat. Same thing could've happened if Carl had been walkin' on the steel and slipped between the beams."

"Yeah, but he wouldn't have been breathin' smoke."

"Clyde doesn't always think things through all the way."

"Well, somebody is gonna have to do it," Ellis said through his new teeth. "Because that fire ain't gonna be the last problem around here."

Malcolm was getting uncomfortable with this kind of talk. "Did you hear that Sterling's gonna get married?"

"No shit."

"Guilty as charged," Sterling said.

"So let us come to the wedding," Ellis suggested. "You got to have guests." Sterling had told the crew enough for Ellis to conclude that it would be either the crew or nobody. "You'll get a blender, maybe even a toaster oven out of the deal."

"I'll bring my wife," Malcolm offered.

Sterling stroked his chin as if he were carefully considering the matter. "You guys can come but I want the toaster oven." It was agreed that a toaster oven was a fair demand and that anyone who showed up would have to dress right and act civilized.

Lizard finally made his appearance and started talking over our conversation. "Clyde's movin' us into another new area. Good news is that the street mats will be removed and we'll be working in the open air. Bad news is that there will be power cables runnin' through everything. Be careful 'cuz these lines are laying right on the beams."

"Cables for the job?" Malcolm asked.

"No. These are power company lines feeding buildings around here. High voltage stuff."

"Don't they have them boxed up?"

"No. I told you they're layin' right on the steel."

I was confused. "Boxed up?"

"When you got hot lines runnin' through a job, the company builds boxes around them so you won't knock into them," Ellis said. "Either that or they'll shut off the power at night and let you work around them then. That's the best: overtime for the night work. But it sounds like Elbell ain't gonna do nothin'."

"Clyde says it'll take longer to build the boxes than we're gonna be in there."

"So we're supposed to work around the cables with the juice on?" I asked in some disbelief.

"Clyde says that if we're ..."

Malcolm cut off Lizard. "Careful! That's what he always says. But he's full of it. And another thing: there's no nets in that area. We're gonna be workin' on the top beam. twenty foot drop. We've got to have some protection. If they don't want to put up nets, at least give us some harnesses and steel cables to tie off on."

"I ain't gonna argue with you about that. I'll see what I can do about getting some harnesses."

"What about the power lines?"

Lizard waved his arms in the air to call a halt to the discussion. "Elbell ain't gonna pay us to just sit here and bullshit. Let's go."

"You ain't gonna say nothin' to him about the hot wires?"

"What I'm tellin' you is that ain't nothin' gonna change in the next minute and we've got to get out of this trailer and do some work."

"So you basically agree with him?"

"I agree that you should be careful and that if you are, we should be able to get through this. I ain't sayin' it's the best situation."

The door to the trailer swung open and Clyde Bender walked in. "Why you guys still in here?" he asked impatiently. "You've already clocked in, so you ought to be working."

Lizard came to attention. "We were just havin' a few words about how we're gonna do the job."

Clyde looked like a lopsided bowling pin. "Don't be taking too long with those angle braces. Shouldn't be liftin' out one piece at a time. That'll tie up a crane for the whole day. Cut all the angles loose before you use the crane at the end of the day."

"You want us to cut loose all of the angles before removing any of them?" Ellis asked with an attitude.

"That's what I said," Clyde answered with his own attitude.

"That steel is just gonna be lyin' on the flanges of the street beams. If we hit it, it's gonna fall. Cables all over the place. One of them gets cut through. . ."

"Damn it!" Clyde interrupted. "We're tryin' to do a job here and not take fifty years to do it! You can deal with the situation. Why in the hell do you think that piledrivers get paid so much?"

"I'm not askin' for anything more than what other contractors do for their men!" Ellis shot back.

"Other contractors aren't doin' the piledriving on this

job! If Elbell goes out of business, will that make you satisfied?"

"The way this job is being run, maybe Elbell deserves to be out of business."

"Keep it up and you'll be out of this business too!" Clyde turned to Lizard. "I'll go through every piledriver between here and Mexico until I find men that are willing to work and to stop bitching all the time. It's your job to keep these guys under control. Now do it!"

As I watched Clyde pound his way out of the trailer, I thought that he had actually been trying to convince us that he was an asshole. The message was that he did not have to earn our respect because he already had all the power he needed to get what he wanted. I wondered where was Lloyd on all of this.

"What about bringin' in the Union?" Malcolm asked without moving.

Lizard clapped his hands together and then pointed to the door. "You heard Clyde. Let's go."

Drager, who had stepped back into the trailer, blocked the door. "I've already called Crispin."

"About the cables and no fall protection?" Ellis asked

"Shit no. About Travers and Nesko."

"For why?"

"To get him to take away their permit cards. They got no business being here."

"You're fucked up," Ellis shot back. "Crispin ain't gonna do nothin' because he ain't got a reason to. And if he ain't already heard about what Travers did in the fire, I'll tell him."

Drager flared his nostrils in anger. "All Travers did was to help me pull out Carl. Travers don't give a shit about any of us. The Union shouldn't be wastin' a slot on either him or Nesko. And if you can't see that, you're the ones that are fucked up."

Lizard banged on a locker. "Cut this shit! I'm serious! Either get goin' or I'll tell Clyde to fire your sorry asses."

* * *   ✦

Slowly, we stood up and arranged ourselves in a line. Then we trudged out the door and into the sunlight, which made me dizzy. Lizard herded us towards the new work area. As we rounded a stack of steel, we saw Frankie standing with his archives in his pockets and a look of exaggerated seriousness that created the impression that he was a gargoyle.

"Heard you guys had a fire down here," he said.

"Don't be getting' started, Frankie," Malcolm replied in an uncharacteristically mean tone.

"I told my lawyer: no tunnel jobs," Frankie continued, ignoring Malcolm. "I got a letter from him right here that says that he's appealing." Frankie pulled out several pieces of paper but seemed not to be satisfied that any of them was on point. "Well, here's one that I wrote to the Governor." Without showing the letter to anyone, he stuffed it back into the collection in his shirt breast pocket. "I told my lawyer: no tunnel jobs."

Malcolm took him by the arm to pull him away from us. "Frankie, since this ain't your type of work, maybe you'd better be getting' down to the union hall to see what else they got."

Malcolm kept pulling him away and towards the gate. Frankie twisted in our direction and tried to keep talking.

"OK, I'll go. Like I said: tunnel work ain't for me and it ain't just the fires."

Ellis turned to me and shook his head. "If I ever get hurt bad, don't be rushin' me to the hospital. No point in endin' up like him."

When Malcolm returned, Lizard told Drager and Early to stay up top and then led the rest of us down a new set of stairs along a massive excavation wall. I was relieved that in this area, the street mats had been removed and that therefore we would be working in daylight and open air. The mats had been removed because this section of the project was being finished first so that an intersection of streets could be repaved and put back into normal use as quickly as possible. But before that could happen, the piledrivers would have to dismantle the steel skeleton which previously supported the street mats. This would involve the difficult process of removing large street beams and their bracing steel. The work would be done in stages with the beams being taken out in pieces over a number of days.

The lifting of the street mats suggested to me, as other things misleadingly had, that maybe my circumstances might be turning a corner for the better. But it was only a suggestion which was quickly subverted by a new visible hazard. Just as we had been told, there were high-energy cables on the steel beams. They reminded me of thick jungle snakes hanging from branches. At some locations, they were tied back to whalers and in others they were simply draped over beams and angle iron. During the process of removing the steel skeleton, these cables would have to be supported, stabilized, and worked around in various ways – not simple.

Our orders were to cut and remove the angle iron used as cross-bracing between street beams. I was assigned to work at the end of a beam because that's where the smallest braces were and because I could do the work while steadying myself against the excavation wall. At least, this was my initial thought in giving credit to Lizard for making an effort to protect me, but it was quickly abandoned as I confronted the fact that the hot cables were running along the ends of the beams. I then proceeded to do my job slowly as I could.

At the lunch break, I climbed out of the hole, grateful for the escape. Ellis organized a little party to celebrate Sterling's wedding plans. It was a special banquet with lunch box desserts being used for the festive occasion. Scooter Pies, Mallo Pies, Moon Pies, and Ring-Dings. Ellis ate carefully as if he did not want to jar loose his new teeth. Sterling thanked Ellis for the event and reminded everyone that they had committed to a wedding gift. Sitting in the sun, I appreciated every photon of the light, every molecule of the breeze, and every syllable of the moronic conversation.

My brief reverie was ended when Drager returned to the group. "I just got off the phone with Crispin," he announced. "He's coming down to see us."

"I don't believe you," Ellis said, barely looking up.

"Who gives a shit what you believe?" Drager fired back. "Why do you guys always think you can gang up on me? All I'm tryin' to do is to protect the local."

In about ten minutes, Crispin appeared, working on a toothpick in the corner of his mouth and looking unhappy to be there. He skipped the pleasantries and went right to what he had heard from Drager. "I understand that you got some problems with the punks."

"What kind of problems?" Ellis asked. "I ain't seen any problems."

Crispin removed the toothpick from his mouth. "Drager says that they ain't workin' out."

"That's bullshit. If there had been any real problems, you would have heard about 'em from me. This whole thing is bullshit. Forget the punks. They're doin' fine. You ought to pay attention instead to the way this job is bein' run."

Crispin flicked his toothpick into the air. "Elbell's run into their share of problems and they're behind schedule. Ain't the first time I seen something like this."

"You walked this job? You know what is really going on here? They've got us working next to hot wires. They've got us working without fall protection. They've got us working over junk piles...you know about the fire. They want us to cut away lacing steel and then leave loose on the flange of an I-beam until the end of the day. The list goes on."

"I get it. I get it. I'll talk to them about some of this stuff. But listen to me. Elbell is already losing money on this project. Don't be expecting to get everything you want."

"What are you tryin' to tell us?" Malcolm asked with irritation in his voice.

"I'm telling you that I will talk with them but that I can't raise hell with Elbell over every complaint I hear from you guys."

"Then what are we payin' dues to you for?"

"For one thing, the best damn wages any hourly employee makes in this city! Shit, when I was doing foundation work, we were grateful to have the damn job."

"Whose side are you on anyway?" Malcolm asked sharply.

"What kind of question is that?! I've got a relation-ship with Elbell and I use it to get things done that put dollars in your goddamn pockets. I didn't come down here to get abused." Crispin rattled the keys and coins in his pocket. "I told you that I would talk to them." He turned to leave.

"Hey, what about these permit guys?" Drager shouted after him.

"I'm sick of all of ya," Crispin yelled back over his shoulder.

Ellis spat on the ground in Crispin's direction. "Good working relationship, my ass. That sucker's on the take."

CHAPTER SIXTEEN

Minnie and I had decided that she would pick me up at my place to go to her parents' house for the dreaded family dinner. Before she arrived, I went to my apartment, peeled off my work clothes, and quickly made my way to the shower, which I took in a clean tub, thanks to Crystal. After the shower, I dressed with calculation. I unwrapped a new shirt, saving the pins and paper insert for some unknown purpose. The shirt, which retained its fold marks when I put it on, screamed: "New Shirt!", so I took it off and tried to find something else. Some of my other shirts were on hangers hooked on various edges in the room and were in a rare state of cleanliness, but they needed ironing. I picked up the new shirt off the bed and put it back on, and to balance the effect, selected a pair of pants with no crease in them.

I left the apartment and walked to the curb to wait for Minnie. The air was surprisingly clear, and the golden evening light had the unlikely effect of making the neighborhood look valuable. The brick buildings now were richly colored; their windows reflected a shine of bullion. I could almost feel time move as the shadows lengthened and the air shifted with the breeze. I drifted through the moment in a literal daydream.

Minnie drove up in her Ford Focus. "Sterling and Crystal say that they're going to tie the knot in two weeks," I said as soon as I was inside the car. "They want us to be the witnesses."

"I bet Crystal wears something with a high collar. I

might get myself something new too. This could be exciting. I haven't been to a wedding since my cousin got married two years ago."

"Well, Sterling has invited most of the guys on the crew and their women, so there should be some type of party. Probably a strange one."

As Minnie pulled away from the curb, she patted me on the thigh. "Most weddings are strange parties, so don't worry about it. And don't worry about anything when we get to my parents' house. Whatever they say or do, you shouldn't take it personally because they don't even know you."

* * *

After about six miles, we came into a residential area with small houses set close to one another on orderly avenues. Minnie turned onto a street which had obviously been part of a development built many years earlier. All of the houses were the same distance from the sidewalk and were of the same design, their pitched roofs and porch columns running in a regular interlocking pattern to a vanishing point. Small front yards were decorated with low shrubs and an occasional birdbath or ceramic gnome.

Minnie slowed in the middle of the block next to a man buffing his car at the curb. Two doors down, she pulled over, parked, and announced, "This is it."

I squeezed out of my seat, stood in the street, and waited for Minnie to tell me what to do.

"Harry, don't stand there like a light pole. Come around here and let's go in."

I joined her at the base of the stairs leading up to the porch and then walked up the painted concrete steps. Just as we were about to enter the house, Lloyd came out through the front door.

"Minnie, give me a minute with him," he said, not bothering to use my name.

"Please don't make a scene. Just let us be."

"I just want a quick word with him."

Minnie gave him a firm look and walked through the door.

Lloyd looked directly into my eyes. "I figure that a guy like you is eventually going to move on...that eventually somehow you're gonna break Minnie's heart."

I bit my lip. I had already been called a "fucking tourist" by Drager and now Lloyd was basically accusing me of the same thing. Even if I had wanted to defend myself, I was not sure how to do it.

"I was going back and forth with myself about firing you," he continued. "You're a punk, so no one would challenge me on it, and maybe it would be enough to drive you out of town and Minnie's life. But then you helped save Carl in the fire. I figured that you deserve something for that. That's all I'm sayin' for now, but that should be enough for you to know what's goin' through my mind."

I could not really say "thank you". I just continued to bite my lip.

He gestured towards the door.

I nervously stepped into the house. Minnie was standing in the front hallway with her mother.

"Mom, this is Harry Travers. Harry, this is my mother Cheryl."

179

"Thank you for having me, Mrs. Sollis."

"You're welcome," Mrs. Sollis replied coolly.

I thought that she was better looking in person than in the photograph in Minnie's apartment. Yet the sternness in the photographed face was also in the real one. "Introduce Harry to everyone," she instructed Minnie. "They're out back."

We walked through the living room and dining room on the way to the backyard patio. The living room was furnished with a Spanish-style sofa, a glass coffee table, and a brown vinyl Barcalounger. The dining room was brightened with yellow floral-print wallpaper and furnished in an early American style with a china closet in the corner. There was a smell of potatoes, chicken, and cigarettes in the air. I did not have time to focus on anything as I walked through the house, onto a back porch, down some wooden stairs, and into the yard.

Much of the yard was taken up by an above-ground swimming pool, which needed some repairs. A chain-link fence separated the yard from the one next to it. Crowded onto a patio next to the pool, sitting on a collection of aluminum lawn chairs were the rest of Minnie's family.

An older man stood up, flicked his cigarette over the chain-link fence, and introduced himself as Minnie's father, Dan. Minnie presented me to the other people. There was Barry Sollis, Dan's older brother. Barry's wife, Ginger, could not come to the party because she worked nights at the Post Office. There was Mr. Burt Sollis, Minnie's grandfather who, like his son Dan, was a retired piledriver. And then there was Minnie's brother, Sonny, who had brought with him Rita -- a woman wearing a blonde wig and purple jewelry.

Minnie went back into the house to help her mother. Dan offered me a beer and a folding chair. I sat down and tried to connect with the group.

Sonny got first attention because he demanded it. There was no denying that he was different. His black, slicked-back hair made him look like a grackle. The black polo shirt he had selected for the evening also contributed to the impression that he was some kind of noisy, shiny bird. "I've made more money in a month as a day trader in the stock market than I made in a year at the Kung Fu Center," he declared. "I've already paid back the money I borrowed to get started and yesterday I cleared $3,000 ... that's in one day. I don't know why I took so long to make the move."

"There was nothin' like this when I was your age," Barry complained.

"The great thing is doin' it all yourself and doin' it all for yourself," Sonny continued. "It's the only way to break out."

"Where are your offices?"

"I work out of BK Securities. They rent me the space. I'm trying to put together a fund to manage. I don't see any reason why I can't return 20-30% per year. Why don't each of you put in $10,000 with me as a kind of a test. If I don't give you back $13,000 in a year, you can close the book on the whole thing, but if I give you back the 13K, you put in another 10. What can be wrong with that?"

"For one thing, I don't have $10,000," Barry complained again.

"What about the rest of you? You sit on the sidelines

and you're missing an opportunity of a lifetime. You'll never get ahead. Be grateful you've got a contact like me who can help you out. What about you, Harry?"

I didn't want to point out that according to him the thrill was in doing it for himself-- a thought which made me uncomfortable on two counts. "Well, ah, I don't have $10,000 to invest either."

"What about $5,000?"

"I'm not really ready to make that kind of commitment. Maybe in a year or two."

"In a year or two, who knows where the market will be. You just can't wait around like that."

I didn't want to point out that if he didn't know where the market would be in a year or two, how could he be so sure that he could make 20-30% in it. "Everything has a price, including waiting," I agreed generically as I glanced at Dan, who was lighting up another cigarette but not saying anything. Lloyd, who had joined us, was also silent. He looked tense; the tips of his fingers white from their pressure on his beer can.

"Don't' say I never offered," Sonny said with some irritation.

"It takes some getting used to," Rita volunteered as she inspected her painted nails. I thought to myself: Crystal with some money.

"No one in this family has ever listened to what I say," Sonny grumbled.

"Don't get started now," Dan said. "We don't want to hear fifteen years of arguments."

"You wouldn't treat me like this if I had gone into piledriving like Lloyd did."

"I ain't ashamed of piledriving. It was an honest

living and it paid for this house and kept this family going."

Lloyd held up his hand. "Every one of us, maybe except for Harry, has heard all of this before and he don't have to now, so let's move on with it."

Sonny stood up. "OK, OK. I'll leave."

"No one's askin' anybody to leave," Dan said quickly.

Sonny sat back down in a sullen heap. Dan turned to me. "Minnie tells me you're a college man."

"Yes, but it didn't lead to anything." No use hiding the fact.

"You don't need a degree to be a piledriver."

"That's true; you need something more than that."

Dan nodded his head. "Minnie keeps talkin' about gettin' a degree in somethin' and I keep tellin' her is not worth the debt she'll build up."

Lloyd held up his hand again. "Now don't you get started."

"Dinner's ready," Minnie announced through the kitchen window. Dan went over to his father and bent close to his ear. "It's time to eat." Mr. Burt Sollis turned and lifted his arm so that his son could help him stand up. He straightened himself and then walked over to the backstairs with everyone else following at the same, deliberate pace. I brought up the rear.

As I was approaching the back stairs, Sonny stopped and pulled me aside. "I don't believe your line about not havin' the $10,000. Minnie's not about to waste her time on somebody that don't have resources. It's not her style." Sonny's voice had a contrived confidentiality to it. "But you're the first college guy. I got to admit that's a new twist." Before he could continue, Minnie called out again through the window, "The food's getting cold. Come in, you two."

* * *

The dining room was crowded with unmatched chairs and the table was crowded with large plates. As the serving dishes were passed around, I recognized that my family had never had such a meal, even at Christmas. My parents had never encouraged me to think of myself as belonging to a collection of relatives and ancestors; it was as if dodging the past and less successful kin was the cost of the new money in my house.

Much to my relief, Minnie's parents and their siblings spent the dinner gossiping. An absent aunt was criticized for marrying a much younger man and an absent uncle was derided for his cheapness. But no one tried to disown them, because the discussion assumed its importance from the fact that they were family. The next generation -- Minnie, Lloyd, and Sonny -- listened with varying degrees of interest but said little during the entire meal.

Eventually, Barry pushed back his chair and lit up a cigar. Minnie pulled me away from the table by the hand. "We'll come back when you've finished that thing." She led me out of the dining room, through the kitchen, and onto the patio where the bug light was still on, giving off a yellowish, subtly sexual glow.

I looked at Minnie with slow eyes. Even in her straightforward, plain dress, she was captivating. I looked for something in her eye, something in her smile that would confirm what Sonny had said about her.

"My family," she began, "kind of an assortment, right?"

"They've been treating me fine."

"I know that Sonny is kind of full of himself. What did he say to you when the two of you were coming in from the patio?"

"He as much said that you're trying to find a guy with money so he thought that I should have some dollars lying around to invest with him."

Minnie blinked. "He's got a big mouth. Just because I'm trying to do better for myself doesn't mean that I think only about money. That's insulting." Minnie turned away from me. "I'm going back in." I followed her, irritated with myself for having mutilated that moment with her.

Everyone had moved into the living room, bringing some chairs from the dining room with them. I hid my distress and found a chair for myself.

Sonny said that if he hadn't left on his own to start day-trading, he probably would have been fired from the Kung Fu Center. "They never paid me all of my commissions. They always said that there was a misunderstanding about what new accounts would be covered. But that's chump change now. Screw 'em."

As I tried to listen, I looked around the room. Dan's bowling trophies were set up in a little nest on the mantel. A green glass mint dish was on the other end. House plants sat in a neat row on the window sill. The wall behind the sofa was covered with family photographs. A picture of Grandfather Burt and his now-deceased wife, he looking sharp in a polka dot tie and she in a complicated dress with ruffles on her sleeve cuffs. A photograph of Minnie's other set of grandparents taken in front of a ranch-style house in what appeared to be a

Southwestern state. Photographs of Sonny in a blue suit, of Lloyd in a sports coat with lapels that were too big, of Minnie in a white dress with a flower on her shoulder. In fact, Minnie's parents had not looked at each other during the evening.

Minnie and her mother excused themselves to clean up the dishes. I offered to help but the offer was quickly rejected by Mrs. Sollis. "We can handle everything. You just stay put."

I sat back in my chair and watched the evening drift along with light conversation. Everyone pretty much ignored me. Eventually, Grandfather Burt fell asleep in his chair. Dan loosened his belt. Rita slipped off her shoes and rubbed her toes on the carpet. Moths fluttered against the window screen.

I got up to go to the bathroom. As I passed the kitchen, I could hear Minnie and her mother talking in loud whispers. When I heard my name, I stopped just beyond the doorway and listened.

"Mother, you've got no business trying to interfere like this," Minnie said. "Harry's done nothing wrong, and anything I do, I'm responsible for. Stop treating me like a kid."

"What I'm sayin' is for your own good. Harry isn't your ticket. He's just as mixed up as you are. And what about his family? There's no place for someone like you in a family like that. You'll always be apologizing for something. And there's no place for someone like him in our family. You're just dreaming about how this relationship will work out."

"Be happy that I am. Never did with any man up 'til now."

"I can't believe I'm hearing this! Why did you stop seeing Gene Calistro? He fit in fine with us. Had his business up and running and was good to me and your father."

"How many times did you see him? Three, maybe four. You weren't there when he told me that my books take up a lot of space and that when we move in together, it's going to be a lot of work putting them into boxes and then figuring out where to put them, so why didn't I just get rid of them."

"I'm only trying to save you from grief."

It was unnerving to hear Minnie have to defend her relationship with me. I could not listen any longer, so, as quietly as possible, I moved along the wall and into the bathroom.

As I stood in the bathroom, enveloped in the smell of potpourri, I felt as if I were hiding, acting like a child.

There was a knock on the door. "Harry, you in there?" Minnie asked.

"Yes."

"Hurry up. Other people are waiting."

I ran water from the faucet to make it sound as if I were just finishing up and then walked out to find myself face to face with Minnie.

"You sick or something?"

"No, I'm OK."

I returned to the living room and continued to be ignored in the conversation, which was fine with me. Probably everyone sitting in that room had the same view of me as Minnie's mother, so the silent treatment that they were giving me was to be expected and was obviously better than someone directly confronting me with their feelings. As people were gathering their things to leave, Minnie pulled me aside. "I want you to stay at my place tonight. Don't think about going back to your place."

*   *   *

Minnie was angry yet she insisted that I be with her. She had something in mind and it was more than just reviewing the irritations of the evening. She was going to prove that she had a certain power and that now she was going to use it.

After everyone had said their good-byes at the Sollis', she hustled me into her car as if she were a sheep dog. She wanted me to move quickly and in the immediate direction of her choosing. When she pulled away from the curb, she squealed the tires. By the end of the block, she was exceeding the speed limit. She did not slow down as she approached the intersection.

"At least take your foot off the gas," I said. "You trying to kill us?"

"I've got the right of way." She raised her voice above the sound of the engine so that I would not miss anything that she said. "You heard my mother and me talking in the kitchen, didn't you?"

"Yes."

"I meant what I said." She paused as if to arrange her next words. "But I could have agreed with her on some things and meant that too. There are lots of things between you and me that are up in the air. But I'm not sorry that I met you and I'm not sorry about anything we've done."

I could see tears beginning to form in the corners of her eyes. "Sometimes I feel so cramped up when I'm with my family. My mother has these tight little frightened views of everything. When she talks like that, I want to get as far away from her as possible. But then I feel guilty because she's my mother." She wiped her eyes with the back of her knuckle. "I've got to keep telling myself that it's my life."

She did not say anything else until we entered her apartment. She motioned for me to sit down on the couch and then asked, "What do you think about my books?"

"You say these things out of the blue. Why are you asking me this?"

"You heard me talk to my mother about Gene Calistro. About how he wanted me to get rid of my books. You heard that, right?"

"Yes."

"So what do you think about my books?"

"I wouldn't ask you to throw them away if that's what you want to know."

"If I want to read a book some night instead of going out, will that bother you?"

"No."

"If I have to study every night because I enrolled as a full-time student somewhere, will that bother you?"

"No. Well, maybe yes if it's every night."

"I really meant most nights."

"OK."

"Would it bother you if on some night I wanted to read a book instead of talking with you?"

"Depends on what I wanted to talk about."

"Let's assume that it was nothing important."

"No, that wouldn't bother me. I might even want to read a book myself."

"You like to read?"

"Yes." This was not untrue, but I knew that this was also what Minnie wanted, maybe even needed, to hear from me. "Yes," I answered again, even though I thought that her intense focus on this one matter might be a rare instance of her losing perspective.

"And you heard my mother say that there would never be a place for me in a family like yours? You heard that too?"

"Yes."

"And was she correct?"

"Minnie, there may not even be a place for me in my family."

"So what are you trying to tell me?"

"What I am saying is that maybe my parents might be a little peculiar, a little judgmental. They might make things difficult for any woman I brought through the door, just as they have made things difficult for me at times."

In fact, I had wondered how my mother would react if she ever saw the artificial fruit in Minnie's apartment or how my father would react if he ever saw Arlene's World of Uniforms. How much would their taste and sense of appearances warp their opinion of Minnie? Despite what I had said to Minnie, I was not totally indifferent to what my parents might think. I suppose that, at some level, I still had a desire to impress them. And what about my own taste and sense of appearances? I meant what I had said about the books. But what about the artificial fruit? I was staying at Minnie's apartment, as is. If we lived in a place which was not hers but ours, which both of us had set up, would I tell Minnie that the wax fruit has to go?

"I also heard," I finally continued, "your mother say that there would not be a place for me in a family like yours. So I can put the same questions to you."

"'How many times have I already told you that I'm the one who decides how I am going to live my life?"

Minnie stood up from the couch, then took my hand and pulled me up to stand next to her. She leaned in my direction and let her hair fall on my face like a soft curtain. Still holding my hand, she led me into her bedroom, where the curtains were drawn and the top sheet on the bed was pulled back. The air in the room carried a faint smell of soap.

Without saying a word, she turned to me and began to undress with movements that glided one to another. Her body was an honest, eager offer, maybe even a demand. She straightened with erotic pride, undid my belt, and moved her hand down the skin of my stomach. I pulled her onto the bed and held her with focused strength. And then after our passion had accomplished what it wanted, we loitered gently in each other's arms.

* * *

The next morning, I opened my eyes without raising my head from the pillow and looked at Minnie, who was still asleep next to me. Her lips did not quite touch each other; her breathing came in sighs. I could not take my eyes off her. I was spellbound by the opportunity to watch her at close range.

When she woke up, I pretended to be asleep, staying in bed even after she got dressed. I felt consumed and did not want to take on another day. Minnie called to me several times and when she heard no response, she pulled the covers off the bed. Reluctantly, I got up, put on my clothes, and joined her in the kitchen.

Without saying anything, I put two slices of bread into the toaster and then wiped the top of the appliance clean so that Minnie would not do it herself. As I sat at the table, spreading jam on my toast, the prior evening came back to me in detail. The part before Minnie had taken charge of things and had used her sensual strength to try to override the unpleasantness with her family. I did not want to think about her family, but I could not prevent myself from doing so.

Here I was having breakfast with Minnie, both of us positioned like pieces of domestic sculpture. I was living with her before I had really contemplated living with her, and now I recognized that with Minnie came her family. I could not deny her that. But they would deny me. Her mother had made that clear. She may have attempted to describe her feelings as protective and humble, but, as I heard them, they seemed smug. Final conclusions based on nothing more than fragments of information about me and rigidly narrow opinions about her own family. Minnie's father reinforced this squinty-eyed view by having low hopes for her. Maybe he would have encouraged Minnie to aim higher if he thought that he had nothing to lose. Maybe he would have taken to me if I had smoked a few cigarettes with him. And Minnie's brothers were unwelcoming and sullen, each in his own way. Maybe, as they got to know me, they would change, but that seemed unlikely because they did not want to get to know me.

Minnie was looking down at her cup of coffee, but then raised her eyes and looked directly at me. "I'm sorry about some of the things you heard last night. But don't judge my family too harshly. Give them some time."

"Do you really think that will make a difference?"

"Probably not, but we've got to give them a chance." Minnie sipped her coffee without taking her eyes off me. "You need to find out the details about Sterling and Crystal's wedding," she continued after she lowered her cup.

"Details?"

"Where are they going to have the ceremony? What time will it be? How many people are going to come?"

"Knowing them, I doubt that they will have all the answers."

"Even more reason to ask. It'll remind them to make some decisions. Tell Crystal that I could put together a little party for them."

"Don't get carried away."

"No one is getting carried away. I'm just trying to do something that they might appreciate."

* * *

Sterling picked me up in front of Minnie's apartment. By then the two of us had worked out routines to accommodate our women. He seemed in a good mood as he fondled the gearshift, so I decided to get down to business.

"Minnie tells me that I should ask you about the wedding. She says that she might do a party."

To my surprise, Sterling was ready to talk. "Got a Justice of the Peace. He's all set for the ceremony. You and the guys on the crew will be the audience."

"No parents of the bride?"

"Not possible."

"Well, if you would wait awhile, they could probably make it."

"Wrong. Crystal's father is dead and her mother wouldn't understand much. Crystal told you that."

"I'm not trying to start something here. I'm just wondering why this wedding has to happen so quickly."

"I've got to make her an honest woman. It's a moral thing with me."

"Try out another reason," I said sarcastically.

"OK, neither one of us had anything else planned for the weekend."

"Look, all I'm asking is why would it hurt to wait awhile. See how you feel about each other in a couple of months."

"So what am I supposed to look for?"

"Whether anything changes between the two of you."

"It probably will. For the better."

"What does Crystal think about all of this?"

"Hell, she'll try anything once." Sterling laughed. "She's nuts about the idea. For a few days, she even thought about inviting her sister from San Diego to come out and meet her new husband. Show her that now she had got some respectability."

"Respectability from you?" I turned to look at Sterling. "So you get married, then what? You going to move out of the apartment?"

"That wouldn't make much sense. With you over at Minnie's all the time, we practically have the place to ourselves now anyway. Crystal might want to make a few changes, like getting a new rug for the living room, but nothing that we wouldn't pay for."

"Sterling, you're digging a hole for yourself to make some silly-assed point. So your dad walked out on you. So your mother died before she could enjoy her retirement. That's all done with."

"I've already told you that I'm not hung up on my dad...or my mother for that matter. The wedding is Saturday in two weeks. I'm telling you that I'm going to do better because of Crystal. At least, I'll try. Both of us will try. I'm telling you that we're starting to have a good effect on each other."

I dared one more question. "Is Crystal pregnant?"

"Never asked her. Suppose anything's possible."

That was it. A wedding the Saturday after next. I swallowed hard and tried to comprehend the idea that Sterling was actually going to go through with this. It was like trying to drive a car with a bad transmission. The gears just ground up against each other.

Maybe love played a part in this. The two of them certainly liked to fool around together. In their own sort of spaced-out way, each seemed to want the other. Yet, despite Sterling's apparent sincerity, I could not overcome my suspicion that beneath it all was something selfish. I had read in a magazine that when a dog licks your hand, he is not expressing his feelings for you; he is simply trying to get salt off your skin.

I went back and forth between thinking that Sterling

was mocking the institution of marriage when I wanted to believe in it and thinking that he was promoting the institution when I was afraid of it. I certainly took the topic seriously. At a younger age, I had worried and worried that the pained looks on my parents' faces meant that marriage was destined to be difficult, regardless of how nice the furniture was. But ultimately, I became convinced, strangely enough, that in order to escape my parents' bad marriage, I needed to find a wife.

After what Sterling had been through with his family, maybe he was thinking along similar lines. But sometimes, I wondered whether he realized that some decisions are bigger than others, that you have to worry about the future before you get there. His attitude seemed to be that Crystal was not bugging him now, so he might as well marry her. How would he feel about her being his wife after five years of her hitting him up for cigarettes, nail polish, and a big bar tab?

* * *

Carl walked through the trailer door looking thinner than he had before. Everyone except Drager, who hadn't arrived yet, was glad to see him back on the job and gave him slaps on the back to make the point.

"Hey, you lost weight," Malcolm said.

"I dropped fifteen pounds. Pisses me off. I had a nice gut before all of this."

"You're still too fat," Ellis said. "You probably should have stayed home. Pickin' up a few more dollars ain't worth havin' to show up to a job as fucked up as this one is. You would think that after the fire, Bender would be a little worried about something like that happenin' again. But no, he's got us workin' around live cables down in the hole."

"At least, we finally got some harnesses and tie-offs," Malcolm said. "I guess we have to thank Crispin for that."

"But the cables are still unboxed and we're still leaving loose steel on the I-beams and the junk is still piling up at the bottom of the hole. It's still basically a shit show."

Carl shook his head. "The fire was our accident on this job. Now the odds are running with us. We'll get by from here on out. I ain't sayin' I haven't had a few bad thoughts. Believe me, my wife and I talked about it. She wants me to quit. But what the hell am I gonna do to make a living? Been doing piledriving work for 30 years."

"So get Crispin to send you to another job."

"We've already covered that when all of us decided to come to Elbell. This is gonna be the longest runnin' job in this town for months."

"So move out of the area. It's not as if you have never moved before. I think that you came back because we're such great guys and you missed us. And you wanted to go to Nesko's wedding."

"He's getting married?"

"The big day is around the corner." Ellis put his arm around Sterling. "It'll be good. I figure we can all kick back together. So what if Sterling is a punk. He's part of this crew and he's getting married. I've heard of a lot worse reasons to go to a party. And Drager ain't invited."

CHAPTER SEVENTEEN

To my ongoing amazement, Sterling never wavered and the wedding went forward. On the big day, Minnie and I drove Sterling and Crystal to the Justice of the Peace. They sat in the back seat as special passengers of honor. Crystal wore a frilly white dress with a high collar and Sterling was decked out in a blue sports jacket, white shirt, multi-colored tie, gray pants, and black loafers, all of which he had recently purchased for the occasion.

When the wedding party arrived at the Municipal Building, Minnie started fussing over Crystal in an effort to tidy her up. Waiting for us in the building lobby -- an ornate, marble affair with Ionic columns supporting high arches on four sides were Mr. and Mrs. Malcolm Snipes, Mr. and Mrs. Carl Baltimore, and Mr. and Mrs. Ellis Harding, and Early Ford and his new girlfriend Velveeta. All the men were tamed by appropriate-to-the-occasion clothes and seemed a little self-conscious that their women were with them. Lloyd had declined his invitation.

Mrs. Baltimore wore an outfit with dark blue piping on a cream-colored fabric and greeted us with the same warm, easy-going style that she had shown in the hospital.

Mrs. Snipes' high forehead curved along a graceful arch, which gave her the look of someone who had been well designed. She wore an elegant navy blue pants suit accented with beaded jewelry that she said was from Africa. Her smile formed slowly and faded slowly. On the surface, she seemed serene, but I sensed that beneath her cautious, diplomatic responses she was debating with herself as to whether she wanted to be there. When Minnie found out that she worked as a nurse, she started asking questions that Mrs. Snipes first tried to deflect but then started to answer. Malcolm listened with evident pride.

Mrs. Harding was a thin woman with short, tufted hair and a darting, bird-like personality. Her close-set eyes held a nervous intensity that completed the effect. I thought that her species might be known as Pileated Housewife. She tugged on her own sleeves in apparent discomfort with the idea of attending a stranger's wedding. Ellis tried to buck her up with little jokes, but humor had never been his strong suit. Every ten seconds or so, he would check himself out on some reflecting surface to make sure that his hair, which was combed up from his ear to cover his baldness, was still in place.

Velveeta wore a gauzy blouse which flowed easily over her shoulders and down to the top of a black skirt. She handled her introduction to the strangers around her with a casual good humor. I kept looking for an "I got my sugar daddy" attitude in her but never saw it.

The bridal couple tried to make everyone feel welcome. Mrs. Harding seemed to relax a little when Crystal spoke with her. Sterling led the group on a search for the office of the Justice of the Peace. We found it on the second floor next to some cabinets set out in the hallway and entered the room -- a square one with two rows of wooden chairs in front of a single window covered by Venetian blinds. Dark paneling provided a measure of majesty to the place.

A young couple, who looked as if they were waiting

for attendance to be taken in a high school homeroom, sat in two of the chairs near the window. The boy's youth was accented by his pitiful effort to grow a mustache. The sparse black hair on his lip had no hormones, no experience behind it. The girl had a tiny face that was almost lost in her curled, excited hair. Her voice came out like a chick's peep when she talked with her intended. I thought that they were too young to be there. Not that I was concerned that they were making some sort of mistake. No, it was more like it was embarrassing to be involved in the same process as they were. I was relieved when the Justice of the Peace summoned them into his office.

While Sterling and Crystal waited their turn, they walked in small circles around the room. Although they talked with people, their constant movement made it difficult for any conversation to get beyond a few sentences. Everyone seemed to understand that pre-wedding jitters were at work. Minnie made another effort to tidy up Crystal. Finally, the Justice of the Peace appeared at the door to his chambers and motioned for our group to come in.

The chambers were basically a smaller version of the waiting room except that there was a desk with no paper on it next to the wall. The Justice of the Peace wore a business suit with a fluffed handkerchief in the breast pocket. He was a distracted man who twice called Crystal "Karen" the second time coming after she corrected the first time.

Despite His Honor's distracted air, there was sentiment in his voice. Prior to beginning the ceremony, he said that he wanted to speak with the wedding couple about the meaning of marriage. I was in favor of this and noticed that Sterling and Crystal seemed to be too. She kept pushing her hair back and he would smile at odd times.

"Sterling and...ah...Crystal...yes...Crystal, marriage will have a profound effect on your lives. It should not be entered into lightly. You will have responsibilities of a kind that you have never had before. You will have stresses that you have never had before. But you will also have happiness that you have never had before." Sterling nodded as if to say that he was willing to make the trade-off. The Justice of the Peace nodded back and continued. "What you are about to do here today means something. Commit yourselves to it with more than words." Sterling nodded again. Crystal did not move.

His Honor opened a small black book in front of his chest. "Shall we begin?" He introduced the vows. Then he asked that Sterling and Crystal repeat them. They brought their heads together and whispered the promises. I saw a black tear run from Crystal's decorated eye and a quiver run through Sterling's arm. I glanced at Minnie and saw that she was hanging on every word. The Justice of the Peace closed his book and folded his hands in front of him. "I now pronounce you husband and wife. You may kiss the bride."

* * *

Minnie had planned a reception. It was to be a picnic in a nearby park. On the way to the park, the newlyweds sat in the back of the car, cooing like a pair of doves. By the time we arrived at the park, they were almost in a state of bliss. They held each other's hands and stared into each other's eyes with a dreamy, oblivious, sappy fascination.

The park was a grassy expanse with trees shading a lazy hill that sloped to a ravine. A pleasant retreat at first glance. When everyone got out of their cars and started to search for a place to spread their blankets, the grounds began to lose their appeal. Discarded sandwich wrappers and soda cans junked up the spots which had looked good from a distance. For a minute, people stood around, disappointed. Then Minnie started to pick up the litter around one of the trees. Everyone helped her. Without too much effort, we were able to clear an area and set up our picnic. Ellis placed a wrapped box in the middle of the picnic blanket. Minnie placed a small bouquet of flowers next to it.

After wine or beer was poured into plastic cups, I raised mine to propose a toast. "To Sterling and Crystal."

"Sounds like a table setting," Sterling said with a smile.

"They're your names. What can I do? To Sterling and Crystal." Everyone raised a cup.

"Sterling, open the gift," Ellis urged.

Sterling picked up the box and handed it to Crystal. She unwrapped it carefully and folded the paper into a neat rectangle as if she intended to use it again. She opened the box and took out a toaster oven. Sterling took it out of her hands and examined it closely. "OK, everyone can eat."

Ellis offered several more toasts to the nuptials, and the wine and beer went down fast but then people eased off. No one was in a mood to party hard. They just wanted to relax and enjoy the day.

"So, Sterling, what about your honeymoon?" Ellis asked.

"Maybe when I'm able, we'll go down to Florida."

Crystal curled her arm around Sterling's elbow. "I want to see one of them fish shows."

Mrs. Harding put down her glass. "We went to one of those once. I touched a dolphin on the nose. That was before we had kids. I'm glad we did it because we haven't been anywhere since."

"That's not true," Ellis said with no tension in his voice. "We took a real nice trip with the kids up into Canada. You enjoyed it."

Mrs. Baltimore wiped her mouth with a paper napkin and then turned to Crystal. "Be careful where you stay on your honeymoon. We ended up in a hotel room right next to where the kitchen help went out for a smoke. Heard way too much about other people's love lives."

"I agree about being careful where you stay," Mrs. Snipes said. "We ended up in a room right above the dumpster. At night, we would hear people throwing stuff into it and then dropping the lid. After four days of this, I needed to get home to get some rest." She leaned back on her elbow. "And I'll tell you this: good thing that Malcolm married me. I'm the one that finally got him organized."

"What are you talking about?" Malcolm protested with mock outrage.

"Try to explain the time you lost your sunglasses, car keys, and wallet, all in the same day. I found every one of them for you, proving again that without women, men are basically helpless." Mrs. Snipes plucked an olive off her paper plate and popped it into her mouth.

All the women said "amen" to that and the males

tried to construct rebuttal arguments based on the assertion that women created the distractions that caused the confusion in the first place.

The stories and banter continued even after the food was gone. No one seemed in a hurry to leave. Mrs. Harding said that Ellis had mistakenly worn a blue sock and a brown sock at their wedding. Mrs. Snipes said that she had asked Malcolm to marry her because she was tired of waiting and knew that he would never get around to it. Malcolm said that he would have asked her on his own but she talked so much he could never get a word in edgewise.

The sun shifted and allowed its light to come through the trees at a new angle. Sterling leaned back and put his head in Crystal's lap to catch the rays. In an almost posed gesture, she smoothed his hair. Everyone else stretched out on blankets. Minnie and I lay down close to each other with our hands touching.

I felt deeply comfortable. The filtered light created delicate warmth on my skin, the air was at a temperature at which I could not tell where it ended and I began, and by some fortunate circumstance, the indentations in the ground accepted my shoulders and back perfectly. One of those effortless, dreamless naps was coming on, the kind in which you know you are asleep and are grateful for it. I dropped off hearing things I could not see; someone whispering, Sterling and Crystal rearranging themselves, a child on a swing.

* * *

Suddenly, my eyes were wide open and looking at the sky. When I turned on my side, Minnie woke up.

"Are you awake?" I asked softly.

"Yes."

"Want to take a little stroll?"

"OK."

I turned to Ellis. "Minnie and I are going to walk down to the ravine. We'll be back in a few minutes." I stood up and then helped Minnie to her feet. Minnie's fingers curled through mine and took a tight hold. As we walked, her hold relaxed. "Are you going to get a gift for the bride and groom?" she asked.

"I chipped in on the toaster oven."

"No, I mean a gift of your own. You should do it. I'll give you some money and it can be from the both of us."

"Do you think that Crystal will stay with him long enough for me to get one?"

"Harry, everybody's having such a nice time. Don't say anything to ruin it. Don't even think it. They're married now. Just wish them the best. I'll help you buy something nice."

"But what does she want to do with her life?"

"Get by, it sounds like. Don't be so fast to judge her. You can show a little charity towards her. This is her wedding day."

"I've got my opinions, that's all."

"Well, I've got opinions too. I don't like Mrs. Vega who says Arlene charges too much but won't go anywhere else, and I like Crystal." Minnie pulled her hair around her ear. "You know how I say that I've seen livin' hand-to-mouth and there's nothin' to recommend it? Well, it doesn't seem to bother her. Not that I'm intending to live like her, but maybe I worry too much."

Minnie stopped and bent down to pick a dandelion.

She stuck the yellow blossom behind her ear. "Besides, I think that Crystal really loves Sterling. Do you love me?"

I stopped walking and stood motionless for a second. Minnie's question had blindsided me. "I ... I."

"Why can't you tell me straight out how you feel? Are you afraid to say that you could never see us getting married?"

"Minnie, a lot of people take years before they get married. We haven't even been together through a complete change of seasons."

"What do you need the time for? It's either there or it isn't. You're already practically living with me. You see me go to bed at night and get up in the morning. You've seen my moods. You know my body. What's left?"

"I have never said to any woman before that I loved her. I need time to. . . ."

"Is there some problem between us that you're not talking about?"

"No."

"If the problem is that you have trouble making commitments, we're done. I refuse to spend time with an emotional coward."

"No. No. It's not that. And it's nothing about you. I have been trying to tell you that."

"Well, you're not doing a very good job."

I sat down at the edge of the creek that was responsible for the ravine and looked at the opaque water. It appeared to carry little life but nevertheless flowed with an obvious current. I once again thought of Minnie as a current which was carrying me downstream, but then scolded myself for conjuring images instead of focusing on the real person. She did not sit down next to me but remained standing several feet away.

CHAPTER EIGHTEEN

For their wedding night and honeymoon, Sterling and Crystal checked into a local motel that had a room with a gel bed and a bath tub large enough for two. I did not see the newlyweds until the next day when they returned with a slight buzz on. They appeared to be thoroughly pleased with themselves and with their new toaster oven.

Minnie was spending the afternoon with Arlene helping her to redo the store window, which both of them had concluded needed attention, so I stayed with Sterling and Crystal in our apartment. After Crystal excused herself to take a nap, Sterling suggested that we go to the Target Café -- a new dive that had opened in the neighborhood.

"The Target Café?" I asked.

"Ray's is still my home base, but I just want to check it out."

"I thought that you were going to cut down on your drinking."

"I am. I'm not going to annihilate myself."

"Don't you want to wait until your wife wakes up and then go with her?" I thought that I would refer to Crystal as his wife just to see how it sounded.

"Let her sleep. We'll only be gone an hour or so."

"This marriage is off to a strong start."

"All we're talking about is a measly hour in a bar. It's not like I'm cheating on her or anything."

"Won't she be disappointed when she wakes up and you're not here?"

"I'll leave her a note." Sterling looked for a pen and paper. "You don't have anything else to do. Let's go." Of course, the sad truth was that I didn't have anything else to do.

Sterling found some writing materials and scratched out a note for Crystal. He stuck it in the frame of the bathroom mirror and we headed out the door.

The Target Café was larger and better furnished than Ray's, but the clientele seemed about the same. The nicest feature of the place was the padded, overstuffed leatherette booths. Sterling picked one and settled into a comfortable slouch, and motioned for me to join him. I slid in across from him and moved the little lava lamp on the table back against the wall. After the waitress brought us our beers, Sterling held his glass up to the light as if he were examining a fine jewel. "I hereby call this meeting to order."

As ridiculous as the ritual was, I happily recognized it as something that had not changed.

Sterling adopted a parliamentary pose. "We hereby dispense with the minutes and committee reports. Any old business? I move that we issue a proclamation thanking Minnie again for the wedding party. I think that everyone had a good time."

"Seconded. I have to admit that you and Crystal looked mighty sharp."

"Well, now I'm a happily married man," Sterling said in an exaggerated voice.

"You don't seem much different to me."

"Enough old business. New business: so what's going to happen with you and Minnie?"

"That's nobody's business."

"Knock it off. You asked all those questions about Crystal and me and now you're refusing to answer a few simple questions about you and Minnie."

"I'm not about to do something in a fever the way you did."

"I'll put it in a form of a wager: I'll bet that you're hitched within a year."

"I'm not betting and I'm not talking."

"OK, try this one: I'll bet you that our waitress dyes her hair. A bag of beer nuts."

"I'm not betting," I said again.

"A bag of beer nuts! What are you afraid of?"

"You say she dyes it?"

"Right."

"OK. For beer nuts. Nothing else."

I lost when a ceiling light revealed the dark roots of her bleached hair. Sterling received his free beer nuts and decided that he was on a roll. "Let's go back to that wager about you getting married. I'll lower it to nine months and give you odds."

"No way. I told you I'm not talkin' about it. I move to adjourn this meeting."

"Hearing no second, the motion dies. Besides, if it had gone to a vote, it would have been a tie and the Chair breaks all ties. We stay."

"Crystal is going to be waiting for you. We shouldn't park here."

"Yeah, maybe you're right about Crystal." Sterling wrinkled his brow. "You can resubmit your motion in thirty minutes and the Chair will reconsider the matter."

By the time we arrived back at the apartment, Crystal was not there. She had left a note of her own in the bathroom mirror. It said that she had gone down to Ray's and that Sterling should join her. I read the note to him and he looked pleased. "Crystal knows what she wants and doesn't blame me for anything. I like that in a woman. I'm going to the Oasis to see my wife. A married man has his obligations, you know."

* * *

During the following week, Sterling and Crystal played house. The toaster-oven spiked their interest in the potential for kitchen appliances so they purchased a microwave and a new set of Teflon-coated pots and pans.

On Wednesday night, she made another spaghetti dinner with Ragu sauce and invited Minnie and me over for a little social event. Sterling finally got on board with the idea and reluctantly purchased some matching silver-ware for the occasion. "It's only Harry and Minnie," he had initially protested before deciding that his new bride could win on this one.

On Thursday night, I watched them propped up against the wall, shoulder to shoulder, holding hands, watching sit-com reruns. Maybe they were exploiting each other, but I was beginning to reassess my view that I should be concerned about it. After a while, Sterling removed his hand from Crystal's, then lifted his arm around her, and held her tight. It was almost as if he were confirming that she was really there, as if all the time he had spent in SOL's cyberspace had left him tactilely insecure.

On Friday night, the two of them apparently concluded that they were veering dangerously close to the edge of domestic tranquility, so they went directly to the Oasis, skipping supper. "We can't live like shut-ins," Sterling had insisted. "I want to show her off."

On the following Monday, Crystal found work. Over the weekend, she had read the want ads looking for a part-time waitress job within walking distance or a no-transfer bus ride from the apartment. She found one at a luncheonette with a busy noon-time. "My shift is from 11 to 3, which is perfect because I can sleep in and also have my evenings free to be with Sterling," Crystal told me enthusiastically. "Manny, the owner, talked to me for fifteen minutes, like an interview. I was worried he was going to ask me to fill out some application where I would have to give names of former employers. But after a while, he just said that he thought that I would be good with the customers."

I'll admit that I had not expected Crystal to follow through on her talk about going back to work. With her sketchy history, it did not appear to be in the cards.

"I swear I didn't put her up to it," Sterling told me. "This is something she did on her own. Now she feels she's contributing something to the marriage. I told her that she'd already made the apartment look a hell of a lot better and that she was keeping me company, but she said that she'd decided that for at least once in her life she wanted to buy something for someone else. It's become a point of pride with her."

CHAPTER NINETEEN

Each day of Crystal's first week on the job, she reported to Sterling her tip total and then wrote the number on a tally sheet. $32, $37, $45, $41, $50. On Friday afternoon, she took the cash and her first paycheck and opened a bank account. "Sterling and I talked about opening a joint account, but I said that we could do that later," she announced. "First, I wanted to have an account in my own name. The bank gave me a stadium blanket and a thermos for giving them my business. What in the hell am I going to do with a stadium blanket?"

"We'll put it in the trunk of the car," Sterling suggested. "Use it for emergencies."

"What emergencies?" Crystal asked.

Sterling put his arm around Crystal and she gazed up at him in another one of her poses of loving devotion.

"Time for me to go," I said.

*　*　*

"I'm so proud of my brothers!" Minnie exclaimed when I arrived at her place after launching Sterling and Crystal towards Ray's. Oasis "Lloyd got his promotion and now Sonny has come over to tell me some good news." She gestured in the direction of the living room couch where Sonny was sitting. "He says he's had a really good month. And now he's paid me back what I put in with him plus $750!"

"You invested?"

"Yes, because....well....he's my brother. And now he just wrote me the largest check that I've ever seen in my life."

Sonny smiled smugly. "As they say, it takes money to make money and now I've got it. Thanks to 'The Speed of Light.' It's a software company that went public a month ago. I was able to get a block of stock early on and I cashed out two days ago at $15 a share higher than I bought it for."

I was trying to remain calm. "How did you find out about 'The Speed of Light'?"

"I overheard some people at BK Securities talking about it. I jumped in without even holding my nose. Rita's having her nails done and then I'm going to pick her up and take her out to a restaurant where they have white tablecloths and big silverware. I've been waiting to celebrate like this all of my life."

Minnie put her arm around Sonny. "Success can be an attractive thing in a man."

I was trying even harder to remain calm. Here was a nightmare that I had feared happening right in front of me. Not only had I predicted that SOL would fail, but after I left the company, I actually hoped that it would. I wanted to see Paul Matel taken down a notch ... several notches, and I wanted to be vindicated for having the good business judgment to have left the company before that happened. But now with the initial success of the SOL stock offering, it was even more difficult to figure out why I was working in a hell hole without having to confront the fact that I may have given up thousands of dollars for the privilege.

And to see Sonny rake in the cash on SOL was really

too much. Draining blood from my head was the shocking recognition that now that Sonny had some capital, he might, in my father's words, be able to get people like me to cater to him.

"Harry, you look pale," Minnie said.

I smiled weakly. "I'm fine."

Minnie kissed her check from Sonny. "Harry, you ought to give Sonny a chance to show what he can do for you."

I stared off into space.

Sonny stood up from the couch. "Harry can think about it. I've got to pick up Rita. I wanted to deliver the check in person so that I could see the look on your faces."

Minnie came back to me after she escorted Sonny to the door. "Give him credit for taking risks to make it big. You play it too safe and you will always be buying with coupons."

* * *

I felt as if time were beginning to fold in on itself like some strangely shaped figure with no outside or inside edges. My circumstances were mocking me. If, in the end, a guy like Sonny Sollis could rake in the dough and then call the shots, where did that leave a guy like me? I needed to get out Minnie's apartment.

"Let's go somewhere and stay overnight."

"Where?" Minnie asked with surprise in her voice. "To do what?"

"Anywhere. Just get out of the city."

Minnie seemed flustered. "This is like unexpected.

I'm not really prepared for a trip. I haven't thought about what I will wear or anything."

"We're not talking a Caribbean cruise here. A little drive, that's all."

She looked at me with a wounded expression. "I'll still need some time to pack."

"I'm sorry. Pack. Bring whatever you want to."

I followed Minnie into the bedroom, threw a few things into a duffel bag, collected some items from the bathroom, and returned to the living room to wait for her. Sitting on the couch, I leaned against a pillow to break the strict order of the room and inventoried the neatness all around me.

She came out of the bedroom with a large suitcase.

I looked at it. "You know we're only going for one night," I said.

"There could be a change of weather."

I took the suitcase out of her hand. "Let's go."

As I pulled out of the parking lot, Minnie asked where we were going.

"West. To the country."

When I got onto the interstate heading west, I pulled into the slow lane and let everyone blow by me. I was anxious to get out of the city but I was not going to be hyper about it. After half an hour in heavy traffic, I began to feel differently. The city seemed to be never-ending and the only trees to be seen were accessories for condo projects.

Finally, the buildings thinned out, trees began to appear in large, untended groves, and I felt better. These trees were so tall and thick, so different from the few abused maples stuck into little squares of dirt in the sidewalk in front of my apartment. Now I was looking at hundreds of healthy trees, their countless branches reaching up in complex, overlapping patterns of vitality. Once, I thought I saw a deer look up from where it was feeding and dart into a stand of birches.

Minnie seemed to ignore all of this as if something had come over her. She looked straight ahead down the road, even when I told her to look for the deer.

I had already told her about Crystal's new job, so I thought that I would give her an update as a way of making conversation. "Crystal's collected close to $300 in tips in her first week. She likes her boss. A couple of customers are asking for her when they come in. She's on a roll."

"I told you not to judge her too harshly," Minnie said without moving her head. "Neither one of us has a clue about what makes her tick." Minnie stopped talking and continued to look straight down the road.

I took one hand off the steering wheel and waved it in front of her face. "Is something eating you?"

Minnie waited a few seconds and then turned to me. I caught this out of my peripheral vision but I could not see her face, since I had to keep my eyes on my driving. Finally, she said in a voice I could barely hear above the engine noise, "You didn't like the way I made a fuss over Sonny, did you?"

"Well, I was a little surprised how impressed you seemed to be, particularly after some of the things you said about him."

"I may have gotten carried away with some of my compliments, but he's family and I'm trying to be supportive."

"It's one thing to be supportive. It's another thing to be a sucker."

"He paid me back every penny and then some."

"But someday his luck may run out."

"I think I've got him in focus. And maybe you do too. At least you've met my family. When am I going to meet yours?"

"It's not the same thing. My parents are divorced."

"I could meet them one at a time."

"Easier said than done."

"Just because it might be difficult doesn't mean that it would be impossible. Do they even know that you are seeing me? You never talk about them."

"Yes, I've told them about you." This was true but perhaps misleading because they knew few of the details, which, of course, was due, in part, to the fact that they didn't ask for any. In the rare, recent conversations I had with my mother, she had asked: "Are you still seeing that young woman....I'm sorry... what is her name....Minnie, yes, Minnie?" When I answered "yes", she simply responded: "Tell me if it gets serious."

I looked out the window in the direction of the setting sun, which was slipping behind the low, old mountains of an Appalachian ridge. In the foreground, trees now appeared as silhouettes against the dimming light. "We should be looking for a motel pretty soon."

Minnie seemed to understand what the moment would allow. "What kind of place should we be looking for?"

"A nice family-owned place ... something with a little character."

"Are you going to register us as husband and wife?"

"I hadn't thought about it, to be honest."

"Well, you should."

* * *

I turned off the interstate and onto a state highway in order to find something with a "little character." We soon encountered a sign which promised that the Mt. Laurel Motel was only four miles down the road.

The entrance to the Mt. Laurel Motel was a semi-circular drive bordered by carefully planted marigolds and evergreens. The flowers caught Minnie's eye from a distance and I quickly agreed with her that this place was what we were looking for. The motel was a one-story, L-shaped, white wooden building with an overhanging roof along its entire front. Cars with New Jersey and Pennsylvania license plates occupied about half the parking slots outside the rooms. More flowers, red and pink geraniums in pots, were set next to each door. The establishment was obviously the source of pride for the owners.

Gary and Edith Snyder were identified as the "Inn-keepers" on a sign above the office door. Mr. Snyder adjusted his hearing aid as he greeted me from behind a high counter flanked by a rack of tourist brochures and an announcement that muddy boots should not be worn inside the rooms. "We get a lot of deer and pheasant hunters and they can mess up a carpet in no time," Mr. Snyder said when he noticed me reading the sign. "So will you be staying with us tonight?"

"Yes sir, if you have room."

"We do. Will you be wanting a single king-size bed or two singles or a queen? We've got 'em all."

"A single king would be fine."

"Very good. Fill out this register for me, please. Will you be using a credit card?"

I completed the registration process without ever having to identify Minnie as my wife. I kept this to myself as I unloaded our bags into Room 16 in the middle of the L. The somewhat embarrassing truth was that this was the first time I had ever stayed in a motel under my own name.

The room was generously sized with standard-issue furniture and pastel artwork screwed to the walls in mauve frames. I was a little disappointed that there seemed to be nothing of the Snyders in this room. Nevertheless, the accommodations were clean and in their own way inviting. As I inspected the soaps, body lotions, coffee packets, and other convenience items that had been provided, I recognized another first: this would be the first time that Minnie and I would sleep together in some place other than her apartment. I took some strange satisfaction from this room. It would be ours, if only for one night. I was responsible for us being in it and only the two of us would know what went on inside. I felt close to Minnie as she unpacked her bag and placed some of her things into the glossy-veneer bureau.

For a few brief hours, I was able to unwind. After a nice dinner at a local steak house recommended by Mr. Snyder, Minnie and I retired to our room and watched a movie on the swivel-mounted television. We imitated the love-making scene in the film, taking full advantage of the king-sized bed, rolling from side to side without coming close to the edge.

After we turned out the lights I had trouble falling

asleep. At first, I thought that if the in-the-wall fan/AC were not so loud, I could doze off, but I soon acknowledged that I was keeping myself awake. It's hard to describe what was in my mind. I felt as if I were watching water spread onto the ceiling from a leak in the roof that I could not locate. Rain running along beams and pipes before it actually dripped onto the plaster, making it difficult to find and plug the hole.

In the morning, I saw the first sunlight slice through an opening in the window blinds. I was tired and out of sorts. I dreaded going back to the city and my job. But there was nothing to be said about the topic; I owed it to Minnie to keep my dismay to myself.

CHAPTER TWENTY

A working stiff. That's what I felt like when I forced myself to go to work on Monday morning. And I felt it in a way that went right to my bones. After I walked onto the job site, I noticed Frankie trying to get someone's -- anyone's attention -- outside the piledrivers' trailer. "Hey, don't do tunnel work! I'm tellin' you it's bad shit," he said.

Drager came around the corner of the trailer. I stepped back to put some distance between us. Frankie stepped forward to try to engage him. "Tunnel work is bad shit," Frankie repeated. Drager pushed him in the chest with a quick motion which made it appear as if he were releasing a tight spring in his arm. Frankie's papers went flying as he fell backward through an awkward somersault, rolling over like a circus clown. I stood there for a few seconds, stunned at Drager's assault. Then I bent down to help Frankie, who was sprawled on the ground. I heard Drager moving closer and I looked up to see him a few steps away from me. "You little fuck...." Sterling, who had been following a few paces behind me, stepped in front of Drager. At the same time, Ellis came out of the trailer to see what the commotion was about. Drager backed away and watched as Ellis gave a hand to help Frankie get back on his feet. Drager returned his eyes to me. "You little fuck," he hissed at me again and then turned and went into the trailer.

Ellis, Sterling, and I picked up the rest of Frankie's papers and gave them to him in a stack. "Thanks,"

Frankie whimpered. "But now everything is out of order. Why did he do that? I didn't do nothin' to him." Ellis performed what had now become something of a ritual and escorted Frankie off the job. As I watched the two of them walking away, I struggled to suppress my increasing fear of Drager's venomous focus on me, the only point of which seemed to be to give him an excuse to be violent. Even after Ellis and Sterling went into the trailer, I stayed outside, trying to buy some time for my adrenaline surge to dissipate.

* * *

Eventually and reluctantly, I joined the rest of the crew, including Drager, in the trailer. He was sitting in what was now his marked territory in the back corner where everyone gave him extra space. After a few minutes of tense silence in the trailer, Lizard appeared to talk with us about what Elbell had in mind for the day's work.

"Clyde wants us to take out more lacing steel and he don't want us tyin' up a crane doing it."

"He still wants us to leave the lacing loose on the flanges?" Malcolm asked.

"That's right."

"A piece of steel falls off a flange and cuts into a wire, you got 13,000 volts running through everything."

"We've been over this before and ain't nothin' gonna be changed."

Lizard then began giving out orders in his usual clumsy way. I could not watch him spitting the words from the corner of his mouth.

* * *

All of us worked slowly through the day because we were afraid of the loose steel and the wires. We checked out every situation twice before proceeding, but even that was not enough. Just before quitting time, Early knocked a piece of angle iron off the flange of a street beam. The brace fell ten feet before landing with one end on a soil ledge and the other on a power cable. My tight-lipped account of this incident reflects the way that Early wanted us to deal with it. "Don't say nothin' to Lizard or Clyde or even Lloyd," he pleaded. "Clyde finds out about it, he'll think that I done it on purpose. I swear that I barely touched it. Don't say nothin'."

It was difficult for me to remain silent. The falling steel confirmed for me the crew's fears about what could happen if we followed Clyde's procedure of leaving loose steel on the flanges until the end of the day. But Early's plea froze me in place for a long minute and I just peered down into the hole, feeling at least some relief that the angle iron had not cut through the power cable.

Sterling joined me and then went over to Early to reassure him that things would be OK. "We aren't gonna say anything but we'd better get the steel back up here before Lizard comes around and sees it down there himself."

Sterling and Early picked their way down to where the angle iron rested on the cable and carefully lifted it free. Then they pushed it up in my direction so that I could grab onto it from where I stretched over a beam and then place it back on the flange.

"Let's get outta here," Early said as he gestured for

me to head towards the opening in the street mats. As I moved in the direction of the opening, my furious thoughts returned, this time boiling even hotter within me.

Up top, Early slouched along in the direction of the piledrivers' trailer. His shoulders had fallen forward as if he were in a position for a chest X-ray. The rest of the crew, except for Drager, were still in the trailer by the time Early, Sterling, and I arrived. When we stepped through the door, Ellis asked, "Where you guys been?"

"Just cleanin' up," Early muttered back.

Malcolm looked up from his shoes. "Some kind of problem?"

"Well, ah...ah..."

"Look at us," I interrupted almost rudely. "Cattle being taken to the slaughter."

Carl now raised his head. "Excuse me?"

"We're acting like cattle being taken to the slaughter. Thinking that we can work around the dangers on this job."

"You're a god damn punk," and you're talkin' like that?

"Everybody knows that the angle iron, the wires are really dangerous. We need to do something about them."

Carl shook his head. "Since when did you become an expert? And just what are we supposed to do that won't cost us our jobs in the process? That's the way things turn out, particularly with guys like Clyde and Lizard."

"But what if all of us say that we're not going back into the hole unless they do something to protect us."

Carl took in another deep breath, held it as if to contain his anger, and then released it in a sudden rush.

"How old are you anyway? You got a wife? You got any kids? What do you know about supportin' a family? I need this fuckin' job. You're a punk for Christ's sake."

"Carl! Carl!" Ellis yelled. "The guy saves your butt and now you're talkin' this trash to him. I'm with Harry that we do something. This job is fucked up. And it ain't just Hadden and Clyde. Drager is crazier than a shithouse rat and shouldn't be workin' on this job"

"Most times I ain't gonna say nothin'," Early spoke up before Carl could respond to Ellis. "But I don't like bein' afraid all the time about gettin' killed and about what Lizard and Clyde might do to me if I complain about it. I didn't want to tell you all, but the reason we were late getting back to the trailer was because I knocked a piece off the beam. Right away I'm askin' Sterling and Harry not to say nothin' because I was afraid that Lizard and Clyde would fire me for it. Yeah, I'm scared of this place."

The crew seemed dumbstruck.

"You knocked steel off a flange?" Malcolm finally asked.

"That's right," Early answered. "Barely hit it."

Malcolm looked troubled. "It's those loose angles. Maybe it's time to do something to get some attention."

Carl screwed the cap back on his thermos. "I ain't forgettin' what Harry did for me. But it don't give him the right to take my job away."

"Don't be takin' it so personal," Ellis said. "Harry's not lookin' to take anybody's job away."

Carl put his thermos into his lunch pail. "Well, if you're all so convinced that ya gotta do somethin', I say that at least we ought to talk to Lloyd first before we go too far. Crispin has as much told us already that we're a bunch of crybabies, so we can't be goin' to him."

"Lloyd won't be much help either," Ellis said impatiently. "It's the truth. He'll be looking to save his job too."

"I say we ought to give him a try." Carl wanted an option. "Hell, he knows what's right."

"Sure, he'll listen, but then what's he gonna do?"

"Maybe he'll be able to think of something. I don't know."

"Can't be talkin' to him on the job," Malcolm said. "That'll tighten the screws on him for sure."

"Maybe Harry can work out something with Minnie," Sterling said suddenly. "Lloyd might be willing to go to his sister's place."

Even though everyone knew that I was dating Lloyd's sister, I was steaming that Sterling had brought her into this, but I remained silent.

"Makes sense to me," Ellis said. "What do ya say, Harry? Can you pull it off?"

I glared at Sterling, who smiled back at me. "I suppose I could ask," I finally stammered. I had started this discussion, so I could not cut it off.

"Then I say that we wait and see what Harry can put together," Ellis concluded. "We owe Carl that much."

Everyone nodded in agreement and began collecting his things to leave. As they were closing up their lockers, I could still hear Carl's bitter words. I felt the tightness in my stomach caused by an unpleasant truth. Carl was right: what did I know about what price he might pay for my self-inflated agitation? He was right: I wanted to start something and then drive it pedal-to-the-metal into oncoming traffic. He was right: I was a punk and had no business talking to the veterans as if I knew more about anything than they did. Even though I may have good reasons to say what I did, my disregard for the consequences was arrogant and reckless. It was also thrilling.

CHAPTER TWENTY-ONE

"The Oasis?"

"Definitely," Sterling answered.

We stopped by the apartment to pick up Crystal, who asked, "What about Minnie?"

"I'll call her from Ray's and tell her that I might be late."

At Ray's, all of the booths were full except for one in the back near the restrooms. Even before everyone was settled in, Sterling started talking.

"Crystal, are you listening?"

"Uh, huh." Despite her answer, she seemed to confine her attention and energies to picking threads off her sweater.

"OK, then this meeting is called to order. Any committee reports? None. Any old business? None. The Chair has a quick item. I'll bet you $5, Harry Travers, you can't tell me the exact date that's showing on Ray's calendar. Don't turn around. It's one of those calendars that shows only one day at a time."

I tried to figure out the gambit. I knew that the date was October 20 but that would be too obvious a guess. Ray must have forgotten to change the calendar so it was showing the wrong date. How many days had he forgotten to tear off? But then again, maybe Sterling figured that I would think that guessing the right date would be too easy and that I would try to come up with some other date when, in fact, the right date was showing. "No bet."

"You cheap, timid son of a bitch. Afraid to bet a measly five bucks. I can see you someday committing suicide and your last thought will be to worry about the cost of the bullet."

"I've lost enough money to you already."

"It would have been simple for you to have won. You know that Ray takes care of this place and that he would have today's date up. The calendar says October 20. But you had to think about it too much and make it complicated. That's your problem."

Sterling motioned to a waitress for some beer. "The Chair has new business to discuss. Crystal, are you listening?"

"I already said that I was." She flipped some sweater lint under the table.

"I'm quitting the Elbell job. I'm through with pile-driving. I'm done. Enough of Drager ... Lizard ... Enough of working with bad shit all around me...this whole situation is getting too ugly." He looked directly at me. "I listened to you trying to convince the guys to do something and I'm thinking it's time to check out."

"No argument that The Lizard and Drager are dangerous, but to just ..."

"Dangerous? They're not even fully evolved."

"But to just give it up cold?"

"Sure. Not as if it's some big loss. Yeah, I said that I wanted to learn how to build something solid. So now I will have to find something else solid to build. Now I know enough to see that I'm not cut out for piledriving despite what I may have said before we got into this. I've got enough money for Florida and now I'm ready to spend it."

"On what?"

"Betting on the horses in Miami. I've already told you."

"I'm trying to make a basic point here."

"I am too. What do you know about gambling? You're afraid to bet on the simple stuff. I'm looking for a challenge. My own type."

"Talk to him, Crystal." I was getting desperate.

"It's his life, honey. I hate to see him give up that good construction money, and I would hate to give my job...I mean I just started. But it's his life. And where he goes, I go."

Sterling looked satisfied. "Crystal and I are just going to walk over the horizon together. Kind of romantic, don't you think?"

"Walk over the horizon together? Yeah, and the world is going to turn out to be flat and you're going to drop off the edge."

A waitress put a pitcher of beer on the table. I poured myself some and watched the foam roll over the lip and down the side of the glass.

"I figure I should stay for another week and get a full check," Sterling said. "Then I'll have an even four thousand to play with. It's OK if you want to stay here and become a real piledriving man."

"And what are you going to become?"

"I just am." Sterling pressed back his shoulders.

Crystal looked up from her sweater. "Harry, you think Minnie would be interested in going to Florida? We could make it a foursome."

I shook my head. It was such a bad idea that it had to be discouraged immediately. "Minnie's got her family here. I don't see her doing something like that."

"Well, then, when Sterling doubles his money, I'm gonna send her a box of grapefruits. She's been real decent to me."

I looked down at my beer. The head was gone except for some dried foam on the glass. "Four thousand. How far are you going to get on that? You're still focused on that thing about your dad leaving and your mother dying before her time," I finally said.

"You can't keep trying to explain everything about me on the basis of my mother and father. Did you ever occur to you that maybe I'm just a born fuck-off?"

"Sure, but you can't stop there."

"Why not?" Sterling closed his eyes, took a long swallow of beer.

"Sterling, four thousand dollars! It's going to be gone in no time."

"I said that I would find new work."

Crystal sat up straight. "Harry, you won't say it but you still remember that night here when me and Dawn left you guys with the bill for the drinks. Right? And you think that I'm going something like that again to Sterling. Right?"

"Well, I…"

"That was lousy. I admit it. But I didn't know Sterling then."

"That makes a difference?"

"Definitely. I'm not gonna cheat somebody I know. And now I know him. Better than you. He's my husband you seem to be forgetting."

* * *

Minnie was waiting for me in front of her building. We started off down the street, shielding our faces from the wind as it picked up grit from the street and blew it against us. This was a wind of a departed summer, of harsher conditions yet to come.

I spoke loudly against the air. "The men on the crew were wondering if we could meet Lloyd at your place to discuss what's happening on the job."

"Why Lloyd? Why my place?"

"Carl thinks Lloyd might be able to help us get something done about the situation. Everything seems to be going to hell all at once. The work is really dangerous and then there is this guy Drager. He's scary strange. People are nervous to be around him."

"Is it really fair to Lloyd to get him involved in this? He doesn't have control over any of this or he would have already done something. I'm sure of it."

"We've got to talk with him. He knows more than we do. The men want it. There aren't a lot of options. We thought that Lloyd would come to your place because he would feel more comfortable there. Will you help us out?"

"I guess you can use my place. I'm just worried where all of this is heading."

We came to the end of the block and stopped to wait for the traffic light to change. A car with a high-gloss paint job passed in front of us, the driver with one hand on the wheel and one hand holding a cell phone to her ear, yakking in a way that suggested that she was living hysterically. I wanted to move as soon as the car went by, so I pulled Minnie to cross the street against the light.

"What's the hurry?" she asked.

"It's uncomfortable out here."

After Minnie jumped the curb on the other side of the street, she started talking again. "So why did you and Sterling have to go to Ray's first thing after work?"

"So he could tell me that he's quitting piledriving and eventually going down to Florida. Plans to go to the track with the cash that he's saved up."

"What about Crystal?" Minnie slipped her hands together, almost as if she were concealing a prayer. "What did she say?"

"She didn't argue with him."

"But they've got to have more in mind than betting on horses."

"He will probably gamble until his money runs out. After that, who knows? But maybe they're going to be happier on the road than hanging around here and trying to be normal."

"Crystal may be more normal than you think. She cleaned up your apartment pretty good and now she's got a job."

We stepped under an awning for the entrance to a small grocery store. Just at that moment, a hole in the flat-bottomed clouds above us opened and sunlight fell where we stood. The shadow from the awning cut Minnie in half. My eyes had difficulty looking at her in two lights. She stepped forward out of the shadow, which allowed me to see a furrow just above her brow. Her concerned look in the candid light hinted at how she would appear in middle age.

"How do you feel about all of this?" she asked me.

Ever since leaving Sterling and Crystal at the Oasis, I had been trying to sort that out. I had no right to complain about his decision. He had never promised that the two of us were going to be tight for life. His only infraction was to have been around when I had been willing to follow him and to do things just to see where they ended up. And he was right: the job was turning evil and nothing more was to be gained from it and a lot could be lost. Time for both of us to cash out. "Things are happening too fast," I finally answered.

"Why can't you just quit like Sterling and that will be the end of it?"

"Not for the other men on the crew, it won't."

"We're talking about you."

"No, we're talking about the crew. Why do you think that I asked you about using your apartment to meet with Lloyd. I'm in the middle of this now."

"Because you put yourself there."

"Maybe that's true, but it doesn't make it any easier for me to back out now."

"Yes, it does. You really think that the rest of the crew won't know what to do without you?"

"That's not what I'm saying."

"What are you saying?"

"Nothing more right now. Talking isn't helping me with this."

"What will help you?"

"Can we just focus on the crew meeting with Lloyd at your place? Are we all set with that?"

"You're not going to be able to avoid confronting all of the realities by focusing on only one detail."

"It's not a detail and I need to know for sure whether we can use your apartment."

Minnie shook her head. "When do you want to do it?" she asked with resignation in her voice.

CHAPTER TWENTY-TWO

The next morning on the way to work, Sterling ran on about how he could double his money in thirty days at a Florida dog track. He was doing a big psych job on himself and I was not going to discourage him. If you're going to do anything important in life — and at that moment winning at the dog track seemed to be important to him — you've got to have illusions. So if Sterling was trying to fool himself into thinking that he could beat the odds, so be it.

What about me? Before any of this, experience had come to me in a few, lazy, run-on sentences with bland, ambiguous adjectives; now things were happening to me in rapid exclamations with a blunt, emphatic vocabulary. I was trying to learn a foreign language and there would be no dropping the course. Or so I thought.

* * *

As I stood outside the supervisors' trailer, I could feel the cool air slip over the edge of my collar and down my chest. I brought my arms close to my body and stuck my hands into my pants pockets to stay warm so that by the time I found Lloyd, I was hunched over.

"You're not dressed right for this weather," Lloyd said as soon as he spotted me. "You got to wear layers."

I tried to adjust my collar to block the wind. "Lloyd, you got a minute?"

"Maybe."

"The guys on the crew need to talk to you. Not here. Not now. Later at Minnie's. I've already set it up with her."

"Talk about what?"

"About the job. Clyde. Hadden. Drager"

"I can't tell Clyde what to do."

"We know that, but Carl wants you there."

"Why isn't he askin' me? Him or one of the older guys?"

"They wanted me to do it. I guess because they know that I'm seeing Minnie."

Lloyd scanned the job site as if to see where Clyde was. "When is this supposed to happen?"

"Tonight after work if you can make it. The longer we wait, the bigger the chance that Drager or Hadden will pick up something."

"I still don't understand why I'm talkin' to you about this. You're a punk. Maybe I would talk to Carl, Ellis, or Malcolm about this, but not you."

"So what are you saying? That I've got to go and get one of them to talk to you?"

"Yeah, that's pretty much what I'm sayin'."

"Then, I'll do that," I said and walked away to find Ellis. For obvious reasons, I was not going to look for Carl.

By the time I located Ellis and then the two of us were able to find Lloyd, it was almost time for the shift to start, so Ellis had to talk quickly and Lloyd had to listen quickly. Because I had already told Ellis about my earlier conversation with Lloyd, he basically repeated what I had already said.

When Ellis was finished, Lloyd cupped his hands and

blew into them. "Too damn cold to be standin' around chewin' over this thing," he said impatiently. "I don't see any point to this. You sure that the senior men want to do this?"

"Yeah," Ellis said.

"I'll show up but I'm not stayin' long."

At various times during the rest of the work day, I sensed that the crew was thinking about the upcoming session with Lloyd. Not much was said but I suspected that Ellis and Carl, in particular, were rehearsing in their minds what they would say. I was too. Initially, I felt a need to pull back, go easy on everything to show Carl that I understood what he had said to me. I even thought that I shouldn't say anything at all and just let Ellis or someone else do all of the talking. But then I worried that the opportunity with Lloyd would be wasted. Of course, I kept my thoughts to myself. When I finally asked Early if he knew what he was going to say, he simply answered that "I won't know until I get there."

* * *

No one arrived on time at Minnie's. Sterling and I arrived first and then waited in her living room wondering whether the others had changed their minds about coming. I was relieved when the buzzer sounded and Minnie opened the door to find Malcolm, Early, and Ellis standing there. She welcomed them in and directed them towards the living room. I stood up and shook their hands.

"We getting' formal?" Malcolm asked with a look of amusement. "A handshake just for walkin' through the door?"

"I'm glad to see you, that's all."

We sat down and waited for someone else to show up.

"Don't be surprised if Carl is a problem again when he gets here," Malcolm said. "A few years back, he was out of work for so long he ended up on food stamps. It's like there's nothin' he fears more than being unemployed. I think he'd rather be injured on the job than not have one."

"He's said all of this to you?"

"Yeah. Basically. I was tellin' him about some of the times when I sat on the bench for months and about how restless I got. My wife was working so we got by, but we had lots of arguments about money. Carl's wife never worked outside the house. It was a lot tougher for him."

"Lloyd will probably skip tonight," Ellis said. "He doesn't want to get into a mess with us."

"He said he'd be here," I answered.

"If I had been made foreman of this crew instead of Hadden, I would get in Clyde's face about what's goin' on. Lloyd could do the same thing."

"Even if it meant losing your job?" Malcolm asked skeptically.

"Yeah. Even if it meant puttin' my job on the line. That's why I'm here tonight. For sure, my wife ain't real happy about it. But I asked her straight out whether it ever occurred to her that I might be able to do a better job than some of the morons who get the titles? I got new teeth now so I don't see no reason to keep my mouth shut."

"You guys ready to go to another weddin'?" Early asked. "Velveeta says that she doesn't want me hanging around with her like I'm 'Uncle Early.' She wants to know if I'm ready to commit. Commit to her and her kids."

"Don't be askin' me to give you the toaster oven," Sterling protested. "It's mine, fair and square."

Malcolm slapped Sterling on the shoulder. "So as the only newlywed on the crew, you got any advice for Early?"

"He doesn't need any advice from me, but I'll give it anyway. Marry her. She's better than you deserve."

Minnie brought in some beers and a bowl of pretzels. She handed the bowl to me. There was no coffee table to put it on, so I just went from man to man with it. Malcolm put two pretzels on his index finger. Ellis waved me off and then changed his mind and took one.

Carl arrived in the predicted bad mood. Although he was polite to Minnie, he was surly to the rest of us.

"Where's Lloyd?" he asked.

"He's on his way," I said.

"I'll give him five minutes. If he ain't here by then, I'm puttin' the evenin' to better use."

"Carl, don't bullshit us." Ellis said, "You know you ain't got nothin' better to do. This is probably the first time you been out at night in two years."

The door buzzer sounded again. "There's Lloyd now," Minnie said as she went to let him in.

Minnie returned to the living room with Lloyd at her elbow. He dipped his head awkwardly to us. Minnie had brought in her kitchen chairs so that there would be places for everyone to sit. She took a position next to Lloyd as if she were about to speak on his behalf.

The beer and pretzels kept everyone busy with their

hands. I hoped that Ellis would say something to get things started, but, unfortunately, he was struggling with something stuck between his gums and his dentures. Finally, I said, "I guess you know why all of us are here."

"So then, let's hear about it," Lloyd said impatiently.

Ellis took his finger out of his mouth. "Probably shouldn't be eatin' pretzels. Ah, Lloyd, things been pretty bad since you left. You seen it and you heard us always talkin' about the odds and about how we're due."

Before Ellis could continue, Carl moved forward in his chair. "You know I don't make a big deal over chicken shit," he said. Carl seemed anxious that Lloyd not think that he was a troublemaker.

Ellis cut him off. "This new guy Hadden don't have it today and he ain't gonna get it tomorrow. He ain't right for this job." Ellis pushed up on his new teeth with his thumb. "We're still workin' in the wires just like before. We got loose steel layin' around on the flanges of the street beams. And with Drager around ... See what I'm sayin'?"

"I've talked about it myself, but Clyde says he wants it done that way to save crane time. Claims it's a lot more efficient."

"But I ain't never seen it done that way before ... with all those wires runnin' along the sides of the hole."

"I've seen it done that way. I ain't sayin' that it's the safest, but I've seen it. Clyde keeps sayin' that if you're careful, the job can get done safe and quick. In fact, the quicker it gets done, the less time you have to spend climbin' around on the steel, so his way is actually safer."

"You know that's bullshit."

"I'm just tellin' you what Clyde told me. He got you

the harnesses, didn't you? He and Crispin will work things out for the job, and that includes Drager too."

"Do you really believe that? If they can slide by, they will. And both of them are trying to slide by Drager too, even though he's getting weirder every day. Who knows that he is not going to end up like one of those psychos who goes after his co-workers with an AR-15. He needs help. Somebody should do something."

Lloyd wiped his face with both hands. "As I said, Crispin's real tight with the Elbell people. So he ain't gonna do anything about the wires. And he is probably trying to keep his distance from Drager, but I'll talk with him and Clyde about getting Drager off the job." Lloyd sounded like he could have said much more. "There's some good Union people up the line but eventually they're gonna have to deal through Crispin. As for Clyde, if he thinks you're tryin' to make him look bad, he's gonna get even somehow. And I won't be any help to you." Lloyd wiped his face again. "I've tried."

"Don't run for cover so fast," Ellis said.

Lloyd flinched. "Look, I said I tried so don't be givin' me shit."

"No one is trying to abuse you," I interjected too quickly. "We're frustrated, that's all."

"I don't think that Ellis or anyone else on this crew needs you to talk for them," Lloyd fired back at me. He then turned to the others. "I'm tellin' you that I've done all that I can about the wires and the loose steel. You don't like the situation, walk."

"But we don't want to walk," I said. "That's why we wanted to talk with you. There must be something more that can be done."

Lloyd looked at me as if I were a complete imbecile. "Didn't I just say that I didn't want to hear from you? Didn't I just say that I had done all that I could? What do you want me to do? Pay for another crane myself?"

Ellis put a hand in front of me to prevent me from saying anything else. "We would settle for a few improvements," he said with an edge still in his voice. "Box up the wires. Do two or three crane lifts during the day instead of just one at the end of the day. Harry's right: something more can be done."

Everyone stopped eating pretzels. Lloyd did not say anything. Minnie looked at him out of the corner of her eye. Ellis waited for a response. I kept my mouth shut. Lloyd still did not say anything.

"I got an idea," Sterling suddenly said. "Why don't I raise some hell. I'll go to the good people at the Union. I'll go to OSHA. I'll go to whoever will listen to me. By myself. No need for anyone else to get involved. Maybe there'll be some pressure put on Elbell that they won't be able to talk their way out of. And if Clyde finds out that I'm the one pushing this, that's OK."

"Why you lookin' to be unemployed?" Carl asked.

"It won't make that much difference to me. Being fired will just kind of accelerate things a bit."

"You win the lotto or somethin'?"

"Lay off him, Carl," Ellis said. "I say we let Sterling do his thing. Maybe we'll get an inspection out of it."

"And what happens if it comes back on us?"

"I'm willing to take that risk. I trust Sterling to keep us out of it."

"He's a punk. Are you gonna trust a punk to know how to do that?"

"Carl, what are you sayin'?" Ellis asked. "That we should wait 'til somebody really gets fucked up bad." He looked apologetically in Minnie's direction. "Sorry, Ma'am. What I'm sayin' is that this is the place to take a stand." He spoke with absolute clarity. No denture whistle.

"Aw right," Early said, brushing pretzel crumbs off his lap.

Carl turned to Lloyd. "What do you think?"

"It's not right to be askin' me that kind of question. You guys got to decide for yourselves."

"Then it's been decided," Ellis declared.

Carl stood up abruptly. "Not by me."

"Don't make this worse than it already is." Ellis said. "All of us have got to stay together on this."

"I want to hear from each man that he thinks that Nesko should be turned loose. Malcolm ain't told us what he thinks yet."

"I'm with the rest of 'em," Malcolm said. "Let Nesko do his thing."

"Nesko and Travers are punks. Why are we letting punks have a big say in this? I ain't sayin' that they ain't good guys, but we know the business and they don't."

"Carl, you ain't as smart as you think you are and they ain't as dumb," Ellis answered. "Now let's give this lady her apartment back to her."

Carl did not move and began shifting his weight from foot to foot as if he wasn't going to leave. Finally, he tossed a few words of courtesy towards Minnie and headed for the door. With noticeably more sincerity, the rest of the crew also thanked Minnie for her hospitality and then left the apartment.

Minnie started to clean up the pretzel crumbs that

some of the men had brushed off their laps and onto the floor. When I moved to help her, Lloyd grabbed me by the arm. "Let's step outside for a minute." He was silent until we were on the street in front of the building.

"This whole thing has gone too far. Now you've got everybody worked up. This is your doing. You must feel pretty fucking important now. But you don't have a clue about where this is going." He inched closer. "Stop trying to pretend that you really want to be a piledriver. Tell Minnie it's over. Leave."

"Nothing's over and I'm not leaving."

"Did you hear what I just said?"

"I heard every word."

"What part didn't you understand?"

"I don't understand you standing here lecturing me. I've never forced anybody to do anything. You're insulting the crew. Talking like I have some kind of power over them."

"I'm not insulting them. I'm just trying to protect them from you." As he had done before with me, he walked away with an abruptness which made his words hang in the air.

My legs, arms, everything felt weak as I climbed back up the stairs to Minnie's apartment. When I knocked on her door, she opened it quickly as if she had been waiting there, stepped aside to let me in, closed the door, and then leaned on it as if to seal it tightly. "I'm glad that's over," she said.

"This has been a difficult evening." My mouth was dry and the words stuck to my tongue.

"Lloyd wasn't treated right. You were hard on him."

"Well, he was hard on me too."

"Maybe you deserved it, jumping in the way you did." Minnie moved away from the door and circled me. "Something's really bothering you."

"Nothing you don't already know about."

"What did he say to you?"

I could not look at her. "He said that I should clear out."

"Why?"

"Because things are starting to get really tense and he thinks that I've got something to do with it."

"You do."

I did not want to argue the point with her, perhaps because I hoped she was right. "But I can't walk away now. How would I ever face those guys again?"

"Why would you have to? That project is going to get built no matter what and ten years from now nobody will remember how it got done."

"That's ten years from now. How about what happens tomorrow?"

"It'll happen without you. So you should be getting on with your life. You don't want to be a piledriver forever."

"Do I just have to take your word for it?"

CHAPTER TWENTY-THREE

Sterling made a big production of it. He spent several hours composing his letters. He began by just talking, with Crystal writing down his thoughts. He figured that this was a good idea because her handwriting was neater than his. Then he decided that her script was too feminine for a letter to be signed "Sterling Nesko," so he started to write out the letters himself. Line by line, he scratched out the crew's complaints and a few choice insults as points of emphasis.

For a while, I read over Sterling's shoulder as he wrote. I even made a few suggested word changes, but when he ignored them, I went to my room and threw myself onto the bed. I lay still for a minute or so and then closed my eyes. When I felt weight bend the edge of the mattress, I looked up and saw Crystal reclining at an angle near my feet. She was looking off to the side while propping up her head with her bent arm.

"You still don't like me," she said in a whisper which made it sound as if she might be talking to herself.

"Not true," I answered.

"You don't know for sure. How could you? I don't even know for sure whether I like me."

"Don't be too hard on yourself."

"I'm just telling the truth. The funny part is that because Sterling has never asked me to change, I want to change more than I ever have in my life. I don't want him to have to make allowances for me."

"I noticed that the towels in the bathroom now match

the bathmat. That's a first."

"I've never had someone like Sterling in my life before," she said. "Most of the other men I've been with were creeps. Usually, they were cheatin' on their wives. They were just using me, so I used them. But Sterling wasn't cheatin' on anybody and he didn't mind that I needed a little help to get on my feet."

I sat up straight in bed. "I admit that I had my doubts at first, but I think that the two of you are good for each other."

Crystal turned around and drew her legs up underneath her. She was now looking directly at me. "I want you and Minnie to feel good about us. Meeting Sterling was the first piece of real luck I've ever had."

Sterling walked into the room with some envelopes in his hand. "They're all done. Signed, sealed..."

"And I'll deliver them," Crystal said, standing up from the edge of the bed.

"It can wait until tomorrow."

"It's OK. It's not that far to the Post Office. The walk will do me good. Might stop at the Oasis on the way back. You want to join me?"

"Actually, I'm kind of tired."

"Then I'll skip the Oasis."

She took the letters out of Sterling's hand and patted him on the cheek. "I'll be right back."

Sterling lingered in my room after she left. I rolled to the side of the bed and put my feet on the floor. "She says that you're the first real luck that she's ever had."

"Glad she feels that way. I'm lucky myself to have found her. I feel like I was due. Some people are born to be beautiful or handsome. Luck. Some people, sometimes the same ones, are born into wealthy families. Luck. Some people never get sick. Luck. For my mother, luck became kind of a religious thing."

"What do you mean?"

"Well, she thought that all luck had to come from God. You know how people talk about 'God-given talent'? Well, for her, that was a reference to what she was up against. But she never gave up thinking that God would eventually favor her too, even though he had ignored her when He decided who was going to be beautiful, smart, athletic, whatever, and that she just had to give Him the opportunity to shine His grace upon her."

"How?"

"By buying lottery tickets. By pure luck that only God would determine, there would be big winners who would never have to worry about money again. Live the life they wanted. Be charitable. Feel special in God's and everyone else's eyes. Buying lottery tickets was what gave her hope. Maybe that's why I like to gamble. But I'm not going to be stupid about it. It's more like: you can't win if you don't play."

* * *

The next day, the wind was strong. It bent branches, rattled windows, and snatched hats. The forecast of showers had me praying that the rain would appear early enough in the morning to get us sent home without working, an escape, however temporary, from Drager, Lizard, and Clyde.

As Sterling and I drove to the job, light gray cumulus clouds were being replaced by dark gray stratus that promised a storm. On our way to the Elbell gate, a drizzle began to fall and I became more hopeful that we were about to be spared. Standing at the gate were Lizard and Frankie -- a sufficient distance apart so that they would not have to talk to each other. Lizard waved us away. "Rain day. No work."

"What about show-up pay?" Sterling asked.

"You never set foot on the job so you don't get it."

"No one called us not to come in."

"You never checked your text messages? You never checked the forecast? I'm not puttin' you in for the hours, so just turn around and go home."

It began to rain. "Let's go," I said.

Sterling turned up his collar and bent into the wind as we started to walk away. I stopped and looked back at Frankie, who still stood at the gate, making no effort to protect himself from the weather. "Hey, Frankie," I shouted. "You need a ride?"

He looked up at me and gestured slightly as if he needed more time to think it over.

"Come on. Don't stand there."

He moved slowly in our direction.

"Pick it up. We're going to get soaked out here."

He moved a little faster until he finally caught up with us. "You're the punks, right?"

"Right."

"I'll remember this. I'll tell my lawyer about it."

"No need to do that," I said. Frankie looked younger and even a little neater than I'd previously thought of him. His hair was cut, although not evenly, and his face was shaven, although not completely. He needed a change of clothes, but they were in better shape than the outfit he had worn in the summer.

By the time we made it back to the car, the rain was coming at us in sheets. Sitting in the back seat, a damp Frankie gave off the odor of a landfill. I wanted to roll down a window but could not because of the water flowing down the glass.

"Frankie, where are all your papers?" I asked after noticing that his pockets were empty.

"I'm puttin' my case aside."

"What about all the money you were going to get?" Sterling asked as he backed out of his parking space.

"I'm gettin' a janitor's job down at St. Mary's School."

"You actually got a job?"

"Yesterday. I ain't gonna be makin' construction money, but I told you guys I don't do tunnel jobs anyway. Do you think my wife will come back from Ohio?"

Frankie made sense to me, but it was hard to comprehend how suddenly he could sound so comprehensible. "I think you're onto something, Frankie. But why did you come down here?"

"With me goin' back to work, I ain't gonna be able to look after you no more. I wanted to warn you guys one more time to get off this job. It ain't nothin' but bad things can happen there."

"You told us before," I said somewhat impatiently.

"I know but you guys don't seem to be gettin' the message."

"I think we got it. Where do you want me to take you?"

"Anywhere you guys are going would be OK."

Sterling looked at me in a way that said that if Frankie stayed with us all day, it would be my fault.

"Why don't we take you home? Just give me the directions."

"I'm livin' with my sister now." Frankie swallowed hard. "Don't got a place of my own anymore."

Sterling followed Frankie's directions. "I know I ain't right in the head," he added. "I'm going to try to hold down this job, but I'm not givin' up on my case."

We pulled up in front of a four-story apartment building with a damaged canvas awning over the front door. Frankie got out of the car and then leaned back in through the open door. "I worry about you boys, but you're on your own now."

CHAPTER TWENTY-FOUR

The wind and rain stopped in the late evening of the second day. The next day the still air was so clear that it seemed to magnify everything I saw on the way to work. By now, the sights were familiar, and in their own way, reassuring. I recognized many of the shop employees or business owners as they did their early morning work, but I did not know any of them personally so I could not expect any acknowledgment of my driving by. It was disappointing because I wanted to be recognized by them. In the clear air, I could see the sharp profile of the man at the newsstand stacking his papers. Everything around him was also sharply outlined. The letters on the sign: "*Central News,*" the flowerpot near the door, the cases of bottled water waiting to be carried inside and put into the cooler. All of it was vividly in focus for a second.

It was one of those crystalline fall days which heighten your senses to the point where you understand instinctively, deep within your body, that sunlight is necessary for life. It was not a day for men to die.

You can't really go into each day thinking that it is going to be your last one. You can't live each day to the fullest, whatever that means. So on most days, you go to work, shop for groceries, or clean up the house. If you live long enough or you expect a specific death, you can prepare for your departure, settling accounts, organizing your affairs, retiring your regrets, clarifying your love for some people, maybe even thinking about some last words. But not the men I saw die on this day.

* * *

Drager was standing in the trailer waiting for me. He was without affect, no snarling, no wild eyes, no bulging veins. He motioned for my attention. "I'm done warning you," he said in a voice loud enough for others to hear.

Ellis looked up at Drager. "We're workin' around hot wires. We don't need any shit."

"Who asked for your opinion?"

Ellis stood up from where he had been sitting on a tilted bench. "What I'm sayin' is that we don't need any more torque on the nut right now. Leave the punks alone."

Drager's face did not change. "Don't be orderin' me around. You ain't never been made a foreman."

I could almost hear the muscles in everyone's necks and arms tensing. "I'm tryin' to get along here," Ellis said slowly.

"You must have shit for brains. This is between me and Travers. You got no say in it." If either Ellis or Drager had said another word, the air in the trailer would have shattered.

Before that word was released, Clyde Bender stomped into the trailer rubbing his glasses furiously. Lizard was at his side, hovering near him as if he were an acolyte in some sort of primitive religion. Clyde put on his glasses and glared at everyone through dirty lenses. "Somebody from the Union ... not Crispin ... is coming down here because he got some damn letter from Nesko. Some government inspectors will probably show up too. So you got Nesko to thank if this job gets shut down. And if we're fined anything, it's coming out of your paychecks."

Clyde looked at Sterling. "You and that permit card are about to part ways. Now I want this crew to finish up the last bays so we can get the angle iron out of there."

"So there won't be anything for anybody to see?" Sterling asked.

Clyde smirked and then ordered us to leave the trailer.

Outside, Lizard stepped forward and stood in a puddle left by the previous day's rain. Standing in the water, he looked like a dimwit even before he started to talk. "I'm puttin' Nesko, Travers, Harper, Ford, and Drager down in the hole doin' burnin' work. Snipes and Baltimore will be up top."

"Drager and I shouldn't be working close together like that," I said not caring how it sounded.

"I can't be makin' special arrangements just because you think you got some kind of problem. You got an issue with Drager, you work it out with him." Lizard processed his gum with his molars and then seeing that his shoes were in water stepped out of the puddle. Ellis stepped forward. "Traver's right. He and Drager should be kept apart." Malcolm nodded in agreement.

My breathing was getting shallow. With the little brain power that remained to me, I decided that if Lizard didn't do something, I was going to walk off the job.

Lizard looked at all of us as if we were making his life needlessly difficult. "All right. All right. Drager, you work up top. And stay away from Travers. I don't want to hear about any more arguments between you guys. Jesus Christ, you'd think I'm running a nursery school here. Snipes, you work in the hole. You seem to agree with this move, so I figure you should be willin' to trade places."

Malcolm clenched his jaw but did not respond.

So with my heart racing, I walked with the crew towards the ladder which would take us into the hole. Every time I looked at Drager, he was already looking at me, staring as if he were calculating the distance between us so that his strike would be lethally accurate.

As we approached the opening to the hole, Frankie came around the crane and waved his arms towards us.

"Jesus Christ. Now what?" Lizard headed in Frankie's direction as if he were preparing to block him.

I ran to Frankie to keep him from getting close to the crew. "Hey, I thought you wouldn't be coming to see us anymore."

"You're one of the punks that gave me a ride home the other day," Frankie said. "It was raining. I remember that."

"Yeah, you're right. You told me about your new job at St. Mary's."

"Got the morning off because they're doing some boiler work. So I came down here."

"Well, it's good to see you, but my advice is to stay out of the way."

Ellis walked behind me. "Frankie, Harry, and me got to go."

Frankie turned his head towards Ellis. "Did we work together on the Brookfield job?"

"Don't recall it. But, as I said, Harry and me have got to go. You should be moving along too. You don't want to get into trouble here." Ellis pulled on my arm. "No more time for this." Then he looked back at Frankie. "Go on now."

Ellis walked away and I went with him, After a few

steps, I glanced over my shoulder at Frankie. He was still there in the same position, arms at his side, feet facing directly forward, his head level. Ellis put his hand on my shoulder. "We get through today and regroup," he said softly and pushed on my shoulder to keep me moving.

I began to shake as I picked my way down the ladder. I had made a point of going first, so I could watch everyone else come down and then see where they went. Lizard had assigned us specific locations, but I needed to know exactly where they were. As I watched, I tried to figure out how I would be able to get out of there in a hurry.

Ellis and Sterling were on a level below me. Early and Malcolm were on the same lower level but off to my right. I was on the top of a beam, five to six feet below street level. Even though I had the easiest access to the exit route from the hole, I felt uncomfortable with the arrangement because I could not see Drager. I knew that he had been assigned to work up top, but that didn't mean that he couldn't slip down into the hole for a few minutes and get to me.

Slowly, I began to set up my torch. Below me, I could see some angle iron lying on beam flanges -- leftovers from the prior day's work. My uneasiness about working in this location grew stronger. If I started burning the steel and put my shield down, I would have no peripheral vision; with the hiss of the torch near my face, I would be virtually deaf to other sounds. I didn't want to do it.

I forced myself to light my torch and to go through my established ritual of adjusting the gases so that the flame reached a sharp point. Then I positioned my shield on top of my head without actually flipping it down. I wanted to look around again. Finally, I dropped my shield and put the flame to the metal. My hands were unsteady and my face grew hotter. The flame popped when it hit some rainwater on the steel. I jumped. Breathing hard, I lifted my shield to get cooler air.

I glanced up. I could see someone moving along the approach beam. My muscles tensed as I tried to identify who it was. It was Lizard. I turned down the torch gases and sagged against the steel, laughing to myself that I was actually relieved to see him.

Lizard stopped when he came within shouting distance. "Drager is clocking out early," he yelled. "Says he's feelin' sick. I thought you might want to know. So don't be sayin' I never done nothin' for you." He sounded as if he were also relieved that Drager would be leaving early.

Lizard turned and headed back to the ladder which went up to the street level. I looked around again and saw the other crew members at their stations. I pulled myself back into position to continue working, flipped my shield down again, brought the torch to full power, and pointed it at a piece of lacing steel.

Despite Lizard's message, I still felt anxious, an uneasy sensation that something was not right, a feeling akin to a worry that I had left a door unlocked. This growing discomfort distracted me to the point where I was unable to pay attention to what I was doing, which was the source of even more anxiety. I was breathing hard again.

I pulled the torch away from the steel, turned off the gases, and pushed my shield away from my face. The sun hurt my eyes. I turned my head to the side. Out of the corner of my eye, I caught a shape coming towards me. I turned in its direction and tried to focus on it, but my eyes would not cooperate. I squinted and was finally able to make out a distinctive profile. Drager coming at me.

I ducked down in a frantic hope that he would not see me, and like some kid trying to hide under a blanket, I stayed crouched down. My breathing became more rapid. I could hear the scraping of steel right next to me. He had found me. I stood up to defend myself. "You little fuck," Drager said as he lifted a piece of angle iron and shoved it towards my head. I blocked it with both of my hands and jammed it back into his chest. He lurched back and lost his balance. For an instant, he seemed poised to regain it, frozen in position as if he were in a snapshot. Then he and the angle iron fell into the hole, his agonized voice going down with him until it disappeared into a loud collision of metal and a deafening explosion.

A blast of sparks shot towards me and I jumped behind a whaler and huddled against it, afraid to move as the hot grit sprayed over me. I closed my eyes as tightly as I could. A high voltage hiss came up from the hole. I started to shake uncontrollably and tried to bring my legs closer to my torso. I yelled for help but the sound of my desperate voice bounced off the whaler back into my head, defeated by the high pitch of the wild electricity coming from the hole. The air around me became heavy and acrid. I screamed again. If I didn't get out of there, I was going to die rolled up in a ball.

Suddenly the sparks and the hissing stopped. Maybe I was already dead and didn't know it. Slowly, I opened my eyes. All that I could see were my own legs pushed close to my face. I tried to stand but could not do it. I could hear men yelling down from above. The panic in their voices told me that there was something horrifying in the hole. A new wave of fear came over me.

I tried again to move out of my crouching position and away from the side of the whaler but my legs would not permit it. I took a deep breath and lifted my head a few inches. Then I moved my shoulders back. This seemed to take some of the pressure off and I was able to slowly unbend one leg and then the other. I could still hear the urgent shouts of men now coming from somewhere in the hole. Carefully, I pulled myself up into a standing position. I balanced myself against the whaler, edged over to the street beam, leaned over its upper flange, and I looked down into the hole.

I had to struggle to understand what I was seeing. A piece of lacing steel was lying on top of one of the high voltage cables. More steel was scattered around the cable. Some men from Elbell were climbing down towards this jumble of metal. I focused on the steel and began to make out what they were heading for. Stretched across a beam and a cut cable was Drager, his body smoking, his hands curled in on themselves, and his face fixed in an astonished expression.

The Elbell men stepped over Drager, who was obviously dead, and started pulling away steel to get to another man. An arm, a leg, and then I could see the body. The man's neck was awkwardly arched away from his torso and his left arm was bent behind him. His right arm extended through a pool of blood that had run from his mouth. As if in a desperate attempt to suck in one last breath, the man's mouth stretched open, showing that his teeth were missing. To the side of his body. I saw

Ellis' dentures, chipped and blood-spattered but still startlingly white. I vomited down the side of the beam.

* * *

The next thing that I remember is being carried out of the excavation. I can't tell you much more about how it was done because I was disoriented. But I knew with sickening certainty what I had seen. People, I'm not sure who, tried to ask me a few questions, but I did not respond. Without saying a word, I let them deliver me to the piledrivers' trailer.

Next to the trailer, Carl sat on a toolbox with his head between his hands. Malcolm stood nearby staring into the air. His eyes did not have a far-away look; they had a nowhere look. Early crouched on the ground, rocking back and forth, talking to himself in time with the movement of his body. Sterling was not there. My mind spun. I closed my eyes in order to try to make everything stop, but I was getting dizzier.

I lurched away from the trailer and began pushing my way through the crowd that had gathered at the scene. I squeezed through a group of hard-hats standing in a tight circle and I found myself next to one of the ambulances. Two attendants were pulling a sheet over a body about to be placed into the rear of the vehicle. I saw Ellis' corpse. On the side of his ruined head was an eye pushed out of its socket, staring off in an impossible direction. A fly landed on the eye's glistening surface and walked across the open, lifeless pupil.

I fell back into the hardhats. Someone supported me from behind, but before he could say anything to me, I slipped by him and tried to work my way out of the cluster. I was unsteady and bumped into several men as I made my way to the gate. I stumbled to the curb around the corner from the gate but could go no farther. I sat down on the edge of the street, put my head between my knees.

Someone asked me if I needed help. I said "no," even though I did. Desperately so. Help to stand up. Help to find the strength to do the next thing, whatever it was going to be, just to do something other than sit on a curb with my head between my legs. But I had said "no," even though I knew that I was overmatched by bloody facts.

I sat there a long time...I am not sure how long.... before I felt a tap on my shoulder and looked up. Malcolm was standing next to me. "I been lookin' for you," he said in a quiet voice.

"I'm having trouble. . ."

"You seen them, didn't you?"

I nodded.

"I figured it was gonna be real bad so I didn't want to see nothin'." Malcolm squatted down next to me. "You can't stay here. You've got to clean yourself up. Let me take you home. The job's been shut down."

"Where's Sterling? Did you see him?"

"He's OK. He left as soon as he got out of the hole. Made straight for the gate. I can give you a ride back to your place.. Come on, you've got to get up."

Malcolm pulled on my arm as he stood up. I leaned on him as I got to my feet and then staggered along with him as we headed to his car. He remained silent the entire way. When we reached his vehicle, he turned to me and said in the same quiet voice that he had been using with me, "In God's words: 'I still have many things to say to you, but you cannot bear them now' John 16:12."

* * *

When I walked through the apartment door, I saw Sterling carrying a suitcase into the living room.

"Why did you leave without me?" I asked in as calm a tone as I could muster.

Sterling put the suitcase on the floor and then opened it as if he were getting ready to pack it. Finally, he looked at me. "Because I had to get out of there as fast as I could. Once I heard that we were OK, I split. I'm sorry but I figured that you could find another way back to here."

"You couldn't wait until we found each other?"

"No."

"Why not?"

"I didn't want to have to answer any questions about what I saw...or at least, what I think that I saw."

"You're talking about Ellis' and Drager's bodies down in the hole?"

"Well, yeah, that too."

"What else?"

"I don't want to get you into trouble."

"What kind of trouble?"

"I'm done. I've already said too much."

"Why are you packing a suitcase?"

"We're heading down to Florida."

"You can't just blow town like that."

"Watch me."

"But why do the two of you have to leave so suddenly?"

"I don't want to be around here," Sterling answered in a voice which was too loud for the space. "I've already told you that I don't want to be interviewed about what happened today, And I already told you that I had decided to quit piledriving. I'll give you my share of the rent to cover the last three months on the lease. I'm sorry if this seems like I'm leaving you high and dry, but things have changed. There's no point in trying to change my mind about this."

I walked slowly into my room and closed the door because I felt that I was losing control of myself again. I stood in front of the single window in the room. The outside of the pane had not been washed in years and was barely translucent. Bird droppings, dried rain, and accumulated grime discouraged a view through the glass. Ellis was dead. Drager was dead. Sterling was leaving. I began to cry. At first, a silent tear running down my cheek and then an audible sobbing. Crying for Ellis, for his wife and kids. Crying for myself. Remorseful, debilitating crying. Saltwater running into the corners of my mouth. Crying even for Drager. I could not get my breath.

I needed to be with Minnie but I could not let her see me in such a condition. After a long struggle, I was able to stop the tears only by refusing to think of Sterling and Ellis in any specific way. I could not allow their faces to appear before me; I could not allow myself to hear anything that they had ever said. I steadied my breathing and wiped my nose. I had stopped the sobbing but not my mind from spinning around the unbearable fact that if I had quit piledriving and had simply gone onto other things, Ellis, and yes, Drager, would still be alive. There had been no point to my staying, despite my stubborn insistence that it was somehow necessary.

But I also knew that if I did not talk myself out of this conclusion, I was a goner. I told myself that Ellis and Drager were killed by electricity and steel and that I was not responsible for the loose angles and exposed cables on the job. That Drager was coming at me and that I had to protect myself. Nothing that had happened...nothing... was the result of any conscious decision or intention on my part to harm anyone. I tried desperately to keep focusing on these thoughts. I had to. Standing alone in the room, wiping my eyes, I knew that there would be no end.

What would I say to Minnie? I tried to decide what I could tell her when I realized that I had not told her anything about what had happened and that by now she would have learned about the accident from some other source. She would have every right to be upset with me. But how could I have talked to her earlier? I had to find a way because I could not stay in the apartment any longer.

* * *

"Lloyd called to tell me that he was okay and that you were too. Why didn't you call me earlier?" Minnie said in a quavering voice when I reached on her cell phone.

"I'm sorry. I was in bad shape. I'm sorry." I took a breath. "What else did Lloyd tell you?"

There was no answer.

"So then you know about Ellis Harper?"

"This is...so...awful," she finally stuttered. "Meet me at my place."

When I arrived at Minnie's apartment, tears were streaming down her cheeks. I put my arms around and tried to hold her, but I could not do it for long and had to leave the room. I stood in the kitchen and she in the living room. I could not suppress thoughts of Elli's wife and family, but my agonizing was insufficient to their grief. No family should have to suffer such a loss. How could they endure it? Heartbroken but unable to do anything but carry on? Afflicted with sorrow but relying on faith that their pain would serve some larger purpose?

Minnie walked into the kitchen. "We should cry until we're dry," she said. "No reason to hold back." There was something in her stricken face that said: "Come to me."

Minnie let me stare at her for a few seconds and then said softly, "Can you talk about it?"

"No."

"Just take a deep breath and tell me what you can."

"Deep breathing isn't going to make any difference.... I'm sorry but I can't....Sterling and Crystal are leaving for Florida."

"Today?"

"The accident..."

"I know that what happened was horrible, but..."

"More horrible than you can know...leave it at that."

"But for them to up and leave like that....What did Sterling say? Did you try to change his mind? What about Crystal and her job?"

"He made it clear that it was a done deal. My tank was empty so I didn't argue with him. I need to sit down. I'm sorry that you have to see me like this."

CHAPTER TWENTY-FIVE

The Union provided information as to the wishes of Ellis' family. Notices were posted on the union website and at the hall, which had become the place for piledrivers from the region to gather to talk about the accident. I made only one brief visit to pick up information about what was being planned for Ellis' memorial service. When I saw Don Crispin, he hesitated in conversation with me and then quickly excused himself.

I don't think that he had intentionally put our lives on the line even though he had turned his back on the crew when we needed him. To me, he seemed simply to have acted on the basis of his own experience in the business and if Elbell rewarded him with a few dollars when no one was looking that did not mean that he would send men to their deaths. Maybe now he was struggling with the fact that his risk calculation had not included anything like what had actually happened. Maybe he was a stupid man but not an evil one.

* * *

By the time that Minnie and I arrived at Ellis' funeral, some people had already taken their seats inside the sanctuary. Carl and Malcolm were there, accompanied by their wives. Early was there with Velveeta. So were Lloyd, Crispin, and other people from the Union. When we sat down next to them, everyone nodded but no one said anything. I looked at the casket sitting on a dolly in front of the altar. It was closed with a small spray of flowers sitting on the lid. For some reason, I wondered whether anyone had picked up Ellis' dentures out of the debris and put them with his body. He had paid good money for those teeth and they belonged to him.

Just before the service began, Mrs. Harding, her children, Ellis' parents, and a small collection of adults who could have been Ellis' siblings entered the church. I was surprised at how small his parents were. Old Man Ellis wore a baggy suit, apparently purchased when he had been larger, and a thick green tie that had not been fully tightened and cinched up to his shirt collar. He looked bewildered. I imagined him saying, "Why am I here? Sons don't die before their fathers. Take me home." Ellis' mother looked unsteady and ended up being supported on each arm by her two daughters.

As Ellis' wife walked down the aisle, she acknowledged the piledrivers with nervous distraction. That done, she moved to the front of the church, took her seat, and began to busy herself with her children's clothing.

Mrs. Harding continued to fidget even after the minister began his remarks. Gradually, she quieted her hands and sat back on the pew. Then the tears came. She cried while staring straight forward, not looking at anyone or anything, not wiping away her tears. Hers was a cry of lonely sorrow beyond any condolence.

The minister spoke of "God's will" in an attempt to explain Ellis' death. He spoke of a man who had always worked hard to support his family in an attempt to explain Ellis' life. As I listened, I struggled with the recognition that Ellis' life was being described as a completed event and this brief summary would be the last attention that most of the world would ever pay to him. I also struggled with the recognition that my friendship with Sterling was probably also a completed event. His tone with me before he left for Florida felt as if he were intending to put distance between us ... permanently. Sitting in the church, I almost felt as if Sterling had also died.

I forced myself to suppress these thoughts and to respect the service for Ellis. There was now a bitter presence of mind about Mrs. Harding that was more difficult to witness than open grief. She leaned towards the casket as if to keep her husband company. As if he needed her. As if he, not just his corpse, were inside that casket, about to be lowered into the ground and covered with dirt. Alone forever in the soil. As if he needed her to watch over him.

After the service. Carl, Malcolm, two other piledrivers from the union, and Ellis' brothers served as pallbearers to remove Ellis from the church. As the pallbearers carried the coffin down the church steps, they appeared to struggle with the weight of their load, rearranging themselves and their holds on the brass rails before sliding Ellis into the back of a long black Cadillac.

After the grim limo pulled away, the piledrivers stood together for a few moments in an irregularly shaped huddle. With the gray sky above us dully reflected in our eyes, we looked at each other but said nothing.

Malcolm loosened his tie and undid the top button of his white shirt. "Why ain't Clyde and Lizard here to pay their respects?"

"I'm here to represent Elbell," Lloyd said.

"I'm not talkin' about the company. I'm talkin' about them."

"This shook them up too."

"Then why ain't they here?" Malcolm asked again. "And where's Nesko?"

"Left town to head down to Florida," I answered.

"That was quick. He should be here too."

"It had been on his mind for a while. He wants to start over down there. He meant no disrespect to Ellis."

"I guess there ain't gonna be no funeral for Drager," Early said.

"Who would go?" Carl asked.

"Somebody should say a prayer for his soul," Malcolm said. "Christ Jesus came into the world to save sinners. Timothy 1:15."

"This might be the first time I've felt sorry for the son of a bitch," Carl said. "Actually, I heard that they found some relative, an uncle, to claim the body. I still can't figure out what the hell Drager was doin' to get killed like that. He was supposed to be workin' on top. And Hadden told me that he clocked out sick just before the accident." I held my breath in fear that Carl's comments would work their way to me. "Well, one thing's for sure, there was no way he was going to survive 13,000 volts running through his body."

Carl's comments hung in the air. Everyone looked drained and in need of the privacy of his own vehicle. "Time to go," Malcolm said.

Lloyd started for his car, but then turned and motioned for me to come over to him. I responded reluctantly. When I came up to him, he pulled on the back of his neck with his left hand before he spoke.

"Everybody's just assumin' that Drager slipped off the beam and so far I haven't come forward to say anythin' different." He spoke as if his words were pieces of ice. I went cold myself. I was hearing what he said next even before he started talking again. "I know that Drager was looking to get back at you somehow. Maybe he was going to try to take your head off. Maybe you had to do something to protect yourself. Maybe Nesko saw what happened."

I stood motionless in front of him, with the tips of my fingers growing colder and colder as the blood left them.

"Right now," Lloyd continued, "I don't know nothin' and I don't say nothin'. So why don't you follow Nesko down to Florida before I change my mind."

I still did not move. I still did not speak.

"You ever think about what's gonna happen to Minnie in all of this? Do you ever think about anybody other than yourself?"

"I think about her all the time," I finally said.

Lloyd turned away from me and headed towards his car. "I think about her all the time," I repeated to the back of his head as he walked away from me.

As I rode out of the church parking lot with Minnie, I withdrew into myself, afraid that anything I said would be the wrong thing. I focused on the rain drops accumulating on the windshield, as if each one contained a universe. Then Minnie turned on the windshield wipers and erased them. I closed my eyes, listened to the wipers squeak across the glass.

CHAPTER TWENTY-SIX

During the night, my eyes were propped open by hectic thoughts that gave me the feeling that I might be going insane. I left the bed and went to the couch in Minnie's living room, agitated by a mixture of guilt and fear. When I was able to focus, I tried to figure out what, if anything, I was going to do about Lloyd's blackmail threat. I could deal with it simply by leaving the crew. Yes, Lloyd also wanted me to walk away from Minnie, but I could refuse, would refuse to do that, and still give up the job. Same question over and over: why couldn't I simply decide to quit piledriving?

Maybe I was simply overwhelmed and could not think straight. But if I had been overwhelmed by events, it was because I allowed it, maybe even wanted it to happen.

This is just another one of my superficial summaries, this time applied to myself. But what if it is at the surface where the most accurate explanations can be found? What if what I see others actually do and what others see me do is, practically speaking, the only really solid information we have to work with? What if the search for deeper causes or meaning is, in the end, nothing more than a speculative, maybe even self-deceptive exercise in avoiding the observable truth? At 3:00 a.m., Minnie came out from the bedroom to check on me, but I insisted that she go back. Eventually, an eerie calm came over me.

I was awakened by the morning light. Bright, direct,

rude in its lack of consideration for my particular circumstances. On the window glass, I could see the beginnings of frost near the edge of the frame. The temperature in the room was cool but I was warm under a blanket that Minnie had put over me.

When she got up, she kept her distance because she knew that I had had a rough night. I did not say anything to her until we sat down for breakfast. "Elbell wants us to report back to work tomorrow."

"Why would you go back?"

"We've talked about this before."

"But that was before the accident."

"I need to go back."

"No, you don't. For you to go back would be like doubling down on this awful situation. This is the time for you to recalibrate everything."

"Drager told me that I'm nothing but a fucking tourist. Lloyd said that I'm just passing through. If I don't go back, it'll be just another failure to add to the list."

"Who cares what they said? Don't get intoxicated with living dramatically."

"But I'm telling you that not showing up tomorrow wouldn't feel right to me."

"Wouldn't feel right to you? You have to have a better reason than that."

"I don't. But that doesn't mean that it's a bad reason."

* * *

Going to work the next day was almost impossibly difficult. Returning to the site of the horror, traveling there by myself, knowing that Sterling and Ellis would be missing when the remnants of the crew gathered in the trailer, knowing that Lloyd might deliver on his threat put me in a bad way. Everything was made worse by addled reconsideration of my decision to come back. Now I had a new fear that my thinking...if you want to call it that...was like trying on shoes that were one size too small.

Frankie was standing by the gate to the job site when I walked up to it. "Why didn't you come by and pick me up for the funeral? I wanted to go," he said with hurt in his voice. "It weren't right for me not to go."

"Frankie, I'm really sorry. I fucked up. Why aren't you over at St. Mary's?"

"I called in sick. I never should have left you guys on your own like that. I knew something bad was going to happen."

"We all knew. Don't be singling yourself out." I wanted this conversation to end. "Got to report in. I'm real sorry about the funeral. I really am."

After passing through the gate, I took a route I hoped would minimize my chances of running into Lloyd. On the way, I stopped and looked into the hole. Everything had been cleaned up. You couldn't tell that anything had ever happened.

By the time I made it to the piledrivers' trailer, what was left of the crew was already there. It was the first time we had been back on the job since the accident and it showed. Our faces were taut. We seemed smaller, as if the deaths had not only diminished our numbers but had also diminished each of us individually. We were not a crew anymore just an assortment of dazed survivors. Carl, Malcolm, Early, and I sat silently on the benches unwilling to look at each other.

The morose awkwardness was broken by Lizard's entry into the trailer. "Listen up, you guys. There's an OSHA man to talk with you about the accident. He says that there ain't to be any supervisors present. Just you and him. So report to the blue trailer and somebody there will tell you what to do next. Travers, Clyde says he wants to see you in his trailer."

"What for?" I asked.

"That's for him to say. Come with me."

I did not want Lizard's company. I let him walk ahead of me so that we would not have to talk to each other. Several times, he looked over his shoulder to make sure that I was still following him.

Clyde's trailer was divided into two sections. The outer office had two tables covered with blueprints, vendor invoices, and other papers. The inner office, apparently Clyde's, contained a small wooden desk with some chairs around it. Waiting in the inner office were Clyde and Lloyd. With all of us in the office it was so crowded that Lizard had to stand.

It took a few seconds for the chairs to be arranged. Without greeting anyone, Clyde began to talk in a heavy tone that suggested that his words had been rehearsed.

"We got a problem on our hands here. Two men dead. Government inspectors. The whole thing is tragic."

My chair squeaked as I shifted uneasily.

Clyde started fiddling with his glasses. "The accident was caused by faulty work procedures. A piece of angle iron fell onto a cable and there was an explosion. You know the rest. We think that you weren't careful enough when working with the angle iron. The cables would not have been a problem if you had watched what you were doing."

"If I had watched what I was doing?"

"It's our conclusion that you knocked the steel down in the hole."

"Me? Based on what?" I looked at Lloyd with as much challenge in my eyes as I could muster.

"We could tell from where the steel fell that you were the cause," Clyde answered before Lloyd could say anything.

"I didn't do it. Drager did it."

"That's not our conclusion."

"Drager was supposed to be working up top. He was supposed to be clocking out early. So what was he doing down in the hole? If he was supposed to be working down in the hole on the I-beam, why wasn't he wearing a harness and tied off? The angle iron came down when he slipped and fell."

"Obviously, he slipped and fell. But that was after you knocked the steel off the beam."

"You're blaming me for the accident?"

"I'm not going to argue with you. I'm telling you for the company to do nothing after two men have been killed is unacceptable. So you're fired. Your discharge slip will say that the reason is 'negligence endangering life.' Here is your final check." Clyde handed me an envelope with "H. Travers" written on it.

I jumped to my feet. "You can't fire me! We were taking out the angle iron just like you told us to! Hadden saw everything we were doing on the day of the accident and he didn't say to change anything."

"I told you that I'm not going to argue with you. The

fact is that you couldn't handle this job."

"You knew what we were doing and you knew that we thought it was dangerous." I turned in Lloyd's direction. "I know for a fact that Lloyd told you that it was dangerous. You knew everything! The whole idea was to get us to work as fast as possible even if we had to cut corners."

"You seem to know a lot for an apprentice."

"Lloyd knows I'm right and you know I'm right."

Lloyd's face was pale, his expression pained.

"You can't be firing me," I repeated.

"You're already fired!" Clyde shot back. He stood up, pushed his way by me, and walked out of the trailer followed by Lizard.

Lloyd, who had been leaning back in his chair,. dropped forward so that all of the chair legs were on the floor. "So you think that you can line me up against Bender and then take me down with you."

"No. I just told the truth."

"What was said in that meeting at Minnie's was supposed to be confidential. Everybody understood that and now you're trying to fuck me." Lloyd stood up and kicked the chair aside. "And by the way, Clyde had already made up his mind to fire you by the time I got here. He made the decision on his own.....before I ever talked to him....I was still considering whether or not to keep my mouth shut. It don't make any difference now one way or the other. You're fired. So get off the job."

"Where I'm going is right next door to tell the OSHA investigator everything I know."

"Whatever."

"Elbell is just trying to make me a scapegoat." I stood

up myself. "Why are you going along with this? To save your job? To destroy me so that I will leave Minnie? Because I remind you of that college woman who left you? Is that it?"

"What are you talking about?! Who told you about her? Minnie?"

"Yeah. And when she did, she was feeling sorry for you. I was too."

Lloyd's jaw tightened. "You don't know jack shit about me and I don't need any pity from some punk who is on his way out."

"And you don't know jack shit about me. If you want to be miserable, that's your business. But don't expect me to just walk away and pretend that I was never here."

* * *

As I made my way towards the blue trailer after leaving Lloyd in Bender's office, I felt humiliated. Whatever my confused thoughts were about the job; I was sure that I did not want to be fired. My discharge made me feel completely dispensable. I was just a punk who could be abused without a second thought. But also twisting my insides was the sense that I deserved to be let go. I had stayed on the job, asserted myself, and become a lethal, vain agent of tragedy. To my very core I understood this, but I still could not bring myself to accept my dismissal.

Frankie was sitting on the front steps to the blue trailer. "A government man is in there now. I wanted to be around to help if I could. Why aren't you in there with 'em?"

"I've been fired. You better go on over to St. Mary's

or you're going to end up the same way."

"I can't. I've already called in sick." At that moment, Frankie was thinking more clearly than I was. "You been fired? Why?"

"For causing the accident."

Frankie snapped his head back. "I don't know why they would blame you. They should blame the guy with the tattoos. That guy who knocked me down. He did it."

"His name was Drager. I told the company that he did it. But they don't believe me."

"You helped me, so I'm ready to help you," Frankie pushed himself off the steps and stood up. He adjusted the old hard hat that was pulled down over his tangled hair. "I saw the whole thing."

"You saw the whole thing?"

"I was standing at the edge of the hole looking down when it happened. I seen Drager going down there after I seen you go down there with the other guys. I told all of you that you should stay out of there. I said: 'no tunnel jobs for me.'"

"I remember that you said that."

"Well, I tried to tell people what I saw the day that it happened but no one wanted to listen. I know people don't want to pay attention to anything I say, but I've always taken my medicines and I've missed only two doctor's appointments."

"I remember you telling me that too. Just tell me about the accident."

"Like I said, I seen the tattoo guy...the mean guy... go down into the hole. I knew that wasn't right because he didn't go down with the rest of you. Kind of waited around and then went down by himself. Wasn't wearing a harness. Didn't seem right to me. So I watched him. Even went down a few steps on the ladder into the hole. Something wasn't right."

"Go on."

"He slid along a big H-beam to where you had set up. That didn't make sense because he didn't have any tools or equipment with him and no one was doin' any riggin'. He was up over the top of you. Sometimes my eyes ain't so good. I've got glasses at home, but I don't wear 'em that often. I used to have a case for 'em but lately I can't seem to find it."

"Frankie, you were telling me about how you saw Drager over the top of me."

"Right. He picked up a small piece of steel from the flange and lifted it up over the beam like he was gonna drop it on you. With that steel in his hands, he put himself into an awkward position. Then he lost his balance and fell backwards and down he went. He knocked off some loose angle iron with his foot when he fell."

"Did you see anything else?"

"Nope." He looked straight at me, or at least as straight as he could. "I seen enough to know that that guy fell on his own and if he hadn't, he would have hurt you." There was something new in Frankie's voice and face which I can only describe as suggesting cunning.

"Are you willing to tell the OSHA man what you just told me?"

"That's why I'm here. I told you that I wanted to help."

I grabbed Frankie by the shoulders. "Just sit tight here for a few minutes."

I let go of Frankie, jumped up the steps to the blue trailer, knocked on the door, and then stepped inside. The conversation stopped. The OSHA investigator started to stand up, but Malcolm motioned for him to sit back down. "He's OK," Malcolm said. "He's on the crew."

Carl pointed to a chair. "You better sit down. You look like shit. What happened with Clyde?"

"He fired me."

Something like a collective moan came from the men.

"I figured that's what was comin'," Carl said shaking his head.

"We'll back you up," Malcolm offered. "You've got options. The Union. OSHA. You'll get your job back." Malcolm turned to the government investigator. "You got to take his case."

The investigator, a bald man with a finely trimmed beard and a thin nose, put down his pen and squared off the papers in front of him. "I don't know what his case is yet," he said.

"I've got a man waiting outside who saw everything," I said. "You should get him in here before he leaves."

"Who?" Carl asked.

"Frankie."

Carl rolled his eyes, started to say something, but then stopped.

Malcolm nodded his head to the investigator. "You should talk to him."

The investigator looked irritated. "All right. Bring him in, but I'm running this investigation, not you. I'm not trying to be a hard ass. But at the end of the day, I have to walk out of here with an organized file. What's your name anyway?"

I identified myself and left to get Frankie.

When we returned, Frankie took off his hard hat and addressed the investigator as "Your Honor." I watched the government man to see whether he would dismiss Frankie as a flake, but he didn't change his attitude. Frankie sat at the table where everyone was sitting, folded his hands in front of him as if he were in school, and then repeated almost word-for-word what he had said to me. As I listened to him, I concluded that he had memorized the key phrases in preparation for this moment. When the investigator asked me what I saw, I answered that the only thing I saw was Drager a second before he fell.

* * *

The investigator made notes of what Frankie and I said and then took down our contact information. It was the first time that I had ever heard Frankie's last name: Trotta. I waited for the investigator to give his opinion of the information we had provided him; I wanted instant vindication. But the government man simply completed his paperwork on us, suggested that if I wanted to pursue a case on my discharge, I would have to file a complaint with his office, handed me a card with the relevant address and telephone number on it, and then told Frankie and me that we were free to go.

"Is that all you have to say?" I asked, still hoping to get some type of endorsement out of him.

"I'll pass on my notes, but someone else will have to do the full investigation. Do I think you have a case? Maybe."

The investigator's tone was appropriately official, but nevertheless, I felt humiliated again. Politely, perhaps by necessity, I was being told to leave. As I looked around the room, Carl avoided eye contact with me. Even though Malcolm and Early did not avoid my glance, I felt separated from them. They, along with Carl, were still piledrivers; I wasn't.

As Frankie and I stood outside the trailer, I felt that people were staring at us as if both of us were pitiful losers. Maybe I imagined it, but I don't think so.

"Did I say enough in there?" Frankie asked. "Or did I say too much?"

"You did fine."

"Is everything over now?"

"No. Remember the man took down your address and phone number. Probably somebody else is going to ask you to go through the whole thing again."

"I can do that."

"Thanks again, Frankie," I said as I shook his hand. "I guess we should get out of here."

Frankie took a step, but then came back and shook my hand again.

"Thanks again," I repeated.

"You want to walk out with me?" he asked.

"You go on. I have to pick up a few things from my locker."

"I can wait."

"No. You go on now."

Frankie shook my hand a third time and turned for the gate. He kept going.

* * *

"Now what?" I asked myself as I stood on the sidewalk outside the Elbell fence. "I've been shit-canned. Now, what do I do?" Every option that came to mind was rejected. The energy behind my initial outrage at being fired was draining out of me. Going to the OSHA office to file a complaint could wait a few days until I organized things better in my head. Going to see Minnie at work: bad idea. Calling my father: a worse idea.

I squinted into the sun. Out of the corner of my eye, I could see pedestrians check me out as if they were saying to themselves: "Why is that guy just standing there?"

Once again, I longed for Sterling's company. A rowdy prankster, who would answer the largest philosophical question you could put to him by ordering another round in the bar. I needed him to invoke Robert's Rules of Order to convene a meeting in which the two of us would discuss new business.

I walked down the street to look for a liquor store. I didn't see one so I changed direction and headed down a side street to a different main avenue. In the middle of the block, I could see a sign for a grog shop extending from the side of the building. When I walked up to the front of the shop, I saw a placard which displayed an internally contradictory advertisement for "Premium Discount Wines and Spirits." The establishment was empty of people except for the clerk behind the counter, who was fiddling with his cell phone. He did not look up as I went to a shelf and picked off a bottle of Jack Daniels.

"Any returns?" he asked with his head still down when I took the bottle to the counter.

"No," I answered as I handed him some cash. I hoped that he would start a conversation with me, just so I would feel slightly less of an outcast. But he gave me my change and immediately went back to his text message.

Carrying the whiskey out of the liquor store, I walked like a delinquent, head down, stooped forward, afraid to be recognized, mortified to be killing time on the street at that hour. I needed somewhere to go. I could not go back to an empty apartment, whether it be mine or Minnie's; it would have magnified what I was trying to make smaller and manageable. Maybe I had been too quick to reject the idea of going to Arlene's to see Minnie. But I could not just walk in and tell her that I had been cashiered. I decided that I would drive over to Arlene's and then wait in the car until Minnie's lunch hour to actually see her. While I sat in the car, I could collect myself.

The plan was a good one only to the extent that it got me off the sidewalk and into an enclosed space from which I could still see people. I drove slowly on the way to Arlene's. I parked so that the car would not be directly visible through Arlene's front window. I reached for the whiskey bottle. I spun off the cap and drank from the bottle derelict-style. The whiskey stung, but I took another swig, even though I recognized that if I kept it up I could make a bad situation truly pathetic.

Thoughts appeared out of nowhere like pictures projected onto a cloud. Image after image came forward, identifiable but with no more substance than vapor. Faces and more faces. Sterling, Ellis, Lloyd, Minnie, Carl, Mrs. Harper, Early, my father, Carl's children, Malcolm, Drager, Lizard, Clyde, on and on they came forward in a relentless procession.

Then one appeared that had no name and was not

even a real face. It was that strange painting of the man smoking the snake. That damn card that Sterling's dad had sent to him and that Sterling had carefully saved. The man with a snake between his fingers like he was holding a cigarette. A man who looked to be at ease with his own weakness and who was not unacquainted with sin. In fact, he inhaled temptation. How could he have a halo over his head? Why was I remembering this confusing portrait and getting increasingly upset in the process?

At noon, I called Minnie on my cell phone and told her where I was. She said that she would come to the car. She arrived in a minute and got into the passenger's seat. "You look awful," she said. "Do I smell alcohol?"

"I've been fired."

"Thank God!"

"Minnie, I love you."

She blinked.

I tried to stay under control. "Did you hear what I said?"

"Yes, I heard. Say it again when you're in better shape."

"I know what I'm saying."

Minnie shook her head. "But look at you."

I straightened myself as best as I could. "I know what I'm saying. I love you."

"I heard you...I heard you."

Minnie put her arms around me. She held me close to her and rocked me gently. I could feel the warm dew of the tears on her face. "Shhh-h-h." She stroked the back of my head as she swayed with me. "Shh-h-h. No more talk.

Shhh-hh-h." I closed my eyes and with an open hand, ran my fingers along her body, tracing her smooth contours over and over again as if she were a worry stone.

EPILOGUE

Minnie and I were married within six months. You're probably thinking that I got married because, at the time, I was at sixes and sevens, maybe even desperate. Not true. My head was clear; my heart was full.

I admit that the decision to proceed with a simple civil ceremony may have been hasty. It was kind of an elopement without the stealth. Minnie eventually grew to regret her impatience, but she never conceded that she was at fault. "My family pushed me to the limit," she said. "I warned them to stop, but they wouldn't listen." As for my parents, when I told them that Minnie and I had gone ahead on our own and were now married, they had initially sounded relieved that they would not be expected to attend an event where they would have to be in the same room together and put on appearances. But then they sounded hurt that they had not been regarded as essential participants in the ceremony. The hurt was not lessened by the fact that Minnie's parents were also not present when we exchanged vows. We would have preferred to have done it differently but our families made things difficult for us.

My father had no enthusiasm for my marriage. To his credit, he did not whine that the Sollis family was "too different." Instead, he asserted that I was not ready to be getting married and that I needed more time to get my legs under me. This argument was not totally without merit and it forced the two of us to actually talk with each other. I told him that I loved Minnie and tried to explain how much I needed her. He said that I was being naive about the distractions and difficulties of wedlock and that if Minnie and I were really in love, we could wait to get married until both of us were more settled. But then he backed off and confessed that he was not one to give advice because the woman he had been seeing had moved on to a younger and richer man with a 50-foot sloop docked in Sag Harbor.

After my mother completed a four-week stay in a rehab spa in Florida, she indicated to me that she had no particular objections to Minnie. In fact, after the two of them met, she suggested that Minnie use her brand of perfume -- a comment intended as heartfelt. I don't know whether her silence about my readiness to be married was a rare act of self-restraint or a typical act of obliviousness.

The Sollis' were united in their opposition to our plans. Mrs. Sollis spent two days sobbing after Minnie first mentioned the idea and then another two days in an effort to involve other family members in trying to convince Minnie to come to her senses. Lloyd was a willing messenger but to no avail. If anything, Minnie responded to his pleas with even more determination to do things her way. This should not have come as a surprise to anyone, but apparently, it did when Minnie told her family that she was prepared to go ahead without them.

When I had appeared with Minnie at the altar, well actually at the desk of the Justice of the Peace, I was a man with uncertain prospects. Yes, I had filed a complaint with the government and a grievance with the union to get my job back with Elbell. But the process of getting a hearing and a decision was taking time and while I waited, I toyed with the idea of going back to SOL. I quickly concluded that would be an impossibility not only because of the bad blood between Paul Matel and myself, but also because the Company started falling apart as its stock price dropped in the face of poor revenue numbers. There was even talk of lawsuits and fraud charges. SOL was not an option even if I had been foolish enough to try to return to that voracious environment. So I took various temp jobs most of which involved making and collating copies.

While I waited for my case against Elbell to move forward, I also questioned the whole idea of pursuing it. How could I ask Carl, Malcolm, and Early to put their jobs on the line to testify against Elbell to vindicate me? I had not only been blinded by my perverse excitement at defying everyone's expectations but also had become addicted to it. In fact, I suspected that Sterling may have diagnosed my addiction; and that this was another reason why he had to get away from me.

I decided to withdraw my complaints and let Carl, Malcolm, Early, and, for that matter, Frankie off the hook. I had already done much harm and nothing in my case against Elbell was going to repair it. I knew that by withdrawing the complaints, I would also be letting Clyde and Lloyd off the hook, or at least, a hook; they would still have to answer to the government and others for the accident. Yes, I would lose the opportunity for vindication and even revenge, but perhaps I would gain a real opportunity to, as Minnie put it, recalibrate my life.

When I went to the government office to discuss my decision, I was informed that it was not necessary because the case was being resolved in my favor. Elbell was willing to settle the matter by reinstating me if I dropped my claim for lost wages. Lloyd Sollis was being transferred off the pumping station job. Clyde Bender was demoted and Lizard was getting out of the pile-driving business altogether. Apparently, as company lawyers looked into the case more deeply, they discovered problems for Elbell.

Ironically, because of this favorable outcome, I felt cheated out of the internal melodrama and satisfaction of having decided to do something that showed some consideration for others. I also felt a little ridiculous; all of my agonizing about whether or not to fight Elbell had been for no reason.

I could not stew about the situation. Since I had collected unemployment compensation and some pay for working as a temp while I waited for the case to run its course, the money loss due to my firing was limited, which would make it easier to accept the Company's offer. The Union cooperated by giving me a regular card and offering to place me in a journeyman's program. This was not Don Crispin's decision because, before it was made, he had retired and moved to Florida. The word on the street was that he had been forced out by the Union. The fact that Crispin, Sterling, and my mother all wanted to live in Florida was a mind-twister.

Predictably, Minnie was opposed to my going back and she never softened her position. More than once, she insisted that I needed to have some goal other than simply not turning into my father. I answered that my goal was to, for once in my life, be competent in something that was useful and not simple, and at that point, mastering the piledriving trade checked these boxes.

Predictably, my father was also opposed to my returning to construction. "I can't believe that you would want to go back to piledriving after all that you have been through. You're selling yourself short. You should utilize all of your talents while they can still make a difference. At least, you need to find out if you have a talent for making money."

"I think that I can be a decent piledriver," I responded confidently. "Eventually, become a journeyman. It's important to me."

"But even if you become a journeyman, there's a good chance that nothing will come of it. You'll end up totally inconsequential. You might as well put your name on a grain of rice."

When I told Minnie of my decision to accept Elbell's offer, I tried to round the edges on it. "This decision is only for now,"

"Don't lie to me," she responded. "If you go back, you're going to stay for a while." Of course, she was right.

Elbell did not reassign me to the pumping station site. Instead, I was sent to an excavation job for an apartment building. Even though it was, when compared to the cut and cover work, a pretty straightforward project, it was still "3-D", as Malcolm called all piledriving work, "difficult, dangerous and dirty."

I did not know anyone on the new job, but some of them seemed to know something about me and therefore kept their distance. They had reason to be wary since I was still a relatively inexperienced piledriver and carried misfortune with me. They also had to notice that I was taking time to readjust to the rigors of the job. My foreman was businesslike and, in contrast to Lizard, knew his stuff and was a stickler for doing things by the book. He made no mention of my history or of any other topic besides my specific job assignments. That was fine by me.

To be sure, I was still a small fish in a small pond, but I was no longer the smallest fish. When a new punk joined the crew, I talked to him about what he should look out for. I worked on the journeyman's qualifications with interest and energy. I gave attention to the techniques of the older piledrivers. I kept my mouth shut.

Malcolm made an effort to stay in touch with me and I reciprocated. From time to time, we would get together for a beer. He would talk to me about his wife's promotion to nursing supervisor and his son's baseball season, things like that. I told him a few things about Minnie's family and the jobs I was working on. On several occasions, we got together with our wives for dinner out, but we never talked about the accident. Only rarely did we talk about members of the old crew other than to speculate whether Early and Velveeta would ever go through with their wedding plans.

But after one of dinners, he did say that he had been waiting for the right time to share with me his favorite passage from the Bible. It was almost as if he had been waiting to make sure that, in fact, I deserved to hear the special words. Then he continued, "We also boast in our sufferings, knowing that suffering produces character and character produces hope and hope does not disappoint us because God's love has been poured into our hearts. Romans 5:1."

So I worked as a piledriver and at the end of every day, I was tired but not dissatisfied with my circumstances. I felt grateful that I had a trade; that I might become really good at it; that I could come home to Minnie and that, however uncertain, we had a future together.

While I pursued the skills of a journeyman, Minnie pursued the skills of a nurse by enrolling in a community college as the first step in getting a bachelor's degree from a four-year program. Every day, my respect grew for her unflinching ability to deal with what was right in front of her. She did this not with a stock of certainties, for, as I came to realize she, too, had her doubts and concerns about herself and us. But she always overcame them with a confident poise which she displayed by saying, when necessary, "We will figure it out."

I sent money to Ellis' widow and kids. The first check she sent back to me with a short note saying that the money was appreciated but not necessary. When I sent it to her again along with a second check, she kept them both. I heard through the Union that she was having a rough time financially because she had to use a substantial portion of the life insurance proceeds and workers' compensation death benefits to pay off debts that had accumulated before Ellis died. When she moved out of the area to be closer to her family, I tracked her down and started sending checks again.

There is not a day that goes by that I don't struggle with the waking nightmare of the dead men in the hole. They haunt me -- a required specter in my life. My burdens are not ones that Minnie should have to carry.

So I cannot tell her everything.

There were times when I watched myself and thought that Drager might have been right: I am nothing but a tourist, even in my own life. And that my father might have been right that my life would not be one of consequence.

But I now know I am not just "passing through," that I am not completely insignificant. I am married to Minnie and that fact anchors me like no other. And it justifies everything with an illusion -- finally, one that I can sustain -- that my marriage to her sets me apart for a purpose.

So I slept through the night in a chair in Minnie's hospital room after her miscarriage; I sat by her side at Sonny's wedding; I stayed in the car while she attempted unsuccessfully to reconcile her differences with Lloyd; I was welcoming and then inconspicuous when her mother finally relented and made her first visit to our apartment; I took Minnie with me when I visited my mother during her second stay at the rehab clinic.

And every night, I lie next to Minnie in bed, my face in her hair, my chest against her back, my arm around her torso, breathing with her in a perfect temperate rhythm, thinking that it will always be too early to tell what I have become.

END

ABOUT ATMOSPHERE PRESS

Atmosphere Press is an independent, full-service publisher for excellent books in all genres and for all audiences. Learn more about what we do at atmospherepress.com.

We encourage you to check out some of Atmosphere's latest releases, which are available at Amazon.com and via order from your local bookstore:

Twisted Silver Spoons, a novel by Karen M. Wicks
Queen of Crows, a novel by S.L. Wilton
The Summer Festival is Murder, a novel by Jill M. Lyon
The Past We Step Into, stories by Richard Scharine
The Museum of an Extinct Race, a novel by Jonathan Hale Rosen
Swimming with the Angels, a novel by Colin Kersey
Island of Dead Gods, a novel by Verena Mahlow
Cloakers, a novel by Alexandra Lapointe
Twins Daze, a novel by Jerry Petersen
Embargo on Hope, a novel by Justin Doyle
Abaddon Illusion, a novel by Lindsey Bakken
Blackland: A Utopian Novel, by Richard A. Jones
The Jesus Nut, a novel by John Prather
The Embers of Tradition, a novel by Chukwudum Okeke
Saints and Martyrs: A Novel, by Aaron Roe
When I Am Ashes, a novel by Amber Rose

ABOUT THE AUTHOR

Richard Voigt practiced as an attorney dealing with issues of the workplace and has been selected for inclusion in "Best Lawyers in America". He is a lecturer at Wesleyan University's Institute for Life-Long Learning and at the Presidents' College at the University of Hartford. He and his wife Annemarie live in Connecticut.